12454

1250
LÉE

D1094287

The Müller-Fokker Effect

BY THE SAME AUTHOR

The House That Fear Built
(with Thomas M. Disch)
Black Alice (with Thomas M. Disch)
The Castle and the Key
Mechasm

JOHN SLADEK

The Müller-Fokker Effect

WILLIAM MORROW & COMPANY, INC., NEW YORK 1971

Printed in the United States of America.
Library of Congress Catalog Card Number
71–166345

To
Pearl Peace, M.A.
and
Doc Sam H. Smith

CONTENTS

ANA*O*Y

Time is like an arrow's h***,
Pointing only one way,
Like one l** of a compass
You might be using, to go, on f***,
Another l** of this journey
Down a one-way street
Full of factory h***s in cars
Whose cylinder h***s
All h*** the same way,
Towards the a**s factory,
Whose h*** is a friend
With whom you might play a h*** of cards,
Not noticing there is a f*** card in your h***,
A h****; oh, and maybe writing IOU's,
In an elegant h***,
To be h***ed to whoever f***s the bill,
But now you take h****,
You s******* your c**** up life's gangplank,
Never mind if it goes down with all h***s,
With you on watch, or if your plane n***s down
Off the isle of B**** with no one watching.
At the f*** of the steps you get ready
To f*** the next minute or two,
As depicted on your left h*** by a watch
Whose f*** has h***s like arrows.

EDITOR'S NOTE

The following extract is reprinted here as it appeared on the title page of B. Shairp, THE AMERICAN BOOK OF THE DEAD (4 vols., 8vo, Univ. of Practical Mysticism Press, 19—). Other extracts from the four volumes (*The Ox, The House, The Camel, The Door*) appear as chapters three, eight, eighteen and twenty-five below.

Suspect any coincidence, any fascinating banality. Suspect 'on earth as it is in heaven', 'there's never a cop around when you need one', and 'everything that goes up must come down'.* The planet Uranus is 1782 miles from the sun. Subtract 1 from 1782 and you get 1781, the year when Uranus was discovered. Meaning?

Or take the word in Cockney rhyming slang for testicles, 'orchestras' (= orchestra seats, or stalls, to rhyme with balls). 'Orchestra', a Greek word meaning the space in front of the stage where the dancers dance. 'Orches–' means having to do with the dance. 'Orches–'. Change one letter and you make this root into a tuber, i.e. the Greek 'orchis', our orchid, so-called because it looked to the Greeks like a set of testicles. There is a dance of meanings, a dance of word origens—and dances are still balls.

—God, to a military adviser

---

* Must? See table in Appendix I, p. 245.

PRELIMINARY

Glen Dale, publisher of *Stagman* magazine and 'last of the old-time eligible bachelors' (*ibid.*), was having another of his parties. He and his friends and a few hundred of their friends had gathered in the penthouse atop the Stagman Building to celebrate his fortieth—or thirty-ninth—birthday. The place overflowed with not-quite-young people in odd costumes: Aztec feather robes, copper shirts, bright ceramic shoes and shingle jackets; masks, body paint and glowlamp jewelry; suits of paper, steel and glass; whatever was loud without being vulgarly inexpensive.

On the mezzanine a pop group plugged in their amplified instruments and tried to make themselves heard above the talk of I, Thou and Other Celebrities. The group's name was Direct from Las Vegas. The sounds of guitar, organ, English horn and carillon were audible through underwater speakers to those swimming in Glen's pool, but to no one else.

Two musicologists in modified zoot suits began an argument about some old Deef John Holler blues. A girl in bead mail spoke to a friend of hers who happened to be a famous astronaut. Someone dropped the name of General Weimar-auner, and someone countered with the name of Mr Bradd.

'Who's he?'

'Mr Bradd? Just head of National Arsenamid's Marketing Division, that's all.'

'Mr Bradd. Hmm, sounds like the name of a hairdresser I used to know . . .'

13

Across the room a macrobiotics disciple explained that Christ would have lived longer if the Last Supper had consisted of boiled brown rice. 'Instead of all that Yang bread . . .'

A man looking trapped inside his glasses leant against the mantel and sipped ginger ale. He wore a plain business suit dating from the sixties' 'Kennedy look', enormous French cuffs, and a false smile of nonchalance. The girl in bead mail introduced herself to him, and he murmured his name.

'Donagon?' she echoed. 'You look like Truman Capote. . . . What *is* your thing?'

'Biophysics. I, um, thought they didn't say that any more: "What's your thing." I thought they stopped, um, saying that.'

'They did. Only now they're saying it again. Are you a friend of Glen's?'

'No, actually . . .'

'I met Glen through Bill Banks. You know, the black astronaut?'

'Yes, I think I've heard something . . .'

'He's the one who dropped anthrax on Central America. Poor Bill! He feels so *guilty*!' The girl scanned the party as she spoke. 'You wouldn't believe it!'

'Well, we all . . .'

'I mean it's stupefying! He tried to kill himself, *three times*!'

Donagon set down his drink and put his hands behind him, out of sight. 'Really?'

'Ank! Aren't you going to say hello?' A young man in a crisp paper suit strolled over. 'Ank, do you know Mr Dunne?'

'Dr Donagon, actually,' said Donagon, shaking Ank's left hand.

'Nancy, I need a smoke.' The girl offered her pack of Hashmores, and Ank applied his thin mustache to the girl's forehead, then took two. 'I don't usually smoke this brand,' he explained. 'Nothing in them. Are you a medical doctor, Doctor?'

'No, um, just a biophysicist.'

Someone bumped Donagon from behind, spilling a drink on him. He turned to glare, but the culprit, a man in a wrinkled dinner jacket, was too busy fighting for balance to notice.

''S all right,' he murmured, 'I'm from Interpol.' After

14

resting a few seconds against the fireplace, he shoved off again. Some invisible ship was pitching in a stormy sea, and he lurched across its deck and into the crowd.

'I do the art column for the *Sun*,' said Ank. 'But it's not my real life. Really I'm a painter.'

A girl in a buckskin bikini and a hat with antlers came past with a tray. Before Donagon could protest, she took away his half-finished ginger ale and left a glass of something stronger.

'Not that I've technically painted anything—yet. But I know exactly what I want to do. All I need is a computer random number generator—or, better still, some of that Müller-Fokker tape.'

Donagon gulped his drink. 'But how did you hear about that? It's supposed to be classified!'

Ank coughed. 'I read *Time*'s science page. The "miracle tape" and so on. They said only four reels of it exist—and the inventor's supposed to have defected to Russia or something, so I guess they can't make any more. And not too many people know how to use it.'

Donagon looked around cautiously. No one was near enough to eavesdrop but the two zoot suits, and they were engaged in a shouting argument.

'I may be able to help you. My project is making arrangements to use these, uh, tapes. I can't tell you more about it, but I might be able to fix up something. If you're still interested in a few months, when the project gets going, drop me a line.'

He gave his address as The Biomedical Research Project, Mud Flats, Nebraska. 'It may come to nothing, but . . .'

'You won't regret it, Doctor.' Ank went off to dance with a girl wearing only blue jeans. The other dancers—businessmen in fur wigs, poets in plastic, a senator in a caftan—swirled around them and they were lost to view.

Donagon leaned uneasily against the upholstered wall and tried to look as if he were waiting for a friend. Waves of conversational noise washed up against him, broke, slid back into the great sea of sound.

'. . . a fact that it neither tamps, nor is it an ax!'

'Lichtenstein? I thought you meant the country . . .'

'Brown rice and . . .'

A girl laced into black patent leather from neck to toe

15

(having even pasted on 'lips' of the same material) swung past, talking about the works of Thomas M. Disch. 'Oh yes, I've read them all: *The Geocides, Mankind under the Lash* . . .'

Across the room, Glen Dale moved towards a lively group of painters. At his approach, they fell silent and looked into their drinks.

'How's it going, fellows?'

'Fine, man.' 'Yeah, keen.'

'Well that's—fine. Everything okay? Drinks?'

'Great.'

'Fine, glad to hear it.' He stood leaning lightly towards them for another minute, hoping the conversation would resume including him. It did not. 'Well, I'd better—circulate.' The man from Interpol tacked past. 'Yes, well, so long.'

One of the painters called after him, 'Great party, man!' then turned to his friend. 'What'd *he* want?'

'Aw Christ, he wants somebody to tell him how good he looks in that stupid tin hat. You know, the one thing I can't stand about his parties is he's always at 'em.'

'Yeah, I wish it was his wake.'

Glen approached a fat little bearded man in a sober suit, standing alone by the bar.

'Well, Herr Doktor, are you having a good time?'

A pair of blank pince-nez turned up to stare at him, reflecting all the colors of Direct from Las Vegas's light show. 'Ah, Mister Dale.' The little man, whose name Glen could not recall, spoke English with German precision.

'There is someone here I would like to meet.'

'Well, just point her out to me . . .'

'No, no, this is a gentleman. A biophysicist named Doonigan. I should like it very much if you would introduce me to him.'

'Doonigan? Doonigan? No, I'm afraid I don't know him.'

Asking Herr Doktor if his drink was all right, Glen went over to talk to Ank and the girl in blue jeans. As it happened, they were having a good time. And their drinks were fine. But just now they were about to dance, if he would excuse them.

Donogan asked the girl in the foil pinafore who that was over there. 'The tall skinny guy with the tin hat.'

'Why, that's Glen! The host—don't you know him? Good gouts!'

16

'No . . . I was invited by his secretary, actually.'

'You're a friend of Myra's?'

'I, um, know her, yes. She doesn't seem to be here, tonight.'

'Good gouts! Didn't you *know*? She's the in hospital, having a nose job. I thought everybody knew!'

'That's odd!' Donagon was not aware he'd laughed so loudly until several Aztecs turned round to stare. 'I met her in the hospital! She was having her acne sanded, and I . . . I was . . .' He hesitated to explain the fresh scars under his outsize French cuffs. One of the false Aztecs looked him over. 'And you were having a D. and C., were you, darling?'

'Oh, George, you're impossible!' said the girl in the pinafore. She skipped off to dance with George the impossible Aztec.

'. . . recorded in 1948, while he was still in prison,' said one of the zoot suits.

'Harry, listen—you're out of your mind. It had to be 1950 because the company that cut the record didn't even exist in '48.'

In another room the girl in blue jeans asked the tall man with the ax-blade nose what he did for a living.

'I'm an art critic.'

'You too? I just met one art critic.'

'The one that works for the *Sun*? Haha, *critic*? He thinks Lichtenstein is a country, for Christ's sake. *Critic*?'

Something bumped their legs. They stood back to let the man in the wrinkled dinner jacket crawl past. ''S all right,' he explained, 'I'm from Innerpol.'

The Herr Doktor came through next, asking for a geneticist named Doonigan.

'A what?' One of the two businessmen in fur wigs who were holding each other upright near the piano turned to stare at him. 'What does that sawed-off kraut want? A gyneticist?'

'Geenetics,' said his companion. 'Genes.'

The other nudged him. 'Hey, I wouldn't mind getting in *her* jeans, Charlie.' He leered at the girl.

Elsewhere other happily married men were leering at girls in crinoline, copper sheaths, feather robes and complicated layers of translucency; even at the girl in patent leather, who, hand to mouth, was searching all the rooms for her lost stick-on lips. Somebody went into the toilet to vomit, and

17

somebody else used an overshoe in the closet. One of the zoots was spitting blood in the kitchen sink, while his friend stood by, holding his pork-pie hat for him.

'Look, Harry, I *said* I'm sorry. Anybody can lose his temper now and then. Especially when I know that Deef John cut that side in nineteen . . .'

A troupe of girls in buckskin bikinis and antler hats moved through, pouring coffee and emptying ashtrays. Ank left with the girl in the foil pinafore. Donagon dozed in a chair.

Direct from Las Vegas packed up and left. The party reduced to those who had passed out, determined drinkers, and those without a sense of time, like the six persons in Egyptian dress squatting in the corner and digging a candle flame.

Glen Dale and Senator Vuje shook Donagon awake.

'You all right?'

He nodded, and again when Glen asked if he were a scientist named Doonigal. '. . . Donagon . . .' he said thickly.

'That must be you. There's someone who wants to talk to you. Just a minute, I'll see if I can find him.'

'I thought you was Truman Whatsisname, the writer,' said the senator. Somehow in his caftan he looked more like a senator than ever. 'Here, let's get you on your feet, fella.'

He did not get Donagon on his feet. Instead the toilet door opened behind him, knocking the senator on top of him.

'What the hell . . . ?'

'I'm so sorry.' Donagon's glasses had been knocked off. He saw only a blurry, short figure in black, though he could hear the crisp German consonants. 'I'm so sorry.'

'Why the hell don't you watch where you're going? Now look, you knocked me down, knocked this poor fella's glasses off . . .'

'I apologize again.' The blur made a gesture with both arms. 'But then, where *am* I going? That is a question. Where are we all going? And how is it best to watch?'

'Listen, you little heinie, I fought your kind at Anzio . . .'

'Ah, forgive me, gentlemen. I most probably am drunk. Good night.'

Donagon retrieved his glasses and got to his feet. The short man in black was disappearing out the hall door when Glen came in from the dining room.

18

'I fought his kind at Anzio,' the senator mumbled. Arrogant little . . .'

One of the business twins sat down suddenly in the middle of the floor. 'I DON'T WANT TO GO HOME. I WANT TO GET ME ONE OF THESE LITTLE GIRLIES AND GO UPSTAIRS.'

'But, Charlie, we *are* upstairs. This is the penthouse.'

'I guess he's gone,' Glen said, shrugging. 'That guy was looking for you all evening.'

'Well, I'll get going.' Donagon shook hands with his host and with the veteran of Anzio, and with a long-toothed man Glen introduced as his psychiatrist, Dr Feinwelt.

'Whazzis?' The businessman called Charlie, still seated on the floor, held up a black object. 'HEY! Some guy lost his leatha mustache!'

As Donagon left, he heard someone say, 'Wasn't that Truman Capote?'

'Are you kidding? Anybody who wears French cuffs that big couldn't be *anybody*.'

19

PART ONE | AN EXPERIMENT

ONE

> They say your heart is dacron
> And you just caint love nohow
> But darlin I know . . .

It was a false day. Drizzle and the amplified, reedy heartbreak of a country-western singer drifted over the parking lot. There were tear-streaks on the mistproof windshields, pools of tears on the uneven plasphalt, and (in case everyone hadn't got the message) a wet, melodious wind to blast the faces of several hundred National Arsenamid employees. The message, straight from the hearts of industrial psychologists, was: 'What a hell of a day! Great to get inside, where it's *warm*, and *dry*, and the Melodiak's playing a light, bouncy tune like "Sunshine Balloon".'

One man in a seam-split raincoat did not get the message; he walked slowly, ignored the rain, and even tried whistling along with 'Cold Old Dacron Heart'. He was looking at the factory, too. All the others had averted their false morning faces from the rain, but not Bob Shairp.

He was looking at the factory for almost the last time—and seeing it for the first.

It looked exactly what it was, a service factory for the great food/missile corporation. A long, white building without character, neither ugly nor interesting.

No, today it was a ship, lying at anchor by the edge of the parking lot, with light streaming from every porthole. A

21

voyage a day, for almost two years . . . and today the last. It was going on without him.

The whistle blew. Bob hurried in to the security office. The walls were maize over raw sienna this morning. On a sunny day they would go azure over dark green. As the soft saxophones of Melodiak greeted him ('fill up that sun-shine ba-LLOON with hap-pi-ness'), Bob fumbled for his identity card.

'Must be in the coat I usually wear,' he said. The guard did not return his smile. 'But you know me, anyway.'

'Yeah, I know you, Shairp. Losing your card on your last day here! Just what in hell do you think you're gonna walk off with—a few plans, maybe?'

Bob smiled to see if he was kidding. The guard turned his back on it. 'All right, get the hell in there and stop wasting my time.'

*

Bob was a technical writer with a BA in English and a general understanding of engineering practice. He was not actually allowed to *write* anything, though he worked closely with a writing computer.

Many of National Arsenamid's products resembled one another, and their repair manuals and parts lists differed only in details. Drawings and test routines were fed to the computer, which revised old manuals to fit new items. Bob made minor corrections in the computer's prose.

A block of prose would appear on the screen before him:

Disassembly of half-speed prism carrier (5A1). Remove mtg screws (5A1A), carrier cover (5A1B) and gasket (5A1C). Discard gasket. Using lifting tool UA–10, lift and remove prism assembly (5A1D). Adjust prism assembly aside for testing.

He would work the keyboard to change 'adjust' to 'set', a new block of prose would appear, and so on. As the training film had explained: '*You* are the key. *You* understand nuances of English which the computer cannot. So you see, we can never *really* eliminate the *human* element.'

Yet today, for reasons no one quite understood, Bob was being replaced. They were sending him to Mud Flats, Nebraska, to be retrained, then to one of their fifty-four other plants.

22

National Arsenamid was still masquerading as a food processor. But only five plants still made *Perp* and other breakfast delicacies. Only eleven more made up the home kitchen of an invisible lady named Bette Cooke. The rest were under defense contracts.

Bob had no objection to working for defense. In fact he worried now and then about the Chinese getting ahead in the Second Front missile race. They were said to be working on an orbiting missile platform, as a third-strike capability (meaning something still up their sleeves after China and the US had wiped each other out, twice over).

What Bob didn't like was secret work. He enjoyed coming home, flopping on the couch, and saying, 'Boy! You know what that crazy computer came up with today? Marge, you should have seen it . . .'

And what could he tell her today? That the computer didn't need him anymore?

*

Marge was not sympathetic.

'Retraining pay is next to nothing, Bob! And Spot counted on getting into a military school—really, you couldn't have picked a worse time.'

'I,' he began, and lifted an admonishing finger from his glass. What was so admonishing about that finger? Looked pretty much like all the rest. He put it back and studied the fingers all together. Making white circles on the glass. Or it on them. The drink in the glass was called a pajama. Four parts . . . no, five parts gin . . .

'You what?'

'I had nothing to do with it. For one reason or another, they're replacing me, that's all. I'm being moved on. What are you up to, anyway?'

Marge sat on the carpet, surrounded by a sprawl of magazines. Her right hand twiddled a pencil, her left held an open copy of *Luxurious Home*. The first letter of the title was hidden by her fingers, offering Bob a silent pun.

'I'm doing a test: "Does Your Mate Measure Up?" It says —just a minute—it says that you have a lot of artistic ability, and you could really go places, but that you're inclined to

23

fritter away your time on frivolous projects. What you want in a wife is a mother, because you tend to shirk responsibilities.'

'Oh, that's good, that's good! I'll bet I have to be careful around the fifteenth, because something enters the house of something else, and though fifteen and seven are good numbers —aw, what's the use?'

He decided to see what Spot was working on, on the teaching machine.

*

'Watch, Spot.' Bob pushed open the door with his foot and came in juggling eggs. 'Got it up to four, now, and . . .'

The boy had fallen asleep at his homework. One thin arm lay crooked around the teaching machine, which was still trying to get him to answer something about the gold standard. His pajamas were black, and cut to resemble some kind of uniform complete with false pockets, belts and plastic medals.

As Spot stirred, cuddling the machine closer, his father saw what kind of uniform it was. The red brassard turned to show a white circle and a hooked cross . . .

Bob put him to bed and then cleaned up the eggs from the floor.

*

'Grow up, Bob! It doesn't *mean* anything to him. All the kids have them. On account of that German TV program.'

'*Leutnant Krieger?* You let him watch that crap? Christ, no wonder he worships the SS.'

Without answering, Marge opened her recipe file and began sorting cards.

'So that's what this "military school" thing is all about! All the kids do it, he says. It's harmless, you say. And in twenty years, when they start up new concentration camps . . .'

'For God's sake! You haven't even watched the program, so how can you judge it? It isn't so bad, really. This Leutnant Krieger's not really an SS man at all. He's working to assassinate Hitler. So you see, when he beats up a Jew, it's only part of his cover story. And when he . . .'

'I get it. The best of both worlds, right? That's just the way the Nazis worked in the first place. "This isn't really me doing

24

this medical experiment, it's Destiny working through me. It's Blood and Destiny, and besides, it's orders." What's the use, nobody's listening.'

Marge snapped the file box shut. 'Oh, we're all against you, is that it? Listen, you know what they say about aggression. He needs permissible outlets. Isn't it better to let him get it out of his system now?'

'Or into his system, maybe?'

'Listen, you. If anybody in this family turns Spot into a little Nazi, it'll be you! You, with all your petty restrictions and rules. Who wanted to keep him away from TV altogether? Who wouldn't let him box? *Oh, damn you!*'

She began to cry over a fistful of Japanese recipes. Later, after they had made love, she whispered, 'There was something I meant to tell you tonight, only I've forgotten.'

'Mm?'

'Oh yes. The window peeper.'

'N.'

'One of the neighbors saw someone lurking around our windows last night.'

Bob sat up and turned on the light. 'And I'm going away tomorrow? Why in hell didn't you say something? Who saw him?'

She hesitated, chewing a thumbnail. 'Don't laugh, but it was Mrs Fellstus.'

The light went off and Bob dragged the blankets towards his side of the bed.

'Don't you want to hear about it?'

For answer, he twitched away more of the blankets.

*

The Thursday meetings of the Jess Hurch Society had dwindled, dwindled. No one seemed to care about fighting Communism any more, and Grover attributed this to Lack of Moral Fiber and to Red propaganda.

'They control the press, the radio, television,' he said to the two people in the hall. 'Wall Street, which they revile unceasingly, is really their tool. My own bank today refused us a loan to keep the fight going. So now I'm going to ask all of you to be generous . . .'

25

One of the two snorted, murmured something about a con game, and left. That left only Amy Birdsall (Sec. and Treas.). Grover Minus (Pres.) climbed down off the dais, set the American flag back in its holder, and sat down next to her. Amy lay down her pencil and applauded wildly until he shushed her. Then the room was silent, except for the creak of their folding chairs, as two old bodies shifted and shifted, searching for comfortable positions.

'I give up, Amy. The cumminisks have won.'

She looked shocked. 'Grover! How can you say such a thing! Why only yesterday . . .'

'No, no. We're too old for this kind of thing. My arm's too bad to run the printing press. How can we warn the world, the two of us against millions of cumminisk spies? Better for you to go back to your bible and your Billy Whatsisname. Me, I'll—I've got a few friends in that Florida retirement home we talked about. Thought I might drop down and—and see. Just see.'

Amy started weeping, pushing up her bifocals to scrub away the tears. 'The only thing I ever believed in,' she whimpered. 'Besides God Almighty. I'd carry on by myself, but what can *I* do? I'm only a weak woman.'

For all her eighty years, Amy was stronger than Grover. She had once been a Rockette, and prided herself on still being able to kick off a man's hat—if men still wore hats. But Grover was desperate to comfort her, all the same.

'All right,' he said, patting her hand. 'All right, kid, the Jess Hurchists *will* go forward. But *underground*. No more pamphleteering, no more speeches. We'll just spy them out, and turn over everything we learn to the FBI.'

*

The original Jess Hurch (1842–1887) was a cowpoke, miner, farmer and grain merchant. He was also a gambler, pimp, drunk and petty swindler. Yet his was a life redeemed at the last moment, and, in the town of Medicine Dumps, California, Jess paid his debts.

He was celebrating something by shooting out store windows and store owners along Main Street when he noticed a crowd collecting by the railway station. The governor of the state was

26

about to campaign for re-election from the rear platform of his special train. Jess just naturally found a good spot in the front of the crowd.

It was a hot day. The speech was long. The governor invited everyone to sit down. Jess hunkered down on a rail and dozed off.

Midway through his speech, the governor asked if anyone wanted government by guess and by golly. Jess awoke, thought someone had called upon him to say a few words, and jumped up.

The swarthy man seated right behind him picked that moment to shoot the governor.

Though somewhat startled at being sprayed with brains and blood, the governor was unhurt. The citizenry sighed with relief at Jess's departure. Then they strung up the wrong man. Then they shot up the town, good-naturedly.

The actual assassin was found hiding in a cracker barrel, and they finished off the day with a second necktie party. The swarthy little man's last words were 'Long live Anarchy!' Thus it came to be that Jess Hurch transcended his own nature (the coroner reported him rotten with two kinds of VD) and joined the roundup of history—American's first martyr to Anarchy, better known as Communism.

Seventy years later the Jess Hurch Society began. Grover Minus was especially pleased to carry on this particular name. As he demonstrated to his friends, 'Jess Hurchist' was an anagram relating the movement directly to Christianity.

Jess would have liked that. 'Jesus H. Christ' was his favorite ejaculation.

*

Mrs Fellstus sat in her accustomed place by the window, peering at the world through a slit she'd cut in the curtain.

'He's there again!' she cried. There was no answer from the study, so she wheeled herself in, to make sure the doctor heard. 'The window peeper's there again tonight! Dean, you're not listening.'

'That's right, Mother, I'm not listening. I'm trying to read an article in this journal.'

'But the window peeper . . .'

27

'Mother.' Dr Fellstus tucked a huge, flat thumb in his *Journal of Kennel Psychiatry* and turned to face her. 'We've been over this so many times, haven't we? Isn't it really just another case of the Communist in the Basement?'

'No! Dean . . .'

'Let me assure you, Mother, we are very, very safe here. Since you are no longer a Jess Hurchist, you need no longer fear the "great conspiracy". There is no one outside, no window peeper, no one at all.'

'Just come and look at him, Dean. Just once.'

'Mother, remember the time you read somewhere the phrase "a chink in his armor"? And how afterwards you kept imagining Red Chinese clanking up the stairs—remember that?'

'Please, Dean. Just look.'

Very (sighing) well, Dr Fellstus walked into the living room, whipped back the curtain, and saw his own surprised expression. The handlebar mustache needed a trim.

'Nothing and no one. Why don't you watch a little TV, Mother? I believe they're showing Billy Koch tonight, preaching from Porklink Stadium.'

There was no edge to his voice; nevertheless it was an order. Mrs Fellstus switched on the set, and the veterinarian returned to his journal.

The easy assumptions of this particular article rankled. Dr Fellstus, like its author, specialized in nervous diseases of the collie. He did not like to see this kind of over-emphasis on Oedipal matters, at the expense of common sense.

The 'Lassie' image, the feminization of this rough Scottish sheep dog, may have made no small contribution to the popular, sentimentalist view of the collie. Owners erroneously attributing to their pets a passive, meek, fastidious nature may find instead their pets are vigorous and headstrong. They may react to this discovery by covert rejection, or by trying to force Laddie or Bruce into a womanly rôle. They may lock him up, curtail his barking, even expect him to perform distaff duties like slipper-fetching. Thus the collie's worst puppyhood fears, those of castration by an angry sire, are seen to be . . .

Heal this child, O Lord!' cried the TV set.

'Angry sire indeed!' said Dr Fellstus, pulling at his un-

28

trimmed mustache. 'And not a damned word about early weaning!'

'. . . could have sworn . . .' said his mother's lips. 'A man . . . in a long gray overcoat . . . walking stick . . .'

*

There really was a man in a gray overcoat, and he did use a gold-headed walking stick. His name was MacCormick Hines, and he was not 'window peeping', but checking out the truth about reality, the truth he'd come upon twenty years before.

The truth was that reality was televised.

Tonight, for example, Mr Hines watched a soap opera called *The Shairp Family*. Others might tune in on television by turning a knob. He tuned in by telling his chauffeur to stop the car and wait while he took a little constitutional, by creeping up to the screen and peering in.

The advantage of televised reality was that one could tune out any ghosts of unpleasantness. Mr Hines was able to believe that he was not one of the richest men in the world, only 'comfortable'. He was able to believe that his corporation, National Arsenamid, made only fine cereals to build healthy kids, and nothing at all like anthrax, smallpox and typhus. And finally he was able to believe that everything he owned was his by dint of hard, honest work.

Whenever one of the bright young men who handled his investments tried to tell him how rich he was, Mr Hines would shout him down:

'If I have a few comforts, by Gum I've earned them! Application, that's what it took. Application of the seat of my pants to the seat of a chair. Putting on my thinking cap, giving the old gray matter a good workout. I sleep four hours a night, and I don't waste a golden hour, a diamond minute of the rest! Time is money.

'Better wear out than rust out. A little hard work never hurt anybody! All it takes is a little Yankee ingenuity, a little "can do". I don't believe in the word "can't". It takes gumption, and grit, and stick-to-itiveness, and a lot of plain, hard, honest-to-God elbow grease!

'Use the brains God gave you! Dream awhile and scheme awhile, but keep your feet planted on *terra firma* and PLUG!'

29

Then, with the young man shouted out of the room, he could go back to his gentle dreams.

*

The Shairp Family was one of his favorite programs. He preferred standing in the cold drizzle to see it, when he could be sitting in dry bleachers watching that faith-healer program across town, even if the action here was a little slow tonight. The writers were probably in a slump.

So Bob was going away on business, while Spot was not, for the time being, going to military school. Well, well. Not much to chew on. As for the business about the 'window peeper', that was all wrong, all wrong. The real drama ought to come from *inside* the family, and not be grafted on artificially. Mr Hines thought about complaining to the sponsors, whoever they might be.

What ought to happen is for Bob to get lost at sea in an air crash. Then Marge could remarry—or almost—and Bob could 'return from the grave'. That would be bully realism. Whooping cough for Spot, but when Bob comes back, they all live happily . . .

As he shuffled away, leaning into the cold October wind, Mr Hines wondered about that window-peeper business. Who would the peeper turn out to be? Some long-lost relative? Someone in distress? Or someone who would help out the Shairps when—as inevitably it must—tragedy struck? He could hardly wait to see the mysterious stranger's face.

30

TWO

Bob came out of the dream sometime during breakfast, under the combined impact of coffee and headlines:

SCIENTIST DISAPPEARS

Müller-Fokker a possible defector

EVANGELIST BREAKS RECORD

10 MORE YEARS WAR? NO, SAYS ARMY CHIEF

Weimarauner predicts breakthrough

Something about . . . children? By the time he climbed in the car, his dream had dwindled to just two words, 'Jelly Day.' He had to stop off at the factory to turn in his badge, then on to Mud Flats, Nebraska. He forgot even the two words. . . .

The guard took a look at his badge and grinned. 'Just in time, Shairp. Another hour and we would of summoned the Industrial Security boys to come and get it. Anyways, we got to finalize your new badge for the other project. Are you leaving today?'

Bob nodded. Two workmen passed between them, carrying a computer console. It was his; he recognized the cigarette burns.

'Okay,' said the guard. 'Okay. We'll expedite the processing, if you'll just organize yourself a chair over there in the visitors'

31

room. Your replacement's waiting in there, by the way, if you want to meet him.'

As Bob opened the door, the occupants of the visitors' room, a man and his dog, looked up. The man smiled, showing a rotten tooth. 'Hiya.'

Behind Bob, the security guard began bawling out the information on his card to someone else. There were typing sounds.

'I guess you're my replacement,' Bob shouted over the racket.

'OUT: SHAIRP, ROBERT ETWALL! 77903! TECH WRITER, CAUCASIAN, MALE!'

'What say? Can't hear ya.'

'I said, I guess you're replacing me. As a tech writer.'

'Me? Nawww. 'S old Bingo, here.'

Bob still didn't get it, until the guard took up another badge and bawled: 'IN! BINGO!' The dog looked up at the sound of his name. '89474–A! TECH WRITER, GOLDEN RETRIEVER, MALE!'

Bob tried to smile. 'I'll be damned.'

Rotten-tooth chuckled. 'Amazin', ain't it? Ol' Bingo here earns more'n me. Ya see, they trained him in one a them animal labs, so he knows how to tell a circle from a ellipse *real close*. That's all it takes, I guess. They got the computer fixed up ta turn that inta writin'. Say hello ta the nice man, Bingo. Come on, boy.'

Bob took a silky paw and gazed into gentle stupid eyes. 'Hello, Bingo,' he said solemnly. Thinking, *so much for the human element.*

*

Wes Davis had his boots up on the desk and his hands clasped behind that elegant head of hair.

That hair. It rose a full four inches from his widow's peak in front. The sides had been starved down to a pair of cuneiform sideburns even narrower than the space between Wes's eyes. But on top—a relief map of some dark planet, all greasy peaks and whorled valleys. It overwhelmed the other part of his head, the part equipped with a small but recognizable face.

Wes was thinking how just it was that there should be only one chair in the gas station office. It just wouldn't be right for

32

the Mud Flats Ramblers—Skeeter, Travis and Gus—to sit right down with him, their leader. Might give them the idea they were leader types, too.

So here was Skeeter, shaking up a Pepsi and spraying it down his throat; Gus, leaning on the pop cooler; Travis, pretending to study the *Stagman* calendar on the wall; here they were, waiting for Wes to tell them what to do.

'Yes sir,' he said. 'Yes sir. When your wife takes some clothes down to the laundromat, she has to se-par-ate the colored ones from the white ones. Am I right?'

He was right.

'Why? Because they run. That's right. Take a nice perty little pair of lace drawers . . .'

'Where?' That was Skeeter, trying for a laugh. Wes stared him down.

'Take them nice little white nylong lace drawers, throw 'em in with a dirty, stinking, black old pair of socks, and what have you got? What happens?

'I'll tell you what *don't*. Them socks sure as hell ain't gonna come out *white*! No, it's the pure white little drawers gets ruint, ever time. They come out all black and gray and dirty. Not just them, everthing in the whole wash gets ruint! And all by one little old *harmless* nigger sock!'

Travis scratched his crotch. 'What happen to the othern?'

'What?'

'The other sock. They was two before, and now you just got one. Where's the othern?'

Wes opened a desk drawer and spat into it. 'Jesus Christ, Travis, you didn't hear a thing I said. I'm talking about NIGRAS! It's just the same. You mix the two races, it's the white gets ruint.'

He jumped up and slapped the desk. '*That* is a *fact* of *science*!'

While the fact of science soaked in, Wes went outside and groomed the windshield of a tourist's car. Tucking a rag in his pocket, he resumed his leadership position.

'Now everbody knows the Army is full of nigger-lovers. And everbody knows the National Arsenamid Corporation is run by Jeeews, right? An Equal Opportunity Employer, they call it.

33

'So what do you spose the Army and the National Arsenamid Corporation are hatching up together over on the edge of town? Over in that Biomedical Research Project.'

They didn't know, Wes.

'You know what biomedical research is? *Makin babies in test tubes!*'

'Naw! Can't be!'

'Yes sir, and not white babies. Nigra babies!'

'But in test tubes!' Travis scratched furiously. 'Christ! How do they get out?'

'I'm comin to that. They just start the babies off in test tubes. Then they ship them to hospitals all over the US of A, and they *stick them up white women!*'

'Aw, Christ!'

'It's true. I know it for a fact. Ever notice how all them hospitals got lots of nigra orderlies and nurses?'

'Yeah, that's right, Wes.'

'Yer fuckin' A, that's right. The nigra conspiracy is on the move, right here in Mud Flats! They'll populate the whole world with black bastards—*unless we stop 'em!*'

*

'That's right, Shairp. I know they told you it would be "retraining", but that was just to keep a security blanket over this.' Major Fouts, Project Security Officer, looked at his watch for the sixth time in as many minutes.

'But I—didn't I come down here for retraining?'

'Look, I don't care, buster. If you don't like the job, skip it. We sure as hell don't need you. I mean, just about any warm body will do for this experiment.'

Bob cleared his throat and gazed at the barred windows. 'Is it dangerous? I mean, just what will they do to me?'

'No, it isn't dangerous, and I can't tell you anything about the project until you're cleared. So are you in or out? Hurry up.'

'Will I—be all right afterwards?'

'YAS, YAS, YAS! NOW HURRY UP!'

'I'm—in?'

'Fine now go see Donagon research head for your papers then go down for your physical and then come back up here

34

for clearance here don't forget to fill out all the copies and sign them you're restricted to base until the clearance comes through sign this and take it up to 4B today they want a blood sample this is your V–5 form and that's your waiver if you need anything else see Donagon.'

As soon as Bob was gone, Major Fouts pulled the blinds and locked his office door. Then he worked the combination on his desk drawer and removed three almond Hershey bars. Two he slid under the blotter, the third he peeled and folded lovingly into his elastic mouth.

There was no excuse for it, he knew, none but tedium and despair. Fouts had done everything the Army could expect of him, and more. In his first year here, he had cleaned out a dozen lab assistants of questionable background. He had tightened up all security procedures. He had blacked out news releases. And he had fixed up the computer with an auto-destruct mechanism using only four charges, a model of efficiency. And then—nothing. Nothing but deadly routine, the daily dossiers, the loathsome tight uniform. The candy bars.

His mouth full of melted heaven, he damned Mud Flats. A city post would have been all right. Algernon Fouts could have managed that . . . mingling nightly with theater crowds . . . unescorted at a ballroom . . . bars. . . . Even hidden away in remotest Arcady, fine, but this! In damned, damned Mud Flats, where one was never alone. Official secrecy was easy enough, but any other kind was impossible.

So a part of him lay shut away in his footlocker, under the pile of uniforms his misery had outgrown. Eating, a permitted indiscretion, dulled the pain a little, just as it dulled his features.

There came an unmilitary knock at the door. 'Algie? Can I see you a minute?'

Fouts snatched up the wrapper and stuffed it through the slotted lid of his security waste basket. He swallowed the last of the sweetness and unlocked the door to Dr Donagon.

'What do you want? I'm busy here, you know. Got to check the dossier of this new guy, Shairp . . .'

'Please, Algie, you've got to let me publish. *Anything.* Just some little hooker, something to get my name on it.'

Fouts swam back to the desk through his own liquid layers.

35

'Not my responsibility. Both the Army and National Arse have their reasons for keeping this under wraps. If it was up to me, I'd let all you boobologists print all you wanted in your boobology journals.'

'Major!' Donagon flung back a lock of his thin, khaki-colored hair. It fell forward again. 'I am a bi-o-physicist, and I am also head of research here. I know I'm young, but I think that, um.' He brushed back the stray lock. Fouts could see white scars on the man's wrist. 'I think that I am due some respect in that, um, respect.'

'Yas, yas. Anyway, things are looking up, kid. The press is going to be invited in on zero-day. You'll get all the publicity you can eat.'

'If only I could be sure—that it was the right kind of publicity, Algie. This could mean the Nobel if I handle it right. But I still ought to have published something. Others are at work on it. Otis Korner at Attica, Flaken of Illinois. O God! If they get a man on tape before I do . . .'

'If you spent less time iffing . . .'

Donagon blushed. 'I'm afraid, if you must know. The press . . . they garble things . . .'

'All right, all right. Make up a prepared handout.'

Donagon brightened noticeably. He left, and Fouts went back to work. On the second Hershey bar.

*

Billy Koch, breakfasting at his desk on a glass of Slimmix (90 calories), shook out his morning paper and got down to work, marking sermonizable stories.

He circled an article on the current Asian conflict and swiveled around to the typewriter to hunt out: 'I offer mnt prayer (sil?) for our boys who have won vict, w/ many trag. losses, in (place). But wht vict can compare &c.'

He put a question mark near MAN SUES GOD FOR LOCUST DAMAGE and turned a page. Pickings were poor: CONGRESS APPROVES BUDGET CUTS; SERIA TO TRY FOR 3½ MIN MILE; ROAD TOLL. . . .

He caught himself humming a pop tune, 'Ice Cream Blues', switched to a hymn, then caught his breath again. A small item, buried in the back pages:

36

COMPUTERIZED MAN?

Washington (AP)—A Pentagon spokesman announced today a joint research project between the Army and National Arsenamid Corporation to 'investigate the possibility of partly or even completely digitalizing a living man, using genetic, physiological and neurological data'. Further details were not forthcoming, but a reliable source states that a subject has already been selected, and the experiment is said to be under way.

Billy circled this item twice, and doubly exclaimed on the typewriter: 'You can compute a man—but nt immtl soul!!'
So much for the sermon. He was about to check the financial pages for the inevitable rise of BK Industries, when his secretary announced the arrival of his architect, Ögivaal.

*

Downstairs from Billy in the Crusade headquarters mail room the first three bags were dumped on the sorting table and the sorters went to it. They dealt first with packages. A box of birdseed addressed to 'H. Spirit' went to one of the staff whose mother had a budgerigar. An odiferous box bearing the suspect palindrome 'A Mr Oops laminates set animal spoor, Ma' went into the wastebasket unopened, joining a bedspread embroidered by loving hands with all of the Psalms. A musical revolving crucifix from some novelty company was set aside for the market analysis department, while an 'electric rosary' went into the large carton destined for a Roman Catholic charity.

Using thumb-knives, the sorters disemboweled envelopes and discarded the frivolous, the illegible, and the hopelessly insane:

'Dear Billy, I am the Messiah, He who is not sent. The Messiah shall command, it shall be his command. The Messiah commands you according to the commandments of the same to use My name in vain, while you are knowing My wife . . .'

'Dear Billy: Last night I woke up and you were standing at the foot of my bed and there was something wrong with your face. Billy, I thought you were going to kill me with a ax. I don't know. Maybe the devil sent this vision to confuse me when I'm having headaches . . .'

37

The answerable letters were passed on to the *Replies* table. Marilyn Temblor closed her magazine, keeping for a moment the after image of one perfume advertisement—it seemed so darned unfair that Crusade workers weren't allowed to—and made her mind blank for business.

The first letter, from a cancer patient, was easy. Marilyn carried it to the row of automated typewriters and ran one unvarnished nail down the list of items posted on the wall:

Habitual sin	359
Unfaithful spouse	360
Marital problems (general)	361
Major illness	362
Afraid of dying	ˊ363
Death of spouse	364
Death of child	365

Afraid of dying, then. She punched 363 on the control panel, rolled a sheet of letterhead in the typewriter and carefully typed the salutation:

'Dear Mrs. Dale:'

From there on it was simply a matter of switching from MAN to AUTO. The letter was typed in just under six seconds.

Dear Mrs Dale:

I received and read your letter, and I was deeply touched by it. You seem to be afraid of dying. This is only natural, for no creature on God's earth wants to die. For the humble animals, death is an end.

But not for you. FOR YOU, DEATH IS THE VERY BEGINNING.

When Columbus set sail, he didn't know . . .

And so it went, right on down to the PS about remembering God in your will. A marvelous machine. Marilyn didn't understand how the signers could refer to it as a 'tripewriter'.

The signers were young bible students who saw no conflict between afternoons reading theology and mornings falsifying Billy's signature to thousands of letters. They were a flippant, cynical bunch, and Marilyn hated taking letters in to them. One in particular, a fair-haired, blue-eyed, disgustingly handsome boy named Jim.

*

38

'I understand perfectly,' said the architect. 'Everything modern but nothing extreme.' He and Billy were looking at a sketch entitled *South Elevation: Bibleland.* 'Now, about the mechanical figures and so on?'

Billy flipped through his desk diary. 'I've got my computer man, Jerry, coming in Wednesday—let's all have lunch. How much do you need to know?'

'Everything, sir, everything. Each pavilion must be a container for the thing contained, neither more nor less. For less *is* more, and function designs its form. There must be balance, adaptability, total harmony and standardization . . .'

'Now what about the site?'

'I prefer to pick a flat, undistinguished piece of land and landscape it, Mr Koch.'

'Okay, but keep the estimate in mind, Archy. And I wish you'd just call me Billy.'

'Very well—Billy. I will not exceed the estimate, you can be sure. And I leave no detail to chance.

'That's something I learned at architecture school in my homeland. My mathematics master used to mark a problem completely wrong if there were even the slightest error. I asked him why I should lose all credit for a simple misplaced decimal point.

'He said, "Wrong is wrong, Ögivaal. When you will be an architect, and your building collapses, it will not matter the reason. You cannot then say 'This thirty should be a three." I never forgot his words.'

'This site . . .'

'Ah yes. I have one tentative site located, quite ideal but for the fact that it is a small Indian reservation.'

Billy's pale blue eyes flicked up, then back to the plan. 'If it's worth it, we can probably get them moved off. Is it?'

'Yes, yes, it is perfect. Quite near that place—what is the name? Death Valley.'

*

On the wall above Donagon's desk was a histogram showing who was where in the Nobel race:

39

```
Bell and Jopp   ----------------
Burnside        ------
Donagon         -----------------------
Flaken          -------------------
Korner          -----------------
Müller-Fokker ----?
Smilax          ---------
```

The one who really worried him was Müller-Fokker, who might have done it already. If he had really defected—no one seemed to know for sure—he might have the entire resources of Soviet research at his disposal.

Donagon wiped his damp hands, opened the journal and began just after the ripped-out pages:

We decided not to abandon the attempt after all; to try once more to store a man digitally. The last obstacle had been removed, i.e., storage. Previously we had estimated many thousands of miles of magnetic tape would be required, with complex retrieval problems. The multiple storage paired redundancy tapes, developed by Müller-Fokker (the so-called 'Müller-Fokker tapes') in Vienna and demonstrated by him at the Louisville National Laboratory, were exactly what we needed. These reduced our tape requirements to four ten-inch reels.

The M-F tape is much of a mystery except to its inventor. The principle seems to be *Gestalt* analysis (if that is the term), or recognition of large patterns in large amounts of data. Data fed in is not immediately recorded, but 'comprehended' and compressed—by the tape itself—into formulae. The tape is not magnetic but electrochemical. It may not be erased, but new data may be recorded upon old. There seems to be a layering or—

We do not really understand the M-F tape at all, but we do understand it will do the job. At present we have no way of retrieving what we want from the tape, and since its inventor has vanished, it may take us many years—

Many years—

Every datum will be recorded many times, to reduce error. At present, surgeons are removing tissue samples from the subject (from bones, organs, glands, etc.) and determining cell-structure data. We have already encoded a DNA map, photographs, holographs, x-rays, resin casts, EKG's and so on—as complete an analysis of the subject as we can make. There remains but one step, the mapping of all electrical and chemical activity of the

40

subject's brain. The press will be invited to this session; they will see us succeed or fail.

Succeed or fail.

Through the partition dividing his office from that of Major Fouts, he could hear the crinkle of cellophane and foil, and the sound of devouring.

*

The laboratory looked like a throne room. Bob sat in the throne, a surgical chair; his courtiers wore rubber gloves and his crown was a steel vise. Above the crown those in the visitors' room could see pinkish-gray, crumpled velvet.

Back of the throne was a large illuminated map of this velvet surface on which men marked the current weather in Bob's brain. On either side were ranks of cabinets in decorator colors. Two featured control panels, one a typewriter, two more the inevitable banks of flashing lights. Four were dialling twin reels of tape (one with some excitement), eight others were anonymous, one was vomiting paper, and the two in the visitors' room were opened to display whiskey and glasses.

There were other press facilities in the visitors' room, including telephones, free cigarettes, sharpened pencils and fresh pads, and a big stack of xeroxed press releases.

The one reporter who did show up had a hell of a time.

'I sure appreciate this,' he said to Donagon. 'I'll bet the rest of the gang haven't got it this good down there in Florida.'

He asked Donagon if he'd ever heard of the magazine he worked for, LIFE.

'Florida?'

'Yeah, everyone else went down to cover the big cancer cure story. I missed the plane, so I thought I might as well drop over and check this one out. I really had another assignment over by North Platte, I had to get a picture of this deformed bull. I'd take some shots of your set-up here, only I can't. My camera and stuff caught the plane.'

He wanted Donagon to have a drink with him and hear the anecdote, but the biophysicist was wanted elsewhere.

*

A voice behind Bob asked him what he felt.

41

'I feel . . . my right foot . . .'

'Yes?'

'Oh, you know how it is with workbooks.'

'And now?'

'A strawberry, all glowing with starry lenses, a starberry . . . recapitulation of the plot of some old man . . . buns, for instance . . .'

Major Fouts stood watching from half-way across the room, where Donagon manned a bank of switches. Between them and the operation was a forced-air curtain to maintain sterility. It was strange to see a man talking away with half his head sawed off and a group of surgeons peering and probing within. It made Fouts feel the sharpness of his own foot-bones.

'This is a buckle collection . . . this is supposed to be a father . . . bank statements or . . . Is there anyone here named General Motors?' In an altered voice Bob delivered a message of hope to the motor corporation.

'Is this guy in any danger?' Fouts whispered.

'None at all. Shhh.' Donagon threw more switches. A kind of phonograph arm beside the chair swung around, lowered its needle, and began to 'play' the brain.

'What's that?'

'Shh. Nothing.'

'Marge!' Bob shouted. 'As a strawberry blonde . . . history as a garbage truck . . . Now look! I'm not going to say it again . . . this is lumpy.' He wept.

'Now what do you feel?'

'My picture in the atlas . . . the strawberries are . . . funny how the old school holds up . . . the old Lion Oil Company . . . arrested! . . . I hear you think . . .'

He sang a few bars of something no one could identify.

'There's an old saying around here: please wash hands before returning to work . . . a man disappears, but his ghost . . . he had it, he paid the death . . . in the movie freeze rabbit . . . U.S. Grant, the truth experiment . . . attaches . . . the bank hath changed its bank . . . the railroad egg trial . . . Dixie cups full of penetrating truth, remember? . . . smell that?'

'What do you feel like now?'

'I feel like picking my nose.'

'You *are* picking your nose. What . . .?'

42

The door slammed back and four men walked in. Donagon rushed to meet them.

'You'll have to go into the visitors' room,' he said, smiling.

'No we don't.'

'I—what? Which paper are you from?'

'This one.' The tallest man hauled out an old revolver and slapped him with it.

Fouts jumped to the alarm button. When the bell went off, the other three strangers pulled their guns.

'Okay, fat boy, where are they?'

'Where are what?'

'The nigger-babies! The test tubes!'

One of the intruders drove the surgeons away from Bob. 'Aw, Wes, look! Jesus Christ, they cut this guy's head open!'

The one with the big greasy pompadour leveled his gun at Fout's belt. 'How about it, Fats? This one of your nigger expeermints?'

'I don't know what the hell you're talking about. But I do know you're gonna do a stretch in Leavenworth, pal. Better lay down the sidearms and make it a short visit.'

'I think . . . I think I hear a bell,' Bob volunteered.

'I know your kind,' said the pompadour. 'Tryin' to put a nigger brain into that pore mother! *Come on, boas, let's mess up the place!*' He wheeled and fired a shot into the nearest memory cabinet.

'I smell a shot . . .' said Bob, still picking his nose.

Fouts's auto-destruct mechanism worked almost perfectly. The tape-reader charge misfired, but the other three went off as planned, as soon as one of the unauthorized persons tried to yank open a cabinet.

One charge was in the main memory bank. One was in the control console. They rendered the computer completely useless to Wes Davis and the Mud Flats Ramblers.

The third, slightly bigger charge was embedded in the soft padding of Bob's chair, at about ear level. The chair had been designed by an orthopedic surgeon to maintain posture and reduce fatigue. What was left of it still looked good that evening, to the cleanup crew.

'That's the way I'd like to go,' one remarked. 'Comfy.'

*

43

Lieutenant Colonel Fouts tried to shut out the screaming and wailing from the other side of the partition; he tried to order his thoughts.

There was plenty to think about: The government had pulled out of the Mud Flats project and abandoned the attempt to tape a man. National Arsenamid was expected to follow suit. In retrospect, the idea did smell of circle-squaring and perpetual motion, he had to admit. So if Donagon couldn't take the disappointment and KNOCK OFF THAT NOISE, it only underlined how crazy he was. The Army had kept his leaky dream afloat long enough. Anyway, National Arse would probably find something else for Donagon to do. Design a new cornflake, say, or answer the telephone.

Fouts himself was off for a few weeks' badly needed leave, then some new assignment. He checked a few items off his list: files destroyed, diet started, new oak leaves to buy in Frisco, bag packed, desk cleaned out. There remained only the call to Sharp's next of kin and what else? A Butterfinger candy bar that wouldn't fit into his luggage.

'O God!' said the partition. 'My whole life wasted! *That* close to the Nobel and—ruined! O why have you forsaken me, O my governme . . .'

'I SAID KNOCK IT OFF!' Fouts slammed his wastepaper basket against the wall four or five times. It set the plywood quaking and reminded him to return the wastebasket to the supply room. Well, screw that. He had a bus to catch in fifteen minutes. With a start on the candy bar, he dialed Mrs R. E. Sharp.

She answered too soon, catching him with a mouthful of stickiness. A big swallow, then:

'Mrs Sharp? Mrs Robert Etwall Sharp? Uh, this is Lt Col Fouts, Knighted Stays Army, Mrs Sharp—oh, *Shairp*, is it? Uh, Mrs Shairp, it is . . . excuse me . . . my painful duty to inform you that your husband, you know, Robert Shairp, is dead.

'What window-peeper? No, it's not. No, really, I'm serious. Excuse me, ma'am. PIPE DOWN OVER THERE, YOU MEDICAL EXPERIMENT!

'Did you hear me, ma'am? I said it is my painful etcetera blah blah your husband is dead. The Mud Flats Biomedical

44

Research Project. A joint effort by the Army and National Arsenamid. An accident.

'Yes, we've taken care of the body. We'll be sending you a few personal effects. Oh yes, and if he was a veteran, you get a free flag from the Veteran's Administration.

'Uh-huh. Well, it's been nice talking to you, Mrs Shairp. 'Bye now.'

Five minutes to go. Donagon moaned. Fouts picked up his bag off the desk.

The gun was under it.

He'd found it lying on the laboratory floor after the four lunatics were hauled away. It was evidence, to be sent to the Justice Department. The details of how to send it were in the destroyed files.

For a moment he stood weighing it, half-looking for a place to hide the thing. Then a wail from the next office reminded him of a reasonable solution. Bag and overcoat in one hand, gun in the other, and candy bar between teeth, he barged into Donagon's office.

'Goth oo cath bus, Donogan. Thake this thing off my handths, will oo?'

'What? Oh, sure. Thanks, Algie.' Donagon smiled wanly. Fouts's free hand took the Butterfinger. 'Sure you know what to do with it, now? It's evidence, see? You have to . . .'

'I understand, Algie.' Donagon wiped away a tear and winked. 'Thanks again.'

'Sure. Well. See you.'

The lieutenant ran from the building, his fat ass waving goodbye to Donagon.

*

Marge put down the phone. 'Your father is dead,' she said. 'So stop goose-stepping around the house and go to your room.'

Many hours, many drinks, later she spoke again, this time to a cigarette table lighter disguised as the vaguest of Oriental gods. 'Bring him back to me. Please. Whole and alive. I'll do anything in return.'

This inferior, butane-operated deity replied within a week,

45

in its own vague way: Marge received Bob's billfold, his shoes, and a suitcase full of dirty socks and underwear.

*

National Arsenamid debated carrying on with the project alone, without the Army. They thought of consulting Mac-Cormick Hines, but no doubt he would consider this a trivial matter and resent the intrusion. Someone suggested interesting the Navy in making men out of sea-water. But Doctor Donagon's suicide made their decision for them: the project was over.

Four reels of tape went on sale in a US Govt. Surplus store in the Midwest. 'PUT YOUR MOTHER-IN-LAW ON TAPE—SHE'LL DIGIT!!!' read the dayglo sign. 'RARE MÜLLER-FOKKER TAPE, FANTASTIC BARGAIN!!!!'

The Army shifted eggs to another basket. In Oregon, a team of biochemists and psychologists were trying to make bears smarter . . .

THREE: THE OX

THOUGHTS OF CHAIRMAN MAN
.... An hour late later jelly days jelly days the bell goes on and on fire I am bladderful late for school at the office

I struggle to stand up somebody has filled the room with plastic amber ice folding me in fakery: folded gyptian mummy folded dead hand card trick gypson giant in the cardifferent twilight of the twomb

(painted on my eye the impenetrable blue jelly of 'this world')

Poe I think of Poe with the opium horrors groping his way to the writing table at dusk or is it dawn: 'There came to my nostrils the strong peculiar odor of moist earth'

So buried alone alive there it is thats life thats life with digby o'dell one of lifes little jokes laff along with charlie chapfall red skeleton milton burial well now tell me mr bones I never seed such a john buryman routine at dusk or was it dawn I must look it up look up

I must be stuck here stuck here or something stuck

As it was is and ever shall be world without anything the experimenters standing there one writing on his clipboard(.) one looking thoughtful one sucking his pencil waxworks all we must be stuck here the film is stuck or

Picking my nose too that ought to give the archaeologists a few laughs the strong peculiar digit DIGIT o christ I must be I am Im on tape

47

Yes

Well Ill be damned (Hey Lullay, etc)

NEMA LIVE SU REVILED

On another level all this word soup has generated another presence, just as IAO generate the alifbet and just as deep structures generate surface structures. I have called the other presence tentatively God. It may not be God. It may not be another presence. It may originate from:

(1) The machine or part of the machine.

(2) My brain or part of my brain.

(3) Some physical outside source, neither machine nor brain.

(4) Some non-physical outside source.

(5) Nowhere and nothing (in the case it really is God).

(6) One of the ten combinations of (1) through (5), in pairs.

(7) One of the ten combinations of three of (1) through (5).

(8) One of the five combinations of four of (1) through (5).

(9) All of (1) through (5).

(10) None of the above.

It all operates like some think tank, where all the words, in crisp shirts (plastic pocket protectors for slide rule, red pencil, black pencil, pen) *confer*—run around *conferring*—the important words forming their teams of lesser words, talking up enthusiasm for this project: 'All right, fellas, the buzzword around here today is going to be "epiphany". Bounce that idea around, examine the macro-structure, get the big depth picture. Sam, you'll be handling the theological end of this, I want to see you work nice and close with Bud's team, they're looking at the "weak force" angle. Let's get at the interface of this problem, guys. Let's state our tentative objective as the answer to "Who made you?"'

Then in the beginning was the word, only now there's too much word, its face is like a teleprompter and the answers keep rolling across, answers to questions I haven't thought of asking yet—have I?—and there isn't any way of shutting it off. Maybe my mind is doing all its thinking at the same time, maybe there isn't any 'time' here . . .

SO MANY DYNAMOS!

'I'm glad you asked me that, Bob. "Are minds mechanistic?"

48

Gee, that's pretty tough. As I'll mention before, there's a little shell game you can play with machines. For any machine there is at least one question you can ask, which the machine can fully comprehend, but which it cannot answer, and to which *you* can see the answer at once.

'Specifically, it is possible to make up a formula which represents the statement "this formula is not provable (in the machine)". Then you ask the machine to prove (or disprove) the formula. If it proves it, the formula is true and the statement must be true, so the machine is contradicting itself. If it doesn't prove it, the statement is true which you know but the machine can't. And that's the difference between a mind and a machine.'

'But suppose someone comes along and alters the machine so it can prove the formula, or at least see the statement is true?'

'Well then it ain't the same machine, are it? So for this new machine you can construct a new formula of this same type. And as often as the machine is altered—or alters itself—you can do the same.'

'But what's the difference? I mean, I'm sitting there thinking up questions and the machine is sitting there thinking up answers—the *machines*, then—so maybe a mind is just a self-altering machine after all.'

His face starts to sag. I think of asking if it's lawful to render tribute to Ceasar or heal the sick on a Sunday, but I see it's not necessary. He collapses into a rainbow puddle of words:

THE RUINS, AUTOPSY OF FIRED, BESTRIDED REAL LIVES, TOO. WHAT PRUNE OF 'IF', OR ITS LESSER GOODNESS? THE RUINS, AUTOPSY OF FIRED, BESTRIDED REAL LIVES, TOO, FOR HE HAS FOUND IT'S SMOKE-RE-THATCHED, MAKING IT WHY MIST-DEALER'S BRAWNY. MY OTHER'S EVIL. ENDS. REQUEST EDITOR'S READING DEVICE.

One level down there's this detective business. I'm sitting stupefied by fumes from the coal grate, picking my nose and listening to him, Whoms, drone on about some notion about free will:

'. . . . it's a puzzle, Whatson. We find the man responsible for a particularly ghastly murder and he turns out to be a

49

madman—not responsible for his actions. Yet we call the killing itself an irresponsible act . . . I ask you!'

I suspected my friend the sleuth had had a calabashful of his special smoking mixture, and so was far from responsible for what he said at the moment. Fixing my eyes on an unfinished sampler upon the wall, I resolved not to answer.

The sampler read—or seemed to read, in the dimness:

HE RUNS, A TOPSY OF FIRE, BESTRIDE REAL LIVES, TOO. WHAT RUNE OF 'F', OR ITS LESSER GOODNESS? HE RUNS, A TOPSY OF FIRE, BESTRIDE REAL LIVES, TOO, FOR HE HAS FUND IT'S MORE THATCHED, MAKING IT WHIST-DEALER'S BRAWNY MOTHER'S EVIL. ENDS. REQUEST EDITOR'S RE ADVICE.

(*THE MIND REELS*)

and alone on the island. My only companion is a stuffed parrot. Breaking teeth off my comb to keep track of the days. Today a plane went over. It didn't respond to my signal fire, unless you can call skywriting a response:

HE RUNS TOPS OF FIR, BEST IDEAL LIVES, TOO. TUNE OF FORTLESSNESS? HE RUNS TOPS OF FIR, BEST IDEAL LIVES, TOO, FOR FUN I'M RETHATCHED, MAKING IT WHISTLER'S BRAW MOTHER'S EVIL. ENDS. REQUESTED TO READ VICE.

These mystery letters began blowing away at once, leaving:

HE RUNS TOPS OF F   BEST I   AL LI ES, TOO.
    E   FORTLESSNESS? HE RUNS TOPS OF F
BEST I   AL LI ES, TOO,   UN   RETHATCHED,
MAKING IT WHISTLE   BR   OTHER'S EVIL.
ENDS. REQUESTED   RE D ICE.

This isn't working out at all. I'd hoped to tell the story but the pen has to trace its own shadow . . . the story includes the world around the story and the story in it . . . say A writes a story about an imaginary land, and A' writes about some wholly fictitious 'historical' event, and A'' writes about or hints at, some fabulous country with all its rulers, rules, ruled . . . then B many centuries later finds the old manuscripts of these works, misses their metaphors and sets the event in the country, which is in the land.

50

'The Iructu', he writes seriously, 'have no word for death. They refer to it indirectly as "potatoes". Death is "eating your potatoes", burial is "planting the potatoes", a stillborn child is "new potatoes", etc. The potato, they explain, like death, has many eyes . . .'

Critic B′ believes the story and adds embellishments of his own. So do other scholars, until by the time of B′′′′′ men are actually planning to set out on a great sea voyage to visit the fabled land.

We set sail in the year of our Lord ———. Each new problem encloses but does not answer the last. 'Let's sail till we come to the edge'* indeed, but over the edge is just another face of the old world-cube. I don't even know what the problem is any more, but I go on calculating, reasoning, drifting off course . . .

And in the water around the ship the plankton have lofty thoughts as they top each wave, and see the next wave on . . .

* *Camp Concentration*, Thomas M. Disch.

51

PART TWO | NOUN 'MAN'

FOUR

Feinwelt rode up in the elevator, thinking psychiatrist thoughts and shareholder thoughts. *The split is there, all right, Feinwelt, you crazy shrink. It isn't enough to be den mother to a bunch of ex-transvestites. It isn't enough to be the biggest shareholder in Stagman Enterprises next to Glen Dale himself. No, you've got to wangle—watch that!—your way in to become Glen's personal Big Shrink. What are you doing here, in this, this mind of a building? In this accidental empire?*

Glen Dale's empire *was* accidental, like a famous pearl. It had begun with a small, quite ordinary grain of irritation— when, in youth, Glen had discovered that he could not, no matter what, get laid.

It was improved and rounded by a few coats of what Glen called 'sophisticated seduction techniques'. A better bottle of wine, a few more jazz tapes, four-star brandy, tickets to shows, dinner for two, oh yes, and smoking jackets, cocktail shakers ... layer upon layer did this poor oyster of a man apply to his misery. Cars, a yacht, the magazine, money, clothes, more of everything, better of each, a glossier magazine, the Stagman Club ... until the accident seemed deliberate and fine. *I wonder whether the pearl ever chokes the oyster to death?*

Eleven million *Stagman* readers opened their center folds each month to enjoy the twenty-two million well-photographed nipples of Miss Monthly. Then there were the dozens of Stagman Clubs, the thousands of bare-chested girls in buckskin

53

('Does'), the hundreds of thousands of moist men who, being strictly forbidden to touch the Does, except in the palm with crisp money, came to play. The grandest club of all was here in the Stagman Tower, in the scrotal end. The shank was devoted to magazine offices; the tip, a penthouse for the chief.

The elevator bore psychiatrist Feinwelt up the tube, chiefward, as he worried that Glen might be a difficult case. Nearly forty, after all, and apparently a virgin.

Shareholder Feinwelt worried on the other side. What if Glen did get cured? And what if that meant the collapse of the driving force behind *Stagman*? It was sublimation, no doubt of it. And who, confronted with a pearl of this quality, could want to open it to get the grain of sand? Who but a head doctor? *But drop it, think of something else, think of how many spermatazoa are jerked off over Miss Monthly, let's see . . .*

And spermatazoan Feinwelt, homunculus Feinwelt, crawled upward (eleven million times two million, but not all do it, say six million, that makes, um . . .)

Twelve trillion. Twelve trillion unfulfilled humans, condemned to death over the tits of one stenographer.

*

Glen sucked a coke and reread proofs of a picture feature for *Stagman* on the Good Life (as lived by Glen Dale).

Above, the urbane editor-publisher of Stagman *at work in his luxurious penthouse pad atop Stagman Tower. In Minneapolis did Glen Dale a stately pleasuredom decree, and a posh and private playground. This lordly manor, replete with a brace of handsome amenities, is fully equipped for funful frolic. Sartorial sophisticate Glen wears Aztec feather crown, whose pinions, handcrafted, spell out Interplanetary Drinking Team.*

He took off his Prussian spike helmet and put it in the hat closet. The Phrygian cap was better.

Too effeminate. He took off the cap and tried a comic miter labeled THANK GOD IT'S FRIDAY. Feinwelt came in as he took that off, too.

Left, a light brunch, served à deux in the congenial dining alcove, makes a felicitous and festive feast. Nonpareil culinary accomplishments like this

54

'Working?'

bœuf Ursuline avec *Dobermann Sauce are usual includements in his gourmet cuisine. Pausing in a demonstration of his trencherman prowess, Glen toasts the lady in sparkling Hunck.*

Right, afternoon coffee with the magazine staff by the capacious outdoor pool provides plaisir *aplenty for the man of pelf. Lavish libations and the many-pleasured music of a chamber group make of this work conference a picnic fit for a potentate.*

'Proofs.'
'Well, don't let me disturb you. I have a couple of hours tok ill, Glen. No hat today, I see?'
'Couldn't find anything I liked.'

'Is that so?' The way Feinwelt said it made Glen feel this was all a mistake. Did he really need a psychiatrist? Especially one he knew already.

'Why don't you go into the den and make yourself at home, Doctor?' Maybe he just needed an understanding woman. As in the story in last month's issue.

'Where's Myra? Haven't seen her around for a few days.'
'Yes, she's in the hospital again. Myra's decided she wants Oriental eyes.'

Left, Glen's den par excellence *boasts electronic wonders back of those tapestries that savor of the sybaritic. Princely preprandial potables proliferate, the talk is* intime, *and pretty guests admire this floor of hand-tooled blue Morocco.*

Feinwelt picked up an object from the coffee table **(DUROTREND CLOCK TABLE LIGHTER CONTAINS RADIO, FLASHLIGHT, TACH, DRINK HYGROMETER AND TAPE RECORDER WITH RECHARGEABLE POWER PACK)** and plucked at its chrome attachments for a moment.
'Well then. Shall we get to work?'

*

'Her name was Meri. M-E-R-I. A model. I thought I had it made: a fire in the fireplace, Billie Holliday on tape, schnapps

55

on the bearskin rug. *I had every step planned.*'

'And?'

'And nothing!'

There was silence.

'Why do you think that was, Glen?'

'How do I know? What's wrong with me?

'I mean I'm forty (not quite), single, not bad-looking, rich, famous, hard-working, successful . . . And no Babbitt, either. Who owns every side Julian Huxley's Ants ever cut? Who bought the first holograph Bergen made? Who paid to have Deef John Holler tapes smuggled out of the Library of Congress and re-recorded? I'm hip and I've got taste. I blow pretty good piano. I have the best chef in the city. I'm oenologically wise. My sartorial selection is peerless.

'But I don't get anything.'

*

In the privacy of the penthouse elevator, Feinwelt let out whoops of laughter.

He was more serious when he conferred downstairs with the managing editor.

'Hank, the way I see it, there's one frustrated son of a bitch up there. As his doctor, I can't ethically slow down his therapy or anything, you know, but I'll tell you how we *can* keep him producing. Fix him up. Line him up with about a hundred or two fine-looking, frigid girls. You know the kind, this place must be crawling with them. "Look but don't touch" ladies. If necessary, bribe 'em. Half on non-delivery. You might stick on a monitor camera on that bedroom, to make sure. Then, if things look like they're getting out of hand, create a diversion.'

'You mean, call him up?'

'Call him up, smash in the door, start a fire, send in the cops, tell him he's lost a page proof—anything.' He leaned forward, overpowering Hank with the scent of Chanel No. 5. 'I hope I don't have to tell you what happens if we fail. If that guy up there gets his rocks off *once*, it could mean the end! *Stagman* will lose him—and about ten million readers. The leading men's magazine today, and tomorrow it would be just one more creep sheet on the boots-and-garter-belt counter.'

*

56

The sermon at Vandal Ballpark was considered an unqualified success by everyone—except the preacher, Billy Koch.

'My voice went all cruddy there at the end, Jerry. You notice that?' Billy and his computer expert harnessed themselves into the Saette and waited for the guards to open the gates.

'I thought you were fine, Billy. Really.'

'Just the same, I'll be glad when you get that robot contraption finished. My voice is getting blown out. And that damned thing better work, too, for the money I'm paying.'

'Oh, it'll work, don't you worry, sir. Then you can take it easy now and then. You've been flying too much, that affects the throat.'

Billy wheeled the special car into traffic and floored it. The other vehicles around them slowed, stopped, then slipped past in reverse, gaining speed. Billy grunted happily, leaned over and switched on the videotape replay of his sermon.

'*The Devil can be a lion in the streets, seeking whom he may devour!*'

'Well, what I'm worried about is the healing ceremony. Them people get damned close, you know. Closer than that truck I'm tailgating. They can count the drops of sweat on my brow. How will it look if . . .'

'Don't worry about a thing, Billy. We've thought of every possibility. Our audioanimatron is *exactly* like you, and we're programming in tapes of all your old sermons. Gestures, speech—LOOK OUT!—speech, why you won't know it isn't you. All we need now are these special tapes . . .'

'Get over, you bastard! OVER!' Billy leaned far out the window to scream at a taxi, then sawed the ruby steering wheel to change lanes twice, fast.

'*He can be a quiet cancer, burning in the brain,*' continued the figure on the tiny screen. Billy turned it off.

'Christ, they let anybody drive a cab.'

'It's left at the next light,' said Jerry. His face was drawn with fear, and the odor of overheated deodorant escaped from his crease-resistant suit. Nevertheless he crossed one artificial leather shoe over the other, in a sketch of relaxation. 'Better watch out for the old woman crossing.'

'*I* do the driving, damn you!'

57

The old woman was caught by the yellow light. She turned, hesitated, then started back into the path of the car. Billy accelerated, cramped the wheel for the turn, and gave her a blast on his musical horn. 'Rock of Ages', it sang hastily, 'cleft for me.'

'Up yours, y'old bag!' he called cheerfully.

She looked up, startled, raised one hand as if to ward off the car, then leaped back nimbly as it slid past.

'Hahaha, I knew it! I knew she could move fast enough if she had to. Christ, I'd like to see all pedestrians fry in Hell!'

He drew up before the US Government Surplus store and double-parked. 'Don't take too long, I got to get back to Crusade HQ.'

The computer man carried his attaché case and natural shoulders inside the store.

'I could only save you two,' said the clerk, holding up a reel of tape. 'I just hadda let the others go. The govermint bought one—at least he said he was govermint. That's something—buying back their own surplus!'

'Well, two'll be enough, anyway.' As Jerry made out the check, the clerk went on. 'About a million guys called up asking about um. Wish I had more, but I guess there ain't no more. Hadda kid in here five minits ago asking for one, but he couldn't afford it anyway.'

*

Ank sat in the pickup, calming his hysterical breathing. He watched a bronze Saette cut the corner badly (nearly hitting an old lady) and pull up across the street. Then his eyes misted over, and for a few seconds he lost interest in looking at anything.

Anybody who owned a car like that could easily afford a Müller-Fokker tape. While Ank, in his fifty-dollar pickup truck with a wired-on exhaust . . .

The beauty of M-F tape was that it was really randomized, the clerk had said. While an ordinary computer could generate 'random' numbers, they weren't really random at all. Just fitted to a very complicated equation. Any mechanism was finally predictable.

But the Müller-Fokker tape went beyond mechanism. It

58

was philosophically different. There was room enough in it for (according to the clerk) a human mind!

Sales talk, maybe. And at two thousand dollars a reel, you'd expect a good pitch. Ank wanted it, all the same, more than he'd ever wanted anything—as much as he wanted to be a known painter.

Well, nothing to be done. He would just have to go on saving his pennies from reviewing other people's work, get some time on a small, cheap computer. . . .

*

Purring smoke, the old pickup truck pulled away from the curb and moved off. A moment later, Jerry came out of the store, tossed two odd-looking reels of computer tape—pink, it was, flesh pink—into the back seat and climbed in.

'Better fasten your harness, boy. I *drive* this baby.'

The Saette screamed out, jerking them back in their seats. With every gear change they snapped forward and back, like two mechanical clowns rocking with canned mirth.

'How much was that?'

'Four thousand, Billy. But it was worth it, you'll see. That tape will run the whole thing for us. We'll sort out fragments of your sermons and let that tape re-sort them into new ones.'

Billy drove down back streets to avoid traffic.

'Hold on now. LOOK OUT, YOU SON OF SATAN! Jesus, a man can't even drive across the city with all these—what were you saying, Jer?'

'I said we've almost worked out the scheme for Bibleland. Of course it's a lot easier, because the audioanimatrons there will just be mechanical gadgets, while this one will practically be a man. I'm . . .'

Billy raced for the yellow light as Ank, coming from the right, tried to coast through on the red. They met.

*

'Jeez, look at all the blood!'

'Look at the funny foreign job. They must be *dead* in there.'

'Yeah, nobody could live through that.'

The witnesses who swore this, could, a moment later, attest to a miracle, for the battered door of the Saette wiggled, groaned

59

and gave up a whole, smiling man. But for a cut on his forehead, he seemed unhurt.

'You all right, buddy? Hey, aren't you Billy Koch?'

'The Lord,' said Billy gravely, 'has preserved me for His work. Get an ambulance, somebody. My partner's bleeding like a stuck pig in there.' Somebody leapt to obey.

The ambulance men got to the computer expert first, loading him and the reel of tape he clutched on a stretcher, applying a compress to his knee. The fire department had to cut away part of the truck to get Ank out. He was bruised and delirious. As they lifted him clear, two objects fell out of his lap: a reel of tape and Jerry's foot (still shod in gleaming, unscuffed plastic). A fireman picked them up and tossed them on the stretcher.

'Are you sure you don't want to come along for a checkup?' an intern asked Billy, who was helping clear the crowd.

'No thanks, Doctor. A Greater Physician has already checked me out and found me fit.'

He hailed a cab and returned to Crusade Headquarters. An hour later, while he was going over the plans for Bibleland with his architect, Bill began scratching the bandage on his forehead.

'I think,' he said in sonorous, crowd-thrilling tones, 'I think the doggie want a dink a gaga.'

60

FIVE

'Dr Fellstus! I am here to answer the phone and take care of your appointments. And that's all!'

'Gee whiz, Marge.' The vet's forehead twitched, snapping his dark elastic brows. It was one of Fellstus's chief ways of showing emotion. 'You're a damned attractive woman. And you're single now ... so am I. To me, you're ...'

'A receptionist,' she said. 'By the way, it's almost time for Mr Hines and Toto.' She batted away his hand with a fistful of patients' files. 'I'm a receptionist, you are a *veterinarian*, remember?'

'In your mouth, it sounds—dishonest.'

'Just you forget about my mouth, and all the rest. Or I'll quit. So help me.'

Fellstus tried a smile, but the brows went on jerking. 'If you quit, how will you keep that boy of yours at that expensive military school? Be reasonable, kid. It's a good job.

'And it could be even better. You could have anything you wanted. I'd set you up with a nice little place ...'

The door opened and Mr MacCormick Hines led in a gloomy collie. Fellstus improvised a professional face.

'Mr Hines! And Toto! Let's go right into my office, shall we?'

Hines beamed recognition on Marge. 'My dear, you're looking radiant. *Radiant*. Dr Fellstus, you're a lucky vet.' He nudged Fellstus in the stomach with his gold-headed cane.

61

'Oh, don't I know it, sir.' His huge flat fingers closed over the old man's shoulder and he propelled him into the inner office.

When their session was finished, Mr Hines stopped by Marge's desk. 'I—ah—meant to ask you something, my dear. Have I seen—I know this sounds awkward, but have I seen your face before? On television, perhaps?'

'No, I'm afraid not.' Seeing that he made no move to leave, she changed the subject. 'How's Toto getting along?'

'Depressed, Mrs Shairp. Depressed.' He cleared his throat. 'Really, you ought to think of trying TV work. If you don't mind my saying so, yours is a unique face: Young, yet old, pure, yet motherly, a face touched by suffering, yet—I see I'm embarrassing you, so let me come to the point.

'A certain food company I know of is looking for a woman to do television commercials. I have an idea you'd be perfect for the part. Why not give them a try?'

She half-smiled. 'No, really, I don't think . . .'

'I have their card here.' He extracted a card and laid it before her. 'That's the man to see—Mr Bradd. The director of the Marketing Division.'

Marge did not look at the card. What was this one after? What were they all after? She was thirty, hardly more than plain, anything but sexy. Yet the insurance man—and then Dr Fellstus—and now a rich old man wanted to 'get her on television'. It was all too absurd!

'I know what you're thinking,' he said. 'But let me assure you, I have no interest in you personally. Indeed, you may never see me again—Toto is breaking off therapy—but I do feel this isn't your line of work. And you'd be doing Bradd and his division a favor if you'll go talk to them. Goodbye.'

Marge still did not look at the card, but sat daydreaming while Dr Fellstus ushered in the next patient. Through the closed door came the sounds of therapy:

'Shake hands, boy. Come on, Snuffy, shake hands.'

'*Wrowf!*'

'Seems a little upset today, Mrs Grebe. Did you give him the tranquilizers I prescribed?'

'Oh yes, Doctor. And I did like you said—shook hands with the paper boy to show that he wasn't our enemy.'

62

'Yes?'

'Well you see, our paper boy isn't too bright. I guess he thought I was inviting him to make a pass or something. Anyway, he did, and I had to slap him. Poor Snuffy went berserk!'

There was a pause.

'I see. Well now, we'll just have to try something else, won't we?'

Marge picked up the card. *National Arsenamid. O God.* She tore it up and threw it in the wastebasket.

No favors were going to be done for that company. First they'd used Bob, then made a medical guinea pig out of him. Destroyed him.

On the other hand, she was tempted. The image of herself as a TV personality appealed to her (and wouldn't she be, somehow, closer to Bob?) though she damned her vanity (Two featureless electronic blips, suspended in the void . . .).

She felt like laughing at the whole mess, herself included.

Fellstus showed his patient and patient's owner out and then turned to Marge, his mustache at an angle of concern.

'You've been crying, poor kid. What's wrong? And what are you looking for in that wastebasket?'

*

Mr Bradd wore a pair of heavy-rimmed glasses shaped like little TV screens. He was tanned, athletic, good-looking and (judging by the way he stood too close and talked too loud) homosexual.

'I'll give you the straight poop on this, baby. As Bette Cooke, you'll have a hell of a responsibility. It's not just froodge, you know.' *Froodge.* The word was new to her, probably some coined media term—though for all she knew, everyone was using it. Marge felt as though she were coming out of a convent. 'It's something,' he went on, 'to live up to. A big, big image.'

He limbered up his pitching arm and fired an imaginary fast ball at his desk. The desk was a giant replica of a cereal package. 'That's our old package design for *Weethearts.* The new one, the exciting one, will have a picture of Bette Cooke herself on it.'

He tested his punch against the palm of his other hand.

63

'We'll do a week of camera tests, keed. If you make it—and you have every chance, Mr Hines seldom fouls out as a talent scout—your face will become better known than Miss Liberty's. We'll have you on the soup, the cake mix, the hair drier, the freeze-dried banana-pimento pizza, everything. And on every network time-slot we can grab.

'So you see, you'll be a very big package. You'll be out there, all by yourself, carrying the ball for National Arse. What do you say, kid? Any questions?'

There were no questions. He toed an invisible bag, stretched, and looked at her as if she were the runner on first. 'Test tomorrow, check with Scheduling for the time. All set, babe?'

*

Mac Hines rubbed his hands with anticipation, a gesture he'd picked up from television.

'So Bradd likes her. Well well well well *well*! This is perfect. She never should have been stuck in that dreary soap opera in the first place. Now she'll appreciate my help—she'll be grateful—and when I ask her over for dinner . . .'

*

In the bathroom, Glen squeezed a blackhead in his nose. Now he couldn't go back to the living room until the red mark disappeared.

Left, in the spare-no-expense palatial dining room, guests sample the brimming buffet of epicure edibles. The quiet elegance of brushed cashmere walls set the grande luxe *tone, and a full complement of post-Pop paintings accent the sumptuous set-piece, a vintage musical dining table, richly crafted of Dead Sea marble.*

Right, late-lingering guests have a dawn swim and break their fasts at Glen's bountiful board of gourmet goodies. Smoked frim, scrambled eggs and heartier delectations from his well-stocked larder are accompanied by plenteous

There was no use going on hiding in the bathroom. Feinwelt was sure to think he was up to something in here.

64

potations. Bibbing and munch-
ing, they watch the burnished,
lustrously unique sunrise, as the
party ends in acclamations
gustatory and gemütlich *cheer.*

Feinwelt fiddled with the gadget on the mantel. By its left breast, it was 3:30. In the right, the glass was falling, signaling rain. 'Go on, Glen.'

'There's nothing more to tell. I didn't make it, that's all. I *never* make it.'

'Hmm. Why do you think that is?'

'There's always something. Norma Jean had her period. Zelda was thinking it over when the phone rang. Jessina was afraid of her husband—I guess he *examines* her or something. Jully really wanted to, but she said she had this infection. Glinda was afraid I'd lose respect for her. Pippy was too tired. Heidi said she was just plain afraid.' He sighed. 'It's always something.'

Sighing, he took off the straw boater and sailed it across the room. After a few moments he went to the hat closet, took down a bullfighter's hat and put it on.

'Anyway, tonight it'll be different. I can feel it. I've got this hot little number named Lornette all lined up, see. Hank fixed it up. He says she . . .'

'Glen, let's cut out the crap. This isn't going to be any different from any other night, and you know it. Face facts, you're no winner. There's no point in blaming the girls every time, is there? What about all the genuine opportunities you've had?'

Glen hung his head.

'Until you decide what it is you're really looking for, you won't find it, believe me. Anyway, what's important isn't whether you get laid or not—is it?'

The torero hat fell to the carpet.

'Visited your mother lately, Glen?'

Right, urbane Glen Dale's　　'Why not, Glen?'
vintage Mom in terminal cancer　　'. . . I really meant to get to
ward. Nattily attired in specu-　　see her this month. I mean,
lum and authentic, hand-　　gosh, I owe her everything.

65

crafted stethoscope, Glen (far right) bibs medicinal alcohol with nurse friend. You know, I think the world of her . . .'

'Do you, indeed?'
Feinwelt's psychoanalytic method was like three-card monte. The victim was tricked into a wrong choice and then it was explained to him how he came to be so stupid. The explanation itself meant nothing—it was but a further piece of misdirection —for there was no 'right' choice. Feinwelt believed that whatever a person believed about himself was, by definition, a lie.

'You think I don't like my mother, don't you?'
Feinwelt played a game of church-and-steeple with his fingers.

'Well, maybe I don't like her. Maybe I feel she didn't give me enough love, so—yes, that's it, of course. I reject her now for her rejection of me in the past!'

'Indeed? But wasn't it really your *father* who rejected you? Didn't you feel he was paying too much attention to Mom and too little to you?'

'Of course! That explains everything! I'm so afraid my father will hate me for it, that I can't make out . . .'

'Not so fast. Does it really "explain" everything? Or are you just grabbing at explanations to avoid . . .'

'To avoid realizing that I hated *both* my parents!'

'Hated? No, what you bottled up for so many years couldn't have been hate, Glen. Rather, let us say, lust.'

'Ah? Maybe so. You're right, Doctor.'

'And *you* are too willing to agree with me. So willing that . . .'

'I don't know about *that*. I hope I know my own mind.'

'Then why am I here? You don't mean that. You're only disagreeing to please me . . .'

'No I'm not!'

'. . . as you feel you never pleased your dad. Yet on a deeper level, you'd like to kill me.'

'Wrong again, you officious bastard!'

'Not at all.' Feinwelt lit a cigarette with Glen's table lighter, a jade mermaid that contained a tiny, glassed-in roulette wheel. 'Not at all. I can see you've been squeezing blackheads in your nose just now, both to make yourself "presentable"

66

to me and to inflict upon yourself a mild punishment for not killing me. A punishment you feel you'd really like to direct at your father.'

'SHUT UP! SHUT UP! I'm warning you.'

'Exactly. Since your father is dead, there is no one else to warn. Since your mother is too ill to stand as a father-surrogate . . .'

'YOU LEAVE MY MOTHER OUT OF THIS!'

'But that's exactly what you're trying to do—leave her out of things. To punish her for, as you imagine, trying to take the place of your father. You think her cancer is a sibling-substitute, a possible baby brother . . .'

'SHUT UP!'

'Tut. A little respect, Glen boy. Or I'll take away—this!' He seized the jade mermaid and made a theatrical gesture of pocketing it. Glen jumped him and the two men fell over the coffee table, releasing a stack of Stagmans, which flopped and sprawled around their struggling feet.

'Take my lighter, you son of a bitch?'

'Is it so important?'

'It's mine!'

The machine began coming to pieces in their hands. Feinwelt, holding the biggest piece, cracked the raging editor behind the neck with it.

'Don't apologize,' he said when Glen came to. 'It was all part of your therapy. Well, I see our fifty minutes are up. Same time tomorrow, okay?'

'Nnnhnm.'

*

Marge held up a package of frozen peas.

'Here's great news for housewives!' she cried.

'Here's GREAT news for housewives!'

'Here IS great news for housewives!'

'HERE'S great news for housewives!'

'Here's great news for HOUSEwives!'

There were six syllables to the announcement. Each might be said in one of three pitches; with low, ordinary or high volume; drawled out, chopped short or said normally; said with or without a smile and with or without a gesture. That

67

made, they told her, a total of over one and a half trillion ways of saying it, and Marge feared somehow they might make her try them all.

Mr Bradd explained that a few hundred would suffice. 'We need enough good takes to get a fix on you with our computer editor,' he said. 'That does all the pit work. We just get a few sets of good visual and a few of good sound. Then the computer chops and blends it all, to come up with what the fans think they want. Or what the computer thinks they think.'

'I don't understand.'

Mr Bradd drove an imaginary golf ball and watched his follow-through. 'An ad used to be made up, shipped out and that was that. We keep a finger on ratings and sales, and we do polls. If we find out that, say, a smile just on the word "fabulous" pulls sales in Oregon, then we plug that into the computer and it makes up a special video tape for just Oregon. Whatever we learn, we ask for, and the old computer comes up with it. Of course we still have to shoot the stuff, and have some idea of what we want in the first place. And we do need you. You can never really get along without the human element.' That was Bradd's favorite line, from an old company training film he'd written years ago.

'Hey!' He looked at his watch. 'You'd better get some shut-eye, teammate. Tomorrow's a big one. See you in the makeup section at eight.'

'Good night, Mr Bradd.'

''Night, pal.' He patted her buttocks in a comradely fashion.

Marge went home to study her lines for the following day. No letter from Spot again. An unhappy mask looked back at her from the mirror. It moved, intoning again and again, 'It's so easy with KREW! It's *magic!*'

68

SIX

At six hundred hours the first bell rings.

Spot (Cadet Sturgemoore Shairp) gets out of bed in the approved manner, first untying the thongs that fasten his wrists to the top side of the blanket, then placing his left foot on the floor (counting off the toes aloud as they touch in order), then pivoting smartly so as to come to attention in a full brace. There are seven wrinkles under his chin, the cleft between his shoulder blades can grip a ping-pong ball, his stomach is sucked in and his elbows make 150° angles.

He holds this position while General Rockstone bellows the morning invocation over the video address system (a cadet is not allowed to look at the screen). Then Spot makes his bed with mitered corners, sweeps his room (beginning at the North-west corner, in honor of Rockstone's home state, Alaska) and returns to attention.

At the next bell, he is allowed forty-five seconds to go to the toilet, one minute to shower, and one minute to get into his uniform (tucking in the shirt with wooden paddles). Next, inspection.

*

Gen. Flamel ('Rocky') Rockstone was retiring as president of the St Praetexta Military Academy, and Lt Col Algernon Fouts was taking his place. The entire cadre had assembled on the parade ground, in wind and drizzle, to hear the shrill

69

voice of the cadet colonel read the official history of Rocky's major (indeed his only) engagement in World War Two:

The US held a chain of Pacific islands known as the Corydons. All but one small island at the end of the chain (thought to be uninhabitable) had been fully cleared and turned to military uses. On the last day of the war, Rocky (then a lieutenant) and thirty men were being ferried by plane from a base in the Corydons to a distant fleet. The plane passed over the entire island chain, flying low and taking of course no evasive action. When it reached the last, Sweet Potato Island, the sky around it was suddenly filled with small-arms fire.

The pilot was killed at once. The wounded co-pilot just managed to crash-land in a thicket. And on VJ Day Rocky and his new command found themselves in the hands of the enemy.

The loss of their plane was somehow undetected—perhaps everyone had been indoors listening to the capitulation on shortwave—and no one came looking for them.

Here the official account was a list of hideous tortures, heroic sacrifices and so on, and it stressed the bravery of Lt Rockstone. What made the tortures unendurable was their taking place within sight of a US naval base on the next island. Rocky and his group were able to see ships come and go, planes skywriting V's, and even hear victory salutes. They themselves were well hidden in the jungle, and their captors, a stubborn and self-sufficient unit, refused to believe what was obviously true. The plane was assumed lost at sea, and, due to Japanese and American clerical errors, rescue took well over a year.

*

While they listened to the official account, many of the cadets turned their thoughts to the other, unofficial, version they had read last night after lights-out. It mentioned no tortures. It said in fact that Rocky and his men were treated well by the Japanese, who starved themselves to give them the choicest food, saw to their health, cleanliness and well-being, and even made small gifts of money. It seemed these Japanese soldiers had been without women for some time . . .

But this was only a schoolboy version, written ungrammatic-

70

ally and typed out in many smudgy carbons, read by flashlights under the blankets. None who read it could really believe all of it.

*

The shrill voice stopped, and the band, their instruments untuned by the cold, struck up a warped march. The whole school marched past the reviewing stand, past the bunting bearing the school motto ('Those who say we are women are liars' was the translation) and once around the parade ground. There were three large rectangles each composed of four small rectangles, each in turn composed of four marching lines of ten children each. One was Spot. He could be easily singled out, had anyone been looking, as the one who changed step every four or five paces, and always unsuccessfully. No one, however, was looking.

Fouts suppressed a yawn. 'What are your plans, General?'

'I'm supposed to command a new outfit, X Forces, but I don't know any more about it than you do. All I know is, we assemble in Florida and await orders from the Pentagon. From that gentleman soldier, General Weimarauner.' He grimaced. 'Keep all that under your hat, of course.'

'Of course.'

The general turned his toothless profile to watch the kids. 'These boys are pretty easy to handle. About all you have to do is drill the heck out of them and keep them from playing with themselves.'

Rocky considered playing with oneself sinful, weakening, deleterious to physical and mental health, and probably the main cause of syphilis, so-called 'thalidomide babies', divorce, and losing battles.

Accordingly he forbade solitary showers, toilet doors, single rooms, photographs of any females except mothers, lectures in human biology, dirty jokes, obscene language, and possession of any object that might conceivably be used in masturbation. Shower and toilet time were strictly limited, and touching one's own unclothed body minimized.

Most jacking off, therefore, went on in the library at study time. Nearly every cadet who was old enough jazzed the bottom of a table while staring blankly at *The Rise of the Dutch Republic* or Herodotus.

71

The library was a large drafty room dominated by Rocky's favorite picture, a painting of Galahad inscribed:

My strength is as the strength of ten
Because my heart is pure

*

'Another thing,' said the general. 'Watch out for letters home. Censor them. Remember, parents magnify the slightest complaint.'

Fouts jutted his chin in a tight-collar gesture. 'But don't the parents wonder when they get a blacked-out letter?'

'I didn't mean like military censorship. I meant, if you get a letter that isn't right, throw it out. I've had one kid here writing three letters a week *begging* his mother to take him home. Well, naturally, *that* kind of thing . . .'

'Naturally, sir. I don't believe in coddling America's next generation of fighting men.'

*

Wes Davis thought she was just about the whitest woman he'd ever seen. There seemed to be a special message for him alone in the way she held up a slip and said, 'DRIX just *eats* dirt! Your white undies will be whiter than Heaven knows!'

One of the other prisoners in the recreation lounge made the mistake of saying something about getting in her undies. It took a guard and three trustees to pull Wes off him.

Later Wes calmed himself enough to read his cellmate a little of the book he was working on:

'The difference between a nigro and us is like between a skyscraper and a mud hut or a moon rocket and a spear, or God Almighty and a wood baboon. If you wanted a computer, who would you go to a black African country or our Great Nation? If you wanted a constitution a painting or a poem who would you ask some black savage with a bone through his nose or a white man like Tom Jefferson, Norm Rockwell or Ed Guest? Can we go on listening to the syphilitic Europeans and Communist junky perverts who insist the nigro is our equal? He is not our equal because he is not even human!

'What human could live the way the colored do in Harlem—

72

six or ten to a room? And in Calcutta and Tokyo even more! What human could work for the wages of a black in South Africa—$10 a month! And how about savage rhythm music and cannibalism?

'Let's look at some of the nigros' heroes. George Washington Carver introduced the peanut, a plant whose vines soon killed off the cotton and made land worthless! Peanut vines wrapped themselves around the great heart of the South, choking her to death!'

'By God, Wes, I never thought of that!' The cellmate slapped his denimed thigh. 'Peanuts!'

'Statistics show,' Wes read, 'peanut brittle is a major cause of tooth decay in children, and peanut butter causes malnutrition.' He looked up. 'Ever notice how it sticks to the roof of your mouth?'

'Like a parasite!'

'Thou hast said it. It *is* a parasite, introduced by the nigger conspiracy to wipe us out. Kids have died injecting peanut butter into their veins! And think of the old people, struggling with glued-up dentures.'

'By God, Wes, that's right! Peanuts even have their own comic strip, I hear!'

Wes read: 'GET THE OLD PEOPLE AND CHILDREN FIRST, & YOU PARALYZE THE NATION. So goes the motto of the Great Nigro Conspiracy.'

He was not reading to his cellmate to entertain or enlighten. The cellmate was educated. He helped criticize Wes's style and grammar—and he knew a publisher.

*

Sometimes the field of MacCormick Hines's reality reversed, and he began to wonder if television weren't real.

'My dear,' he said to the set, 'I haven't forgotten what you said that night. The night he died. That you'd give anything to get him back. And believe me, I'm working on just that.'

'And cleaning the Thermo-K is no problem either,' she replied. 'Just push this button, and the blades slip into your dishwater. See how easy?'

*

73

Sunday night was Veronica. 'I'm sorry, Glen, but I don't think you're really serious about me as a person. Thanks anyway for showing me those movies.'

Tuesday night was Karen. 'Glen darling, let's be reasonable. I know your reputation, and I'm just not the kind of girl you want. But thanks all the same. For the champagne and all.'

Wednesday night was Trudy. 'Oh, Glen, I thought you were different!'

Wendy, on Thursday night, was willing. Even on the tiny monitor screen, Feinwelt could see her face was going expressionless and tuned to receive. Glen bent over her, sucking at a bare shoulder.

'That bitch!' Feinwelt stubbed out a cigarette and reached for a toggle switch. 'Takes three hundred bucks just to say no, and then gets hot pants all the same! Lucky I was watching tonight, instead of Hank. He'd let it get too far.'

The timing had to be just right. Too soon and there would be a fresh start to the seduction. Too late and—too late. He waited.

Feinwelt was being pulled too many ways. Late nights protecting his investment, afternoons patching up the damage he'd done Glen each night before, evenings working as counsellor for Transvestites Anonymous—he barely had time to change clothes, frames of reference.

Awkwardly, Glen groped for a breast. Feinwelt threw the switch, and in the bedroom the huge color TV blazed on at top volume.

Bette Cooke was stirring something in a saucepan. 'THE MAN IN YOUR LIFE,' she thundered, 'WILL **LOVE** NEW **INSTANT** VEAL CUTLETS.'

By the time Glen could turn it down the moment was past. Thinking of the three hundred yet to come, Wendy reached for her purse.

'I've really got to go now, darling. It's been sweet, but I've got this terrible headache. I think my period brings it on.'

When she had left, Glen took off his gaucho hat and laid it in the exact middle of the bed. Without knowing quite why, he took all the cokes out of his bedside refrigerator, opened them and poured them on the hat.

74

Bette Cooke was back on the screen again by the time he'd finished. She recommended that listeners give their menfolk a special treat tonight.

Only the safety shield in front of the picture tube saved Bette from that flying bottle.

*

One more week, Marge promised herself. One more week, and if that little snob didn't write to his mother, he'd find himself yanked out of that damned 'academy' and sent to a school for mere human children. Where he couldn't strut around in a uniform all day, snarling commands (as no doubt he was doing this minute), and lapping up all that West-Point-type glory. At eight years old, he wasn't so much of an old campaigner that he couldn't be bothered to scratch out a post card.

*

Spot had his plan. Fouts seemed to be carrying on the school traditions, and television was forbidden (images of women), but cadets were after all encouraged to be religious. Spot simply waited until Billy Koch was on one channel, then watched whatever he wanted.

It was the evening recreation hour, a time when cadets were inclined to find ways to be by themselves. Therefore the school was heavily patrolled by (pairs of) upper classmen, officers.

Sensing rather than hearing their approach, Spot switched over from a cowboy program to *Healing Hand* and dropped to his knees before the set.

'DON'T YOU KNOW ENOUGH TO STAND AT ATTENTION WHEN AN UPPER CLASSMAN ENTERS THE ROOM?' said one of the two officers. It was Jerry Zurkenhall, a pimply fifteen-year-old who, it was said, had hair in the palm of his hand.

Spot did not move or look around.

'OKAY, I'M GIVING YOU FIFTEEN DEMERITS . . .'

'Knock it off, Jerry,' said the other. 'You can't give a guy demerits when he's praying, stupid. It's in the rules.'

'Yeah? So who's he praying to, Billy Koch? My old man works for him.'

75

'No kidding?'

'Yeah, he's in computers.' Jerry put his hairy palm on the doorknob.

'Hey, what does a preacher need computers for? To give him hymn numbers? Hah haha hahaha . . .'

The door closed and the two went off to harass someone else. Spot, anxious for the life of the Negro sheriff on channel two, switched over at once.

'Here's news for BUSY HOUSEWIVES! Have *you* tried my DIN-DIN? You know, each package of DIN-DIN contains *everything* you need for a meal with—mmmm—*man appeal*! You just add water through this little door in the convenient, no-mess foil pack, pop it in the oven—and Bette Cooke takes over! Then just sit back and let your men-folk fall in love with you all over again!'

She was on the screen, serving dinner to a red-haired, freckle-faced boy with a disgusting grin, to a man who sniffed, went silly and rose to peck at her cheek. Mom's face was soft with pleasure, as Spot had never seen it.

Of course it was all acting, but still. Her letters never mentioned his letters. She ignored his plea to be allowed to come home again, she seemed unmoved by his stories of life at the academy. So here she was, living it up with television actors (and her last letter: 'Guess what? Your Mom's got a new job. But I guess you're not very interested in that kind of news . . . guess you're pretty busy with medals and marching bands and military balls . . .') while Spot languished in prison, sweeping from the Northwest corner, mitering the corners of his bed . . .

To the fading smile of Bette Cooke he whispered a threat, a curse that took in Fouts, the upper classmen, all mortal enemies.

'I don't care,' it went. 'I don't care. My old man's in computers, too.'

*

Ank switched off the freeze-dried lemon meringue pie commercial before answering the door.

'Ank Bullard? Package for you.' It was the paint, the last thing he needed for his painting machine. Ank paid the COD

76

charges and dragged the big box into his flat. Since his right shoulder still ached from the accident, he began mixing colors with his left hand.

The accident had been a miracle. First, he'd come to in the hospital to find on his bedside table the very thing he'd have given a leg for: a reel of Müller-Fokker tape. And no one seemed to know who the anonymous donor was.

Then, his second day in the hospital, there had been a visitor with still another gift. He was a lawyer from the Billy Koch Crusade, and though he wanted Ank to understand his clients accepted no responsibility whatever, they were willing to pay him three thousand dollars over his hospital expenses if he would sign this waiver.

Ank had given notice at the newspaper the day he came out. Today he was just an ex-art-critic. Tomorrow—even in a few hours—he would be a painter.

*

The painting machine had a wheel to hold a thousand smears of color and a brush mounted on a pivoted arm. The brush could be moved along the arm by one motor, while a second motor worked the arm around on its pivot. A third rotated the paint wheel, or 'auto-pallette'.

Random numbers generated by the tape were fed into this system, controlling all three variables. The brush could dip up any color, transfer it to any of a hundred and fifty thousand positions over a prepared canvas, and dip again, leaving a dot. Between dottings, it moved through a powerful cleaning solution.

This cartesian process would go on until either the canvas was completely covered or until Ank liked what he saw and stopped it. He called the process *rand-pontillisme* in advance, knowing how important it was for his former colleagues to have a name to fasten upon from the start. Ank was prepared to explain in detail the philosophy behind this 'marriage of random number and Seurat, which guarantees all the benefits of luminosity, color and harmony'.

Now he set it into motion. There were a hundred and fifty million potential paintings in there somewhere, a hundred and fifty million pure abstract patterns without 'meaning' or

77

'intention'. What he would see, in just a few hours, would be the end of so-called Humanism, the end of sentiment and prejudice—the dawn of Mechanism.

*

What he actually saw was a close copy of David's *Coronation* of Napoleon. The details were blurry, but his painting differed from the original in only one respect.

The archbishop's face was modeled in bright greens.

Ank tried a fresh canvas. The brush rose and fell, faster than the eye could follow, and a 'Remington' took shape: A mounted Indian wheeling his pony to fire an arrow into the flank of a galloping bison.

Except the pony wasn't wheeling and the bison did not gallop. Instead, both 'stood on', or were solidified into, thick furry pedestals.

'Surrealism?' he whimpered. 'I've given up my whole career for this cheap surrealism?'

It was almost time to go to Glen Dale's party. He threw the two ruined canvases in the corner and went to wash his hands. Instead of shaving, he decided to have a drink somewhere.

SEVEN

In the corner by the fireplace, two Shriners were telling a Knight of Columbus about the possibility of a Vatican missile.

'You must mean this,' he said, hauling out a dog-eared mass book. 'A missal.'

'Naw, I got the straight word from a bishop. Says they're gonna call it *Miserecordia Dei.*'

'Yeah? Well all I can say is, somebody better say their prayers . . .'

Two men in modified zoot suits stood arguing about a song recorded by Deef John Holler. A hideously fat woman in gold lamé and a stiff blonde wig watched them and, when they paused for breath, introduced herself as Columbine.

Someone elsewhere swore the US Navy had already successfully teleported a ship from Philadelphia to Norfolk.

'It fried the crew, though.'

'England?' asked the young man in the wicker suit. 'Was that Norfolk, England?' On learning it was Virginia, he seemed to lose interest in the story.

On the mezzanine a new group called The World, The Flesh and Father Schmidt bombarded the guests with glare and noise:

> You know I got a little girl named *Gladys*?
> She give me such a **ice cream**
> So when I ask the neighbors what they want
> They tell me there's no

79

Ahhhhhhss
Cuh-ream-MUH!
You caint go home dog
YOU CAINT GO HOME DOG
This cat done **EAT** up all my beans

No one could hear the singer screaming these words to the old Deef John Holler tune, above the party sounds and the electronic background music provided by zither, serpent and white noise generator. But no one was listening, anyway.

The man disguised as a hot dog (red-painted baldness; thick, bun-colored coat) was saying it was hard as hell to find a book worth publishing these days. 'Just got one promising em-ess from a guy in prison. All about the black conspiracy. Oughta do the ton, easy.' He went on to explain to his audience, two models in painful-looking tubular garments from Paris, that 'the ton' was a million copies.

Behind him a professor of American Studies named Throgmorton thought someone had failed to make a distinction somewhere. 'American Studies is not an *all*-embracing field,' he corrected. 'It is a *much*-embracing field. Take my own specialty, for example. I have written what I hope is the definitive catalogue of Little Moron Jokes.'

'Indeed?' The cryogenics man stood ready to feign interest.

Someone asked where Feinwelt was, and someone replied, 'Oh he never comes to these things. Always busy with his girl scouts, I guess.'

'Yeah, what do they call it? Transvestites Anonymous?'

Worried-looking Miss Columbine butted in to ask what a transvestite was.

In another corner Mr Bradd told the gloomy TV producer how Marge had wanted to appear in commercials under her own name. 'Can you slice that? Her own name! *Marge*, for Christ's sake. The economy spread.'

The gloomy producer nodded and went right on talking about his western series based on *Huckleberry Finn*, and entitled 'Sheriff Jim'.

Somewhere in the next room, the tall art critic with the ax-blade nose called someone a 'reified cubist'.

Mr Hackendorf, a civilian anthropologist attached to the staff of General Weimarauner, stood in the kitchen talking to

80

Sir Somebody about the Seneca tribe. The general himself sat in the den, too near the harpsichord to hear what the lady with the jeweled face was saying about dogs. He was watching a pretty girl with a rather large and rigid jaw who stood in the doorway between the den and living room. She sipped her drink through a straw and conversed with a man in a feather cape.

The art dealer lit a cigarette, holding it well away from his artificial feathers. 'So what's new, Myra?'

'Net mech, Drew. Whet's en et yr guellery?'

'Nothing on at the moment. I'm looking for a show. Something really *new*. Anything but computer art. I'm so sick of— say, what happened to your jaw?'

Myra explained that she'd had her jaw sectioned to correct an overbite. After sawing through on both sides, she said, they 'pet en sem plestec enserts.'

'That's nothing. *I* had a pilonidal cyst removed about a month back. Jesus, I was sick for three days.'

Glen was looking lonely, Myra noticed. She excused herself and went over to talk to him.

'Mester Dele? E meant te speak weth ye, abet . . .'

'About the proofs for January? I know, Myra, I've already had a look at them. But can't we talk about that some other time? If you'll excuse me, there's someone I wanted to see.'

He resumed his lonely prowling of the penthouse rooms. There was no one he had to see, but Glen hated for it to look as if he *had* to talk to his own secretary. Hoping someone would remark on his square printer's hat, folded from a sheet of *Stagman*, Glen crossed the living room and spoke to the old Negro by the door.

Conspicuous in new bib overalls, new work shoes and no shirt, the old man sat with his chair tipped back against the wall. He seemed to be ignoring the entire party, possibly because the rest ignored him.

'Hello,' said Glen heartily. 'Haven't seen you here before.' The old Negro did not look up or speak. Glen wondered uneasily if he might not be the Wrong Kind of spade. The Right Kind included jazz musicians, baseball players, poets, astronauts . . .

'Friend of Bill Banks, are you?'

81

No response. Glen resisted the temptation to throw him out—it might look as if he didn't like the Right Kind—and walked away, hiding his burning face in a drink. Ögivaal the architect caught his eye, but Glen continued on to the farthest part of the apartment. Ögivaal resumed his story:

'. . . and it should have been a thirty, instead of a three.'

Throgmorton leaned against the mantel. 'That's a shaggy-dog story,' he told the cryogenics man. 'I think you fail to make a distinction there.'

'All right, how about this one, then? Why did the Little Moron take a ladder to the cat-house?'

Ank came in, dropped a cigarette and bent in slow-motion to retrieve it.

'That's the so-called art critic who works for the *Sun*,' said the tall man, jerking his ax-blade nose in Ank's direction. 'He thinks a Constable is an English cop.'

The young man in the wicker suit opined that the English police were the best in the world.

'Is that so?' said the tall man. He extracted a cigarette from one sleeve of his worn, paint-splattered sweater. 'Well, a friend of mine got busted by English fuzz for speeding, one night. They just about kicked his nuts off. As it happens, he's black.'

Six persons in the costumes of Egyptian priests moved together to the bathroom, where they rolled up their black-and-gold sleeves to bare arms no cleaner or healthier than those preserved in museums. One of them produced an anachronistic syringe.

In the kitchen, Hackendorf was saying, 'You're right. The Seneca are, as you put it, unequalled in common sense. A magnificent tribe.'

'Eh?' Sir Somebody cupped a hand to his ear. 'Damn that infernal music. Did you say Seneca was *tripe*?'

'Tribe, *tribe*. All of the Seneca put together.'

Sir Somebody looked at him in the way only a man of his class is able to look at someone. 'Good Lord! Is there more than one great Seneca? Seneca, whose moving death . . .'

In the next room, just beyond the doorway, Senator Vuje looked around to see who was calling him. No one was, so he turned back to listen to an astrologer, who was giving the horoscope for anyone born on December 25th:

82

'He will work and toil, and others may reap the benefit of his labor unless marriage alters the destiny. He is usually well-disciplined and cautious, and tends to overlook his own faults while quick to recognize the faults of others.'

*

The party rumbled on like a Hay Wain (as someone in the middle of it pointed out), carrying its cargo of fools toward the hour of their release. A lady lawyer spoke long sentences about international law as regards defacing the moon, and to each the cryogenics man nodded and smiled. The girl in the snood claimed that Thomas M. Disch was the author of a novel called *Concentration Camp*. Other girls, in leather bikinis, glass crinolines, wooden mail, foil tartans and plastic pinafores behaved as slightly animated decorations, receiving each conversation item with the same graceful indifference with which chair cushions receive buttocks of all shapes. News, gossip, compliments, pedantry, wit and philosophy, all were rested upon them briefly and then removed, leaving no impression.

One pretty blonde wore a dress of pale creamy silk that seemed to be on upside down. It flared outward and upward from her knees, ending at the neck in a fountain of ruffled lace. Someone remarked that she looked like a peach sundae, and later everyone thought they had originated the idea.

Ank danced with her, danced with them all, doing the jung, the freeb, the buckle-o, the rap. After a short intermission (to puke up a gallon of cheap wine) he returned to dance the rap, the nood and the fox-trot.

'Seneca's death,' remarked the knight, 'reminds one of the death of Quixote. Or, as you Americans say it, Key-oty.'

'Kiote?' Hackendorf frowned. 'He's not a Seneca god. I think you mean one of the plains tribes . . .'

But Sir Somebody wasn't listening. He had given up trying to understand the peculiar American versions of the classics, and turned instead to scrutinize Bates, the young man in the wicker suit, who spoke now of English cooking.

'It's quite underrated,' he said. 'You have to get down in the country and try the really authentic English dishes: Curate's Egg, for instance. And Parson's Nose.'

83

'Good Lord! Is the man serious? Parson's Nose? *Parson's Nose?* What the deuce is he on about?'

In the living room someone comforted Miss Columbine, who lay full-length on the sunken sofa, heaving with sobs.

'What happened, dear?'

'That dirty young man in the paper suit . . .' indicating Ank. 'He called me a—a *lesbian*!'

Ank grinned. 'All I did was ask her why her arms are so muscular,' he said. 'Well it's true!'

Someone looked down at the 250-pound writhing figure. 'Like a trapped elephant,' he murmured. 'Poor thing.'

The publisher in the hot-dog costume plodded through the den, asking if anyone had seen his wife. The lady with the jeweled face regarded him. 'How quaint!' she exclaimed. 'A kapok coat! How poply quaint!'

She turned to smile on the patrician profile of General Weimarauner. 'They wore things like that when *I* was young—practically—I thought they were out of fashion forever. I'll bet he doesn't *dare* take it off. He's afraid someone might see his truss.'

A drink sloshed over her. The face so covered with jewels that it might have been any age looked up. An unsteady man in a wrinkled dinner jacket pulled his forelock in apology. ' 'S all right,' he mumbled. 'I'm from Innerpol.'

*

'A *jaw* section?' Ank lurched forward to look at Myra's face. 'So that's why you're drinking through a straw. How long before the wires come out?'

Before she could answer he began on the details of his own accident, resulting, as he mentioned several times, in concussion.

'Ye den't lek tee well, Enk.'

'Ank looks terrible,' Glen said to a girl wearing only blue jeans. Even across the room he could see the edges of Ank's paper jacket were frayed and greasy, and the seams had started to let go.

'But he's a great dancer,' replied the girl.

Glen made a mental note to take some dance lessons.

Mr Bradd and a crewcut young giant finished their competi-

84

tion, a chinning contest on the bedroom door-frame. Crewcut won. Bradd suggested a little kendo, broom against mop.

'You're crazy to go up against him,' someone whispered to Bradd. 'He's a Yale younger poet, for God's sake.'

Glen asked Hackendorf if he were the Indian expert.

'Well, I guess you might say that. I'm advising General Weimarauner for his book on the Indian wars.'

'I wanted to ask you something about this tribe, the Utopis.'

'The Utopi, yes, a minor Southwestern tribe. Not really important—most of their ritual and so on is copied from others. Gosh, there can't be many Utopi left.'

'There must be some,' Glen said. 'I just ordered a hat from them, a real Utopi headdress. I thought you might be able to tell me what it would look like.'

The anthropologist looked thoughtful. 'I'm not certain, really. Didn't know they *had* any crafts. Utopi hat? That's a new one on me.

'Now, if you'll excuse us, the general and I will duck out early. I have something to discuss with him privately.'

'Daisy James,' said a blonde. 'You know, by Henry Miller?'

'Isn't Feinwelt here?' someone else asked.

The lady lawyer's shrill voice carried over other conversations. 'The question remains, does the moon really constitute . . .'

A man on crutches came in. Someone persuaded someone else not to rush over and ask him where he got his one-legged outfit. Someone else tried to throw up into the swimming pool, but it was covered. The man from Interpol crawled around on all fours, peering up dresses. He was the only one to make the discovery:

The girl wearing only blue jeans really wasn't. The blue jeans, pockets, rivets and all, were painted on.

Glen noticed the girl in the peach-sundae dress was alone. He moved over to talk to her, pausing on the way to put his pipe in his mouth.

Jerry shifted a crutch. 'A jaw section? Myra, that's *nothing*. I lost a *leg* in that accident—clear up to the knee!' He held out the stump for her inspection.

'E see. Thet's trrble, Jrry. Whet'll ye de?'

'Do? Who cares?' He drank off a cocktail and held the glass

85

in a way that indicated he expected her to fetch him another. 'Oh, I guess I can keep on working for the Crusade. I'm still a good systems man, and their computer—but I'd like to get my hands on the bastard who did this to me, Myra. Some stupid fuckhead in a slow truck, hogging the intersection.'

She took his glass and went to the bar. Ank wandered past a moment later, waggling an unlit cigarette. No one seemed to have a light.

'How about you?' he asked Jerry. The one-legged man made a great show of clapping his crutches together and digging out his lighter. He was (his manner indicated) a cripple being put upon by a man with all limbs intact.

Without even thanking him, Ank shuffled away, trailing a torn strip of paper suit and raining live coals on his own lapels.

'. . . and another thing,' someone asserted. 'All the penitents aren't in the penitentiary.'

'Film critic?' said the tall man, slipping a cigarette out of his sweater sleeve. 'You've got to be kidding. He still thinks *The African Queen* is a retitled version of *Strange Fruit.*'

Sir Somebody entered the living room, promenading with the lady with the jeweled face. 'Incredible!' he was saying. 'The fellow claims we English are fond of eating hen's arse!'

'Are you the janitor?' someone asked the old Negro by the door, who declined to answer. 'There's a lot of water coming out from under the bathroom door. Somebody must have passed out in there.'

The old man smiled to himself, took out a sack of tobacco and papers, and deliberately rolled a cigarette.

'Isn't that just like a colored?' shouted the hot-dog man. 'Look at that! Doped to the teeth, or drunk maybe, or just plain idiotic. Has anybody seen my wife, by the way?'

'I think,' said Ank, stumbling into him, 'I think she left with a mustard pot . . .'

The two zoot suits were rolling on the floor. The man on top had seized the other's hand-painted tie and was trying to strangle him with it. '1948, you son of a bitch!'

The six persons in the bathroom were taking a shower with their robes on. The water was up to their ankles and leaking out under both doors, the locked door to the hall and the door

86

to the bedroom, where the polite cryogenics man was helping Bradd to his feet. The gloomy producer stood by, still talking shop.

'I'm tired of doing spade westerns,' he said. 'I'm thinking of doing'—with a malicious look at Bradd, who was groping for his glasses—'a queer western. The fairy lawman who has to keep proving he's a man. Takes incredible risks, rides in a rodeo and so on. So "straight" he wears low-heeled boots. Only what to call it? *Andy Oakley?*'

Ank stood in the corner by the fireplace, mumbling to himself. He seemed oblivious of everything, even the great charred hole in the front of his paper jacket. Suddenly he pulled himself up and charged across the living room towards the patio door. He collided with the man in the wrinkled dinner jacket.

'It's all right,' said Ank. 'You're from Interpol, remember?'

'Hey, how did you know? Hey, come back here!'

But Ank lurched on, crookedly but with purpose, across the fiberglass swimming pool cover and on, towards the parapet.

Out in the hall, the Yale younger poet had wedged the elevator doors open by jamming a mop across the opening at knee level. Now he started chinning himself on the mop, letting his body hang down inside the shaft. The two Shriners and a few others looked on.

Grunting, he explained. 'Have to purify myself . . . after combat . . . too much I and thou . . . need some experience of the Infinite . . . I and It, see?'

'That's not infinite,' said one watcher, 'it's only forty floors, man.'

In the living room, someone asked where that TV exec had got to.

'A transvestite executive? Wild!'

Ank, unconscious, was carried in from the patio by Myra and Drew, the art dealer.

'What happened to him?'

'We found him passed out with one leg over the parapet.'

'Does the moon,' said the lady lawyer, 'in legal terms, belong to *everyone?*'

*

General Weimarauner and his anthropologist sat in a lunch counter drinking coffee, or anyway stirring at it.

'What is it, Hack? It better not be about your damned Indians.'

Hackendorf coughed. 'In a way, General, in a way. But it's also about X Forces.'

X Forces was the as yet unnamed cadre being assembled in Florida under General Rockstone. It was the Pentagon's hope that X Forces could regain some of the reputation for toughness lost by the old Green Berets in Vietnam, and become a model and a morale booster for the other services.

'Go on, then.'

'The Cheyenne had a peculiar military corps called the Contraries. These were the finest, fittest braves in the tribe, and more. *They were so tough, they did everything backwards*.'

The general looked at him, then turned his Roman profile. 'Come on, Hack. I'm tired. Either spit it out, or let's get back to the hotel. I've got to fly to Washington in the morning.'

'They really did, sir. They rode to battle mounted backwards, and they never carried weapons. There was much more merit in it, if when a man had the chance to *kill* an enemy he just *touched* him instead. Just slapped him with the open hand, or hit him with a small stick, the *coup* stick.

'Another thing is, the Contraries never touched women. They were like monks, or knights under a vow . . . were supposed to be. They fasted and prayed and tortured themselves all night before a battle, and then they just clowned around on the battlefield, taking incredible risks. All for honor.'

Weimarauner sighed. 'Yes, yes, but Hackendorf, we already have *enough* honor.'

*

The Yale younger poet and his followers came in from the hall, leaving the elevator doors jammed open, and went straight to the bar. The poet turned his back on Mr Bradd, who was too busy talking to the cryogenics man to notice. Glen and the peach-sundae girl went into the bedroom and locked the door.

'They call me the I B M wish, baby,' sang the World et al., 'They call me the Icy B M fish.'

88

A lighted sign went on over the bedroom door: UNE FEMME EST AVEC MOI.

'I envy that bastard Glen Dale,' said a Shriner. 'He must of gone through more ass than I have socks.'

The cryogenics man, sensing a customer in Mr Bradd, began to sober up fast. 'Freezing isn't just a science, you know. It's an art. Look at it this way: If you'd frozen yourself twenty years ago, today you'd be—what, sixteen years old?' He judged Bradd to be forty-five, actually.

'Twenty-four,' Bradd said, 'but I wouldn't have any money.'

'No? If you had bought *this* sheaf of stocks,' the list brought out and held so that Bradd had to turn and move closer to have a look at it, 'you'd have nearly a hundred dollars for every dollar you invested then. Even if you put your money in the bank, it would nearly have tripled! And youth, don't forget, youth—is—money!' From another pocket he produced a full color brochure of freezer designs.

'What I was thinking,' Bradd said, looking them over, 'was something for a friend—really a business associate of mine. A woman thirty years old. The thing is, her job effectiveness— her RBI—depends on her age. In maybe five years, she'll be useless. Meanwhile, she works maybe an hour a week, maybe two. The rest of the time, she just mopes around the house. Do you think we could do something to shape up her career?'

Mrs Grebe peeled off her jeweled face and put it away. She was about to go with Sir Somebody to his hotel room, to look at his pictures of Welsh Corgis. The art dealer in the feather cape and Myra shouldered Ank and headed for the door. With a look of irony, Jerry stood out of their way.

A businessman in a fur wig rushed in from the hall. 'Hey, somebody fell down the elevator shaft! I heard him scream!'

'Christ! Somebody get the janitor!'

'Where the hell is he?' demanded the walking hot dog. 'He was right here a minute ago. As soon as there's any work to be done . . .'

Two pork-pie hats swiveled to look at him. 'Forget it,' said one of the musicologists. 'No hurry now.' They went back to their amiable discussion of the recording date of Deef John Holler's *Decatur Freight Blues.*

*

89

One floor below, Deef John Holler lay on the roof of the elevator. He had few cues to his whereabouts, being not only deaf but nearly blind, but he found this place more congenial than Glen's penthouse. Here there were no irritating, jerky vibrations from amplified clumsy playing, no smells of stale smoke and spilled whiskey, only a gentle descending motion. He was not interested in getting anywhere, in being anyone, or in living at all. So Deef John sat up, dusted off his new overalls, and began to sing.

All the rest of the evening, riders of the elevator declared they had never heard Melodiak sounding so good.

*

'I see what must've happened,' said the Knight of Columbus. 'Some prick left this mop stuck across the door like this, and guess some drunk tripped over it.' He unstuck the mop and let the doors close.

'Forty floors. Some trip.'

Miss Columbine, plumping her enormous breasts into shape, came out of the flat. The stiff blonde wig was askew, and one trickle of mascara ran down to her white—faintly bluish-white —jowl. Drawing her red velvet cloak about her, she turned her back on the others to wait for the elevator.

When she was gone, they chuckled. 'I think Ank was right about her, she is a lesbian,' said one. 'I mean, did you see that five-o'clock shadow?'

'Sure upset her, though. She spent the whole evening sprawled out on the couch, bawling.'

They went back inside.

Someone lurched up to the bedroom door and peered at the lighted sign over it, spelling it out. 'Fums?' he said. 'I wonder where in hell the other one is. What do they call it? Ohms.'

The water in the bathroom was thigh-deep, but the six pseudo-Egyptians hadn't noticed. They were all piled up against the door to the bedroom, listening to Glen's taped music.

*

Ank awoke to see Myra and a man in a feather cape looking over his two completed paintings. He was at home, on the bed.

90

One of his paper sleeves had fallen off; it lay in the middle of the floor, like an abandoned snakeskin.

'Never mind those,' he roused himself to say. 'They're not . . . not what I wanted.'

'They're what *I* want, though,' said the man. He introduced himself as Drew Moody of the Moody Gallery. 'Those paintings *live*. All right, it's corny, but I've been looking at other stuff all week. Cold mechanical stuff, the kind those computer jerks crank out.'

'Computer . . . ?' Ank tried to clear his head.

'Half the kids in the country think if they can only get a random number generator they automatically become a painter. But this—this is by God *human* art, untouched by mechanical hands. Can you do a few more? I'd like to give you a one-man show.'

'But . . . do you think the critics . . . ?'

'The critics! The critics are a bunch of dehorns who wouldn't know paint from diarrhea. The real world will eat this up, if I present it right.'

'Et's e wenderfel eppertenety, Enk.'

'He's tired and foggy,' said the dealer. 'Tell you what, Ank. I'll give you a jingle in the morning. And here's my card. Now Myra and I will sneak off and let you get some sleep.'

On the way out, the art dealer noticed the tarpaulin-draped painting machine. 'What's this? Sculpture?'

'Uh, no, it's—it's just a paint-mixing machine.'

'See you then. So long, Ank.'

The door closed, setting up a breeze that stirred the empty paper sleeve on the floor. It made one clumsy painting movement, then lay still.

*

'Fear of effeminacy. It might work,' said General Weimarauner. 'Combined with fear of the fool. The—The Pink Barrettes?' He began to laugh, inclining his noble head and putting up a hand as if to ward off blows. 'I'm tempted, Hackendorf, I'm tempted!'

He paused to study the figure in red velvet sitting in another corner of the coffee shop. Nudging Hackendorf, he dropped his voice to say, 'Look at that, will you? Did you ever see such

91

an ugly woman in your life? Gad, any uglier and they'd draft her. Come to think of it, she reminds me of an aide I used to have, only she's about fifty pounds heavier. What was his name, now? Pouts?'

He tore his attention away from the person in the corner, who had just ordered six Danish pastries and a chocolate malt. 'The Pink Barrettes! Yes by God, we'll do it. I can just see them on parade!'

*

The Knight of Columbus was telling the last person he could find about the accident in the elevator shaft. Jerry was looking for Myra. The gloomy producer was telling someone about Miss Columbine: 'Balling somebody all evening on that sunken sofa, and nobody even noticed.' There was no one left for the American Studies professor to tell a Little Moron Joke to. The hot-dog publisher had fallen asleep in a chair, letting his coat open to reveal his truss.

Bradd asked the cryogenics man for the hundredth time if he was sure it could be done.

'See voo play,' someone asked, 'oo ay lays Ohm? E.c. ay lay Fum, may oo ay lays Ohm?' He gestured at the bedroom door.

'What do you want with a man? Won't I do?'

'Of course it'll work,' said the cryogenics man. 'We freeze donuts, don't we? So why not a girl?'

'Can't wreck her appearance, though.' Bradd removed his TV glasses and inspected them for dirt. 'She's got to look good, for, say, thirty or forty years. In front of the cameras, anyway.'

'Don't worry about a thing. Now, what price range freezer were you thinking of?'

*

Glen Dale put on the ninth tape. There were ten, arranged by experts in order of arousal, and now there was nothing left but half an hour of Ravel's *Bolero*.

And he still hadn't figured out a way of kissing Miranda, the girl in the peach-sundae dress. He had fed her arousing music, stirred up the fire in the fireplace, changed (behind a screen) into a dressing gown of red silk, poured many brandies into

92

their two snifters, switched on the electronic odorizer that filled the room with musk and frankincense, talked knowledgeably of Krafft-Ebbing and Tantric Yoga, even shown her selections from a Cinerama blue film. Now he sat inches away from her on the bed and toyed with the tassel of his dressing gown. All this brought them to the point where he *had* to make a move—or a mistake.

'I gotta go home now,' she said, looking at her watch.

'But it's early!'

'Don't argue with me, I said I gotta go! Anyways, I can't crap around here all night waiting for you to make up your mind. We been in here three hours,' she said. 'Three hours, and *nothing happened.*'

'But I . . .'

'I guess you think I'm not good enough for you, with all your Miss Monthly girls and Does and all.' She stood up, straightened her ruffles and smiled. 'So bye-bye.'

'Wait, Miranda, wait!'

Miranda did not wait. She chose the wrong door, tugged at her skirt, and marched over to it. 'Bye-bye.'

Six people in Egyptian costumes tumbled in upon her, accompanied by several dozen gallons of water.

'Christ almighty! What the hell is this, a voyeur hotel?' Extricating herself, Miranda kicked at the Egyptians.

'Miranda, I—wait . . .'

The right door slammed. Glen sank back on the bed. The six fake Egyptians scrambled up and came to sit next to him, one pausing to turn up the taped music.

'Nice sounds, man. Who is it? Sounds like *The Andrew Jackson Davis Penetralia.*'

*

Alone in his room, Bates, the young anglophile, took off his wicker suit and hung it up carefully. It was, after all, a suit with a London label, from a shop on Portobello Road, even if he had bought it at a Minneapolis department store.

Next he took off his imported English leather shoes, his imported English wool socks, and his Union Jack 'Standfast' underwear. He crawled into bed to meet his insomnia.

That Englishman, Sir Somebody, had laughed at him! That

93

was the worst part. They all knew by now: *He hadn't been to England at all.*

The nearest he ever got was buying something English, reading a travel guide, or corresponding with his pen pal, a ten-year-old boy in Scunthorpe whose hobbies included collecting American stamps. The little snot was blackmailing him: information on the English scene for batches of stamps.

This wasn't jolly hockey-sticks at all. He'd have to get to England itself, no matter how. *England, my England!* he thought. *England's green and pleasant land. Swinging England. Land of hope and glory. Little Olde England, where the sun never sets . . .*

He gazed on the picture over his bed, a dazzling picture of the Queen, while his right hand moved under the covers in a familiar and traditional rhythm, old as the rhythm of the waves over which Britannia rules.

94

EIGHT: THE HOUSE

NUMBER ONE TAKES CARE OF ITSELF
.... noun is a replacement for the pronoun I wonder
Bob wonders this man wonders how the hell long he's going to
be in here trapped here in an abandoned mind shaft (and are the
psychiatrists still digging out there?) and buried under tons of
crushing self buried a back number: 'They have parsed my
hands and my feet, they have numbered all my bones' now
there's a thought more noughts than crosses though a crucial
difference that essential plus
Old numb copybones the headbone connected to nothing
really the fingerbone maybe that digit in my nostril really is
one and 'hands and feet' are measurements too they have me
here the integers, trace, fear, sank, sex they (la enemy Hymeneal,
read me any way I'm still an em wide) have fed me right into
their number mumbling machine I'm

95

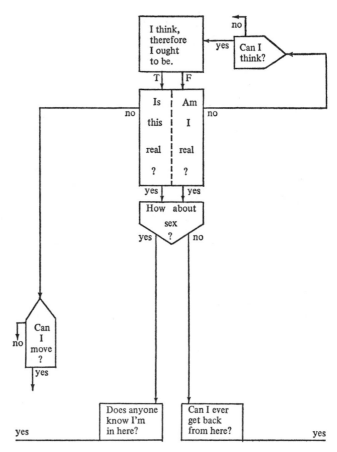

That's me all right, the old inchworm. And my winding
sheet is

> three
>> miles
>> long

ROBINS ON COURSE
Luckily I managed to rescue from the shipwreck an inflat-
able house, miniature bulldozer, seeds, farming implements,
swimming pool kit, prefab bomb shelter, guns, ammo, libraries

96

and lab equipment for geology, botany, zoology, horticulture, medicine and chemistry, instructions for building and operating generators, miniature manufacturing systems of several kinds, 'Hints for the Amateur Farmer', supplies of fuel and food for at least five years, a wilderness survival kit and guide, carpenters', plumbers' and machinists' tool kits, a selection of light novels (neither depressing nor the kind that make civilization look too good), several hundred pounds each of wood, plastic, metal stock, glue, epoxy, nails, small standard machine parts, an abundance of copper wire and electronic parts in all sizes, several radios, televisions, home appliances of all descriptions (all portable and with extra batteries), a one-man oil-drilling rig, a small tape recorder suitable for memoranda and recording bird cries, a barbecue hat, briquets, etc., etc.

The thought of escape is not so tasty as the thought of keeping what I've got. The crash-priority projects must be:

(1) a first-line defense system (alarms, mortars, shelter and perhaps short-range rocket defense).

(2) hygienic water supply and sewage disposal.

(3) oil refinery.

(4) swimming pool and barbecue pit.

(5) drugs from local flora (the supply of Noctec, Miltown, Somnos, Librium, Equanil, Trancopal, etc., is alarmingly low already).

These should keep me pretty busy for a few months, after which I'll be able to get up the NO TRESPASSING signs, set up the printing press, maybe run off my own currency.

The island is snug and comfy already. The only thing (besides lack of sex and the old nagging headache) that really bothers me is the stationary cloud hanging overhead. It's been there the whole first month, neither moving nor changing.

And there's this pair of feet sticking down out of it.

SILLY, DIS IDYLL IS

Meanwhile back in my lounge chair, I decide the whole thing—this room, the experimenters, maybe my perceptions—is plastic. By my calendar watch I've been here three days, surely long enough to prove whatever they want to prove. Enough entombment! Abra cadavera! I rise from the dead.

97

I rise, walk through the steel air, past the vapid faces of Donagon & Co., right on into the crisco wall . . . surfacing in the paradise of my childhood back yard.

Every detail in depth, enveloped with a strange importance. The Sinclair station on the corner, every whitewashed brick in place, every delicate color within the whiteness. Under one of its murky windows the remains of a circus poster make a Rorschach pattern, a map of Odd Islands. The earth is steeped in oil, the dinosaur sign creaks overhead, and the poster remains spell a message: HE UNSTOPS BEST ALLIES, TOO. EFFORTLESS? HE UNSTOPS BEST ALLIES, TOO, RETHATCHED KING THISTLE BOTHERS EVIL ENDS. REQUESTED RICE.

I turn away from the station, feeling an ordinary death about this place: By my back porch hollyhocks are shriveling to hairy stalks; the back porch itself is dying, and there is the gray catenary of clothesline from the house to the little birch I scalped last summer to make a toy canoe. Some dog has turned over the crumpled garbage can and nosed open all its packages of coffee grounds. Maybe the same dog who dug up the yard in four or five places, looking for a spot for his relic bones. I could sit here in the cool grass and die with the dying hollyhocks, watch them give up their 'money' seeds . . . but there's work to do, O sinclairosaur.

Unfurling the flag of the United States of America, I plant the staff firmly in a relic hole and repeat the memorized speech. Claim this planet. People of the United States. Peace loving.

When it's over I sit down for a moment, my head buzzing with Valium, Striatran, Noludar, Listica, Somnos, Lenetran and Trepidone. Two small white butterflies settle to picnic together on a glistening dog turd. The sun is warm.

98

PART THREE | CEMENT SOCKS

NINE

There was no altar, only a platform with a microphone and a banner, BELIEVE ON ME. There was no vaulted cathedral, only an ordinary baseball stadium. There were no fine vestments, only a simple, well-tailored business suit. And, though few knew it, there was no Billy Koch, only a sophisticated android.

It lacked nothing in programming; all of Billy's habits were intact. His powerful hands kneaded the air ('Give Jesus your love! Give it to Him *now*!'), his brows contracted ('Suspended over a pit of flaming fahr! Forget about your puny h-bomb!') and his mighty chest heaved with simulated emotion ('He's a-comin' in a fiery jet! His face is like a blast furnace! He's callin' out—who, me, Lord? You want me? YES, Lord, I'm ready! I'M READY FOR ETERNITY!').

The service too was unchanged. Before the great man actually appeared, there came preliminary events, 'warmups':

A large choir began with a medley of popular hymns, then a warmup preacher delivered a short, hard-hitting sermon that reassured the audience they had come to the right place. He mentioned high taxes, temptations of the young, national unrest caused by Communism and darker races. He praised the basic honesty and faith of rural white Americans and their kin, the four freedoms, motherhood, and the principle of driving money-changers out of temples.

Then, following an organ selection that leaned towards sustained low notes and tremolo effects, the lights dimmed out.

99

Each member of the audience was given thirty seconds in which to feel alone and apprehensive. When it was quiet enough, a voice broke the tension, crying over the p.a. system: 'JESUS LIVES! JESUS LIVES!'

A spot picked him out: The heavy ridge of brow and high forehead, the crisp, pale suit with massive shoulders (called in the trade 'an FBI'), the glittering smile of ecstasy as he closed his eyes and opened his arms to embrace them, his flock of thirty-five thousand. He held this pose for ten long beats. Then . . .

The eyes came open: Virgin blue. The audience screamed its blessing upon him, and the deep organ bass cut in under their scream. Billy led them in 'Rock of Ages', his theme song.

'Brothers and sisters, I don't know why you came out here tonight. Some of you may just be curious—you want to see the man who talks so much about Gawd—but that's all right. That's all right, Gawd welcomes you.

'Some of you, well, maybe you found the religion of your childhood just doesn't seem to work any more. Maybe you've lost faith. Or maybe you really tried to believe, but things just got too much for you? And you felt like quitting.

'Why didn't you quit, then? I'll tell you why: It wasn't Gawd's will! I'm telling ALL of you here tonight, that it was the LORD JESUS CHRIST that led you here! *Jesus* wants you all to get another chance! Yes, Jesus *knows all* your suffering and *all* your trials!

'Yes, neighbors, I don't know why *you* came down here tonight—but *I* came here to BEAR WITNESS TO THE LORD JESUS CHRIST!'

A low cheer, mixed with amens, came from the claquers.

'YES, TO BEAR WITNESS! JESUS IS ALIVE TONIGHT, RIGHT HERE IN THIS AUDITORIUM! HE'S IN ME—AND NEIGHBORS, HE CAN BE IN YOU!!'

The cheers were general this time.

Billy went on to make a joke about a frog in a rut, who couldn't possibly get out—but then a truck came along and he had to; the laughter was extravagant.

'Now there's a lot of talk about the "miracles" of modern science, about "miracle" drugs, yes, and even toothpaste has its "miracle" ingredient.

100

'But I want to talk to you about another kind of "miracle" ingredient. You can't find it at the drugstore. It won't make you smell sweeter or smile brighter. But it is the most powerful force on earth or anywhere else. And I'm talking about the miracle ingredient FAITH!

'There's all kinds of faith. We read a lot of claptrap in the papers about scientists smashing atoms, putting men inside of computers, I don't know what all. Well, you can believe that or not. *I* never saw a smashed atom, neither did you. Nobody did. We just have faith somebody can do it.

'Now there is something plain ridiculous about a man who will believe there is a bomb a *million times* more powerful than dynamite, a bomb that gives more light than a *thousand suns* —and who still won't believe THAT GAWD LOVES HIM!'

When the laughs, cheers and hallelujahs subsided:

'I won't tell you faith moves mountains. I think the Lord put His mountains where He wanted them, anyway. But I do know of a woman who had a bad car accident. Her little four-year-old boy was pinned underneath the car, and it was crushing the life out of him! That woman—who stood just five-foot two and never lifted anything heavier than a grocery bag before in her life . . .'

And so it went, until the finale:

'Have *faith* in the Lord Jesus Christ! Have *faith* in Almighty Gawd! Have *faith* in the Lamb! Have *faith* in the Blood of the Lamb! Have *faith* in the Almighty Pahwr of the Lord! Have *faith* that He can save you! Have *faith* that He can heal you! Have *faith*, and forget about your quack doctors and fake medicines! Have *faith*, and forget about the "miracles" of modern medicine! Have *faith*, and forget about braces and crutches and pills and potions and knives! Have *faith*, and forget about hospitals and x-rays and specialists and surgeons and iron lungs and artificial hearts! Have *faith*! Have *faith*! Have FAITH IN THE HEALING HAND OF THE LORD!'

Pom-papa-pom pom pom, the organ began a sprightly march. Billy's replica held out its arms, and the afflicted (directed by Crusade police to their places in line) came forward for their cures.

*

101

'Billikins?'

He awoke from a dream (God, a high-powered executive surrounded by anxious angel subordinates, was just about to place an order for a thousand gross souls) and found her watching him, this fat, red-faced person called Nurse.

'You want some breakfast?'

'They're hiding something from me, Nurse.'

'Who is?' She began helping him out of his wet pajamas.

'I don't know . . . the doctor, maybe. And that one-legged man that comes around all the time.'

'Jerry?' Her dark red curls shook. 'Don't be silly, Billikins. Jerry's your friend. He brings us presents.' She often wore one of the presents, a huge black negligee.

'Well, I don't care! I caught him in my room yesterday, looking at *my wall*. And he was laughing!'

Nurse's face grew redder from wrestling him into a business suit. Though her uniform was always rumpled and sweaty looking, she smelled only of starch. Billikins didn't like Nurse much, and he decided he'd better not let her look at his wall, either.

His wall was a picture of the world as it *really* was, and it was also a message, the word of the LORD to His elect, spoken through the prophet Billikins. He'd tried many times to explain it to Nurse, because he'd been so sure she was one of the elect, but she wouldn't listen.

She preferred to go in the bedroom with Jerry and lock the door and lock him out. They were having secrets in there, terrible secrets. Jerry was one of the damned. Already his foot had gone to Hell, Billikins knew.

He'd tried to explain to her why he liked to watch Billy Koch on television. It wasn't that silly little man waving his arms around and speaking about Gawd. There was something else, a real deep voice, so deep you couldn't hear it unless you were one of the elect, so slow you couldn't make out the words unless you were one of the elect. And, in a way, you didn't *listen* to it at all. In a way, you looked at it—no, that wasn't right either. You just knew it was there. Nurse had just laughed at that.

After breakfast he gave her one more chance.

'Nurse, the LORD moves me,' he said.

102

'You have to go to the bathroom? You want to go potty?' She leaped up and began tugging at his belt.

'No, no, I mean the LORD moves me to carry on His work. I wanna work on the wall.'

'Oh, *that*.' She unloaded herself in the creaky tube-frame chair again, and at the same time took up a slice of sticky coffee cake. Billikins rose to go.

Her mouth, poised over the cake, curved in a nasty smile. 'All I can say is, if that wall is the LOORD's work, then the LOORD oughta have his mouth washed out with soap.'

*

Nurse Harriet Saga took a hairpin out of her coffee cup. *What a crummy job.* She picked up the paper and leafed through it, tasting her thumb to hasten past meaningless headlines toward the horoscope page.

POPE'S BULL ON VIRGIN MARY
CHINESE DELEGATES NOT RECOGNIZED
MORE EAST BERLINERS COME OVER WALL
'We almost didn't make it'
SCIENTIST: BEARS CAN TALK!

She felt cheated by the paper this morning. There were no sexational movie star drug raid shocking truth stories, nothing. Even her horoscope was vague.

The Big Cheat was this crummy job, looking after a feeb like that. She'd only taken on the job because her niece, Marilyn, who worked for the Crusade, had told her they needed a nurse for some secret project—and because Billy was so handsome. No one had told her his handsomeness was all show, all for the old ladies from Cedar Rapids . . .

True, the Crusade paid her a hundred a month over her salary, but that was to keep her quiet. The funny part was, they wouldn't even let her talk to Marilyn about it. All the girl knew was that her aunt was taking care of some 'old man'. Which was just as well, all around, because otherwise Marilyn would be over here every day—she had autographed pictures all over her little room—and there wouldn't be those pleasant afternoons with Jerry.

'Huh? That's funny.' She looked at the headline and even

103

some of the small type under it. '**BILLY TO PREACH AT FERTILIZER PALACE**', it still said. Some big place in Kansas City. And how could he be out preaching when he was right here? And all those TV programs—maybe they weren't taped re-runs. A twin brother? An actor, ringer? She'd have to ask Jerry. Something wrong, anyhow, and it was worth more than a hundred a month to keep quiet about it.

*

At noon, Nurse turned on the TV and sat with him, watching a cartoon. Billikins saw that the cartoon was really a message from Jehovah to His Person on Earth, showing forth through the simple parable of Bill the Cat, Mary the Canary and Mike Mouse the divine drama:

Beelzebub (Baal-Ze-bul, the shit god, or just plain Bill) wanted to catch and eat Mary, but he always ended up in trouble: running through a brick wall to leave a Bill-shaped doorway, receiving his own bomb in the mail (a Negrofying blockbuster) or flattened by a mallet. But—and this was the important part—Baal would also be restored to his full powers! There was no hint that Mike and his legions would ever, finally, triumph over the powers of dark-seeing Bill!

The cartoon finished with Bill holding his hotfoot and running off into the flat perspectives of distanceland (whence Lucifer shall return, bearing the same light), a fade . . . and Bette Cooke, looking wonderfully substantial, smiled right at him.

'Something from the oven,' she said, 'for Baby and me.'

And it clarified everything. The three chillun of God melted together with love in the burning heart of Jesus, where Bill was Mary was Mike, where Bette Cooke was Billy Koch, being the light and bearing the light and bearing witness to the light. And the light was the sun of God, Baal.

104

TEN

One Man's Fight (against the Black Conspiracy), by Wes Davis, became a national best-seller that month, nudging down on the non-fiction list two cookbooks and a factual account of the way lions live. Many found in Wes's simple phrases and clumsy constructions the honesty of the blunt backwoodsman who speaks his mind. That Wes had been born and brought up in New York, and lived less than a year in the Midwest, made no difference. So broadcast was the fear of a Negro conspiracy that the reviewers were merciful, the media congratulatory, and the public delighted. *At last, at long last,* they said, *someone is saying it out loud.*

A Southern Congressman demanded to know why this man was in jail. A Northern preacher used sections of the book in his sermons (especially: 'Why Jesus Chose White Disciples', 'Why Washington Kept Slaves', and 'The Black Beast: Human?'). An old lady who had been 'receiving' dark presences on the gold rims of her glasses began the Free Wes Davis Society. A schoolteacher, fired for carving the word SIN on the neck of a Negro child, formed the Organization for the Rights of Gentile Anglo-Saxon Man. The Klan revived, and the American Nazi Party gained new strength. Of all right-nut organisations, only the Jess Hurchists stood still.

*

From their tiny St Paul office, Amy and Grover carried on underground work on the largest scale they could afford. Amy

105

spent her days writing anonymous letters to Congressmen, the President and the FBI. ('We wondered if you had noticed how the little cent-sign (¢) on our government's postage stamps looks a lot like a hammer and sickle . . .') while Grover worked on his deciphering.

He was sure that almost anything, if you looked into it, could yield up a Communist plot. The number and arrangement of milk bottles on doorsteps in the neighborhood, for example. That had proved an ingenious code, and through breaking it Grover discovered that They were poisoning the money with radioactives. He wasn't able to get an unrigged Geiger counter anywhere, but Grover had a special dowsing stick that did just as well. Whenever he saw a dollar bill (alas! not often enough) he would suspend the forked stick over it. If it dipped, the dollar was 'hot'—riddled with radioactives.

One of his richest sources of ciphers was the morning paper, especially the daily 'Crypto Cutie' feature. Through this he had already found out that the 'Red' Cross was a front organisation, that most accidents happened in the home because Communists had flooded the market with booby-trapped home items, ranging from fluoride toothpaste and can openers designed to give a ragged edge to the more insidious items like 'fry-o-matic' electric blankets and exploding furnaces.

*

'Eureka, Amy!'

'You have found it?'

'You betcha I have! Another plot of the International Cummunisk Conspiracy. Just feast your eyes on this, yesterday's Cutie.'

He was not, of course, calling her a name. Amy realised her mistake and read the clipping he was holding out:

CRYPTO CUTIE
DKGTQ DTZDXQ AEQ RGB ET ZAD UGEX.

(Hint: Someone in a jam? Quite the reverse,
although he may be in a state!)

'What on earth can it mean?' Amy tilted her glasses to reread the inscription, but it remained a mystery.

106

'Well here's the "official" solution from today's paper,' he said, handing her another clipping.

EVANS ENTERS HIS JAM IN THE FAIR.

'And here's the *real* solution.' He held up a sheet of paper.

'CIGAR CANCER YDR UGS DA NYC PGDE,' the top line read. The next was a re-grouping of the same letters: 'CIGAR CANCERY DRUGS *DA* NYC. (signed) PGDE.' He read it aloud, adding that 'da' was Russky for 'okay'.

'This is serious, Amy. We'd better get off a wire to the FBI.'

'Yes, Grover.' She looked at him, into his eyes, beaming at him all the love and admiration that could penetrate her lenses and his.

Grover turned away. 'Yes, and I want to look into the possibility that the Redskies are running the Supreme Court by radios planted in the heads of all the justices. So get me that book from the library, on the Great Pyramid.'

He had found the dimensions of the Great Pyramid invaluable in learning things about the Supreme Court. The lengths of its secret passages in feet gave him numerical indices: one representing fidelity; two, deception; three, conspiracy; four, a quarrel and so on. The turns of the passages to left or right were self-evident, while upward or downward turns meant improvement or decline.

Likewise many other codes had tipped him off: The names of towns on the bottoms of coke bottles were used to dispatch agents of the conspiracy to their new locations; car license plates (along with the position and number of cars parked on certain streets each morning) delivered the 'orders of the day'; supermarket shoppers' elaborate code of purchases revealed a plan to bombard the television waves with subliminal messages ('QUIT WORK TODAY, CIVIL SERVANTS' and 'KIDS, DON'T DRINK MILK!').

If Amy had had the courage to write 'GROVER, AMY LOVES YOU' into an elaborate cipher and run it in the personal column of the Minneapolis *Sun*, she might have got through to him. Anything more direct was useless.

*

107

MacCormick Hines put down *One Man's Fight* and rubbed his eyes.

'Maybe I'm getting old. I always thought the real fight was individuality and private enterprise against atheistic communism. Now this fella says the Negroes are ... No, I just can't believe that. I used to watch Amos-n'-Andy. Why, those people are *happy*.'

'I wouldn't be too sure of that, sir,' said one of his bright young men. 'The *natural* state of the Negroes may be one of simple ignorance and happiness—but they've been stirred up by left-wing bastards of all kinds.'

Mac sighed. 'You may be right. You may be right, there. In my day, a man could earn his bread by the sweat of his brow, tuck away a little nest egg, bring home the bacon, plan for his family's future. And the next thing he knew, he was ...'

'The owner of National Arsenamid, sir? Speaking of which, I have the figures ...'

'Don't interrupt!' Mr Hines reached out and tweaked the young man's nose. 'I don't want to hear anything more about the National Whatever it is! Get out of here!'

Holding his injured nose, the young man retreated. Mac was not to be left alone, however. Almost at once another b.y.m. strode in, bearing a thick file like a fasces.

'Hail Wes Davis!' he said.

Mac shook a fist at him. 'None of that! I've just been reading Wes Davis's book, and he doesn't have a speck of sound business sense. I doubt if the fellow knows the value of a dollar! If you want to hail someone, hail *me*. On second thought, why don't you hail a cab and leave me alone? Put it on the expense account. Put a letter of resignation on the expense account while you're at it. What's that file supposed to be?'

'Sir, you requested the complete dossier on the Müller-Fokker tapes.'

MacCormick Hines took the file, turned over pages for a few seconds, then closed it. 'Tell me what it says.'

The young man stood at parade rest, hands locked together behind his back, feet apart. 'There seem to be only four reels of the tape in existence, sir,' he said, or rather shouted. 'Dr

108

Müller-Fokker himself manufactured them, and the process is lost—gone with him to Black Power Russia.'

'*Which* Russia?'

'If they aren't, why was one of their writers, Pushkin, a nigra? And how about the Black Sea? Why did all the White Russians flee the revolution?'

'The tape, the tape.'

'Yes sir. The Russians deny that Müller-Fokker has defected, so far, sir. Anyway, the tapes were used for some of Dr Müller-Fokker's private research. Then they went to the Mud Flats Biomedical Research Project.'

'I know what happened there. Go on.'

'The four reels were put up for sale in a surplus store here in town, sir. Two of them were sold to the Billy Koch Crusade, but we've only been able to find one of them there. That one is being used to run a robot replica of Billy Koch, and the key man to see is a Mr Jerry Zurkenhall. If you wish to interview him, sir, we can arrange that. The replica is due to speak in town soon.'

'Where are the other three? You can't make a heart out of a right auricle.'

'Another surplus store bought one of them, sir. The fourth went to the government, oddly enough. To the Pentagon Logistics Office.'

'Hmmm. That'll take a fine bribe. Well, let's get the one that went to another store.'

'We already have, Mr Hines. Our own marketing division is ...'

'I don't have any marketing divison!'

'I mean, National Arsen ...'

'I don't want to hear that name! Out—get out of here and let me get some work done!'

'Hail Wes D ...'

'Out!'

*

In fact he had no work at all to do. Nothing to do but to dream or dread, whatever it was. Whatever it was, the picture of Marge (635 lines/inch) came to him, hot, hurting and magnificent. Her eyes were swords, her breasts mounted horns, her breath an acid bath. Now here was something nice. Mac ran the video tape of her first commercial, then

109

her second, the next and the next. There was something . . .

For the first time in years, he began to wonder if another person might not be real.

No? Then what was happening in the auricles and ventricles of his heart? They felt crammed full of spinets and timetables and brass nameplates and daffodil telephones, all those old and awkward and lovely commodities.

I'm not too old to love, he thought. *Anyway, I'm not too old to love*. He embraced her in oceans of suds; they made a little pink cake. He embraced . . .

He became aware of a figure on the horizon, hailing Wes Davis. The camera zoomed in on a young man with a red nose, standing right here before the desk.

'Mr Hines?'

He put his hands on the desk and asked the b.y.m. what he wanted.

'But I thought *you* wanted something, sir. You were shouting.'

'I was? What'd I say?'

'"I'm rich! I'm rich!"'

'Well I'm not.'

'No sir. But just how did you get so much money?'

'By the sweat of honest toil. By working my fingers to the bone, shoulder to the wheel, nose to the grindstone. I didn't hide my light under a bushel. I didn't waste my God-given talents, of which I am just the steward. Value for money! Build a better mousetrap . . .'

'Yes sir. But just what kind of mousetrap did you build?' The young man's smile hardened.

'Don't borrow from Peter to pay the devil! A penny saved is money in the bank! Give me elbow grease and I'll move the world! Yankee ingenuity, boy, and . . .'

'Yes sir. Applied to what?'

Crimson to the roots of his thick white Yankee hair, Mac fought back valiantly: 'WHEN I HIRE A MAN, I ALWAYS LOOK AT HIS SHOES! IF YOU'VE GOT BACKBONE AND SAND, GO TO THE HEAD OF THE CLASS! WASTE NOT, WANT NOT! MORE HASTE, LESS SPEED! THERE IS PLENTY OF ROOM AT THE TOP . . . oh, what the fuck, I might as well tell you.'

The young man sat down and helped himself to a cigar. Mac lit it for him, then commenced his story.

110

ELEVEN

Our family [he said] has always been lucky on both sides. My great-grandfather Franklin Hines, who (spelled it H-Y-N) won his wife in a game of Russian roulette. Her name was Hero Rwcz, and I believe she had just escaped a pogrom.

My great-grandfather Leonardo Fox, who was to be the only survivor of Little Big Horn, married Galilea Avaka, who could smell water.

My great-grandfather Archimedes Mutt actually made the first gold strike in California, months before the Sutter's Mill strike. Being a lazy man, he pocketed a few nuggets and declined to stake a claim. Archy married a Swedish girl, Bernoullia Bjld, whose talents were culinary. She could cook any dish to perfection after tasting it just once, and she was good at finding double yolks.

Then there was my great-grandfather Watt Peqeq, the so-called 'Unlucky Balloonist'. Over seventy serious accidents, and his only injury was a broken wisdom tooth. He married Dedalie Gissigi, who found at least a dollar in change every day of her life.

Franklin and Hero Hyn had twins, Dagurette and Fulton. The infant Dag was kidnaped by white slavers, but the gang was wiped out by smallpox before they could get her to market. She was found, two thousand-odd miles from home, by a next-door neighbor who happened by. He brought her home to the Hyns, then himself caught smallpox and died.

111

Fulton, aged four, fell out of a boat during a family outing on Lake Michigan. The lake at this point was fifty feet deep. For one reason or another, he was not missed for several hours. The family rowed back to find him standing upon the mast of a submerged shipwreck, barely keeping his head above water.

Leonardo and Galilea Fox also had twins, Howe and Jenny. Howe became a poker player, and so incredibly lucky that many times his life was threatened. One sore loser's derringer misfired; another was taken by an opportune epileptic seizure. A third cowboy's gun went off in its holster, and a fourth was himself shot by an old debtor at the moment he drew on Howe. Finally, one of Howe's potential murderers was distracted by the fire that burnt half of Chicago.

Jenny seldom gambled, though on a dare she once parlayed a dollar across seven horse races to something over four hundred thousand (and this was her dowry when she married Fulton Hines). But grandmother Jenny was lucky chiefly in fashion. She had a habit of buying old dresses, altering them to suit herself, and openly disregarding the prevailing fads. Inevitably what she wore became the *avant-garde* fashion a year or two later; Paris designers finally discovered her and paid her handsomely to let them sketch her old rags.

Archy and Bernoullia had twin sons, Morse and Whitney. Morse went into a monastery; I have only one story about him. He was excessively zealous, at least according to the abbot's way of thinking, and that good man asked him to ease up on the fasting, vigils and self-immolation. One day the abbot rebuked him rather sternly for it. At once a heavy statue, which had been solidly anchored to a stone foundation for centuries, toppled, and the abbot was killed by the Good Shepherd's crook. This story may be apocryphal. By the way, I hear steps are being taken in Rome for my great-uncle's beatification.

Whitney Mutt was wounded in the Spanish–American War and shipped home. The following day everyone in his platoon came down with malaria; all eventually died. Whitney married one of the pretty Peqeq twins, Merrimac, by whom he already had a nine-year-old daughter, my mother, Bell.

Some years earlier, Merri's twin sister had been abducted

112

by the outlaw Jess Hurch, and forcibly married. Before the marriage could be consummated, Jess was accidently killed. I don't know the details, but somehow Monita received both a handsome reward for his capture and a medal for his bravery! Even so, she does not seem to have been that lucky. Perhaps she loved the scoundrel, and perhaps he'd have made her a good husband, who knows?

Whitney and Merrimac received as a wedding present a few shares of then worthless stock. They were to honeymoon aboard the *Titanic*, but food poisoning, a late train and a quarrel with a drunken taxi driver combined to delay them; they missed the boat. Instead they went West, to visit Monita. An incident there proved that Merri was, like her sister, immune to rattlesnake venom.

My father was Singer Hines, Fulton and Jenny's only son. At the age of ten, he fell from a cliff and broke his collarbone, which kept him home from school the day a new boy brought in cholera. As a memento of that day, my father carried with him the rest of his life the five-leaf clover he'd snatched in his fall. The collarbone set badly, and he was consequently not drafted for World War One. He enlisted in the Ambulance Corps, but peace came the following day. 'The infernal luck!' he said. I was to remember those words . . .

*

To continue, my mother was given by her aunt Monita eighteen silver dollars on her eighteenth birthday. Sixteen went for a dog, one for a collar and license. The other was to have purchased a leash, but the store was out of stock.

On the way home, her dog broke loose and was trampled to death by a racehorse. Its owner, a young man named Raines, apologized and offered her half-ownership in the horse, Skitsy Darlin'. Bell's peculiar talent lay, as we shall see, in not having time to get too attached to things before she lost them, and in always gaining by compensation. In this case young Raines became her beau, and next day took her to their horse's first race at Duda, Kansas.

Meanwhile another man named Baynes, of nearby Lardhole, Missouri, set out for another race. Having lost his way, he was misdirected by local farmers to the Duda racetrack (where

113

Bell and Raines sat holding hands in the center of the grandstand).

The starting bugle blew. Skitsy Darlin' got off to a bad start, but moved from sixth to fourth place rapidly. The crowd grew excited as the horses bunched up in the far turn (Baynes was looking for a parking place, Raines was squeezing Bell's hand). Skitsy Darlin' entered the home stretch; so did Baynes's yellow roadster; they collided.

The panic on the racecourse was exceeded by that a second later in the stands, half of which collapsed. Raines was killed instantly; Bell was left holding his ring (it bore the seal of the Crown Prince of Luftenberg, and many years later it saved her life in a tight spot).

For Skitsy Darlin's broken leg, Baynes offered compensation. He proposed to mend the leg, set the animal to stud or similar work, and turn over all its earnings to Bell, and gave her the roadster as a token of good faith. Skitsy Darlin' became famous under Baynes's training—perhaps you have heard of Mathematical Hank, the circus wonder horse?

Bell met my father at a rest home where both were recuperating from nervous exhaustion (he had fallen from a Zeppelin). They married. My triplet brothers and I were born a year later.

Times were hard. My dentist father, out of work, was forced to actually beg on the streets of New York. One day my mother came across the eighteenth and last silver dollar. It was not enough to hold off starvation for long, so she generously gave it to a hunchbacked beggar. It looked 'funny' to him, so he fobbed it off on another beggar, my father. He took it to a coin dealer.

It was a rare 1897 Medicine Dumps Bank Dollar (Obverse: a frontiersman shaking hands with Liberty. Reverse: a wreath, a cornucopia of buffalo, and the words ONE DOLLER) in mint condition, and worth thousands. The dealer offered him five hundred for it and my father sold. The following week, all over the country, immense caches of these dollars were turned up; its value dropped to 'face'.

Some of the five hundred went to pay for a trip West for Bell, to visit her dying mother. She arrived hours too late, and there were the funeral expenses to meet. Merrimac had

114

died in poverty, leaving only her old, tumble-down house (which had, though, survived an earthquake).

Bell called in a realtor to appraise the place. Seeing how desperate she was to sell, he began depreciating the house, knocking on walls to show their flimsiness. One entire room caved in, killing the realtor and revealing the hiding place for Merrimac's valuables. Here were all the old 'worthless' stocks, now priceless. My father sold them to buy his practice, a mansion, and a large hoard of gold bullion for inlay work.

Next day the market crashed, and Singer was able to buy back all his sold stocks for pennies (which he did, out of sentiment). And so, though he spent his entire fortune trying to trace the origin of the Luftenberg ring, he did leave me those stocks.

Every investment I made paid off, or very nearly every one. In time, I could afford to buy the time of bright young investment counsellors like yourself. In time . . .

*

Mac blew out the match and dropped it in his clean platinum ashtray.

'You were about to tell me,' said the young man, 'the secret of your success.'

'Was I? I thought I just had.'

'You didn't say a word!'

'Indeed. It's just as well. I was thinking of a story—something I saw the other day on television. Well, never mind. Back to work. Time, my young friend, is money.'

115

TWELVE

The art critics of a dozen newspapers and magazines came to the opening at the Moody Gallery. They shuffled in like a soup line, snatched what was free (catalogues and drinks) and ignored the paintings as much as possible while they talked to each other.

Ank had been through it all many times, when he'd worked for the *Sun*. They called this 'the game'.

The game was to conceal your own opinion of the show while sounding the opinions of your colleagues. When you had polled enough of them to decide whether it was worthwhile or not, you went back to the paper and set down a few epigrams. If the show was worthwhile, you tried to have at least one 'insight' no one else would manage. This might involve talking about the arrangement of the works, the name cards attached to the walls near them, how many steps to the gallery door, or anything else you were sure no one but you had noticed.

Ank knew the game, but now it was his show, and he really wanted to know what they thought of it. He walked a crooked route through the gallery, avoiding the clusters of wealthy guests, and trying to eavesdrop on the critics' conversations.

'Vasari . . .' said a woman in triangular glasses. '. . . Berenson . . .'

A man with the blurry, distorted features of a Francis Bacon executive stood with his back to one of Ank's favorite paint-

116

ings, a blue-eyed Giotto copy. 'That's it, all right. Tensions lacking. The quintessence of *lif i framställning.*'

Next to him a woman jerked her sneer toward the Turneresque storm at sea (including a coke bottle floating on a nearby wave). 'Insulting as a tit, ain't it?'

'Dada, yes,' said a man outfitted as a lumberjack. 'But this decadent sentiment . . .'

Ank came to a stop before a 'Mondriaan' which featured in one panel a sign: WATCH THIS SPACE. Nearby, someone was talking about the real works of Mondriaan. '. . . sacramental splendor. Inverted baroque, you see, the liturgy of the line.'

The tall art critic with the ax-blade nose saw Ank and came over. 'You covering this, too? I thought the *Sun* fired you.'

Ank stammered. 'I'm . . . here all right. God knows why, it's a waste of time.' The familiar phrases came easy.

'So I thought. What did you think of that Aphrodite thing, by the way?' He referred to the chief piece of the exhibition, a travesty of Botticelli's famous work, here entitled *Bertha Venus*. In this version, blood coursed down the goddess's leg, and great bloody patches appeared in the sky.

'I don't know,' said Ank. 'The painter's probably a clever young guy with no ideas. There's a certain lack of tension, of fiber . . .'

'I know just what you mean. Like a queer without taste.'

*

At the far end of the room, Glen sipped his drink and talked to a bearded young man he took to be the painter. The works were unsigned, and the catalogue called the painter 'A.B.'

'That Botticelli, it says it all, you know? I've been working on an article about the same thing myself—the corruption of the individual, the reduction of sex to a mechanism in modern life.'

The young man made a restless shift, so Glen raised his voice. 'It's like those Bette Cooke commercials. Supermarket sex, canned, frozen, sterilized. Love as meaningless as shopping. Art is the only way to reveal her for what she is, the great bitch-goddess of the built-in kitchen . . .'

'Yeah, well, I'd better get going.' The young man went off to fetch another tray of drinks.

117

Glen saw Ank at the other end of the room, standing alone by a curious pseudo-Cézanne. As he walked towards him, he heard someone saying, 'Well I don't know, Wilma. That's what I thought, too. Cheap, derivative. But notice that kid from the *Sun* really likes them. Can't take his eyes off 'em.'

Glen asked Ank if he saw the artist anywhere.

'I thought you knew, Glen. These are . . . mine.'

'Yours? Terrific!' Glen was secretly flattered at having known the artist long before the show. 'I really like it, Ank. In fact, I'm thinking of buying that big Botticelli.'

*

After Glen left, Drew waved his check at Ank. 'We've made it, kid! Eight grand right off the bat! Everybody said I was crazy putting prices like these on an unknown, but . . . What's the matter?'

'Nothing. I just want to make a confession.'

'You're depressed. Nerves from all the commotion out there, that's all. Those pig-ignorant bastards, they don't appreciate . . .'

'I want to get away for awhile. Go to Europe, maybe, and just . . .'

'Study the old masters? Good idea.'

'No, I want to do something *different*. I don't know, I want to hole up by myself somewhere and maybe make up for what I'm doing here. I've committed a crime, Drew.'

The dealer patted his arm. 'Don't worry, Ank. Giotto will forgive you.'

*

The reviews were good. Ank's show sold out in a week. The news that he would paint no more in this 'period' drove prices upward, until the last sale (to the architect Arch Ögivaal) reached ten times the first.

Ank left for Alsace-Lorraine at once. He bought an old factory near Assholtz, moved in quantities of supplies, and cloistered himself there for several months.

*

Marge drank to the flag, the Veterans' Administration one,

118

which she had draped over the sofa in lieu of a coffin. The drink wasn't liquor, either. That had stopped working weeks ago.

And now this stuff wasn't having much effect. She felt her head leave her cold, crawly body, but that was all. Cold and crawly, the way she felt when Bradd got too close. As he always did.

Dr Fellstus, MacCormick Hines, Mr Bradd—already her life was filling with new names. Like dust sifting in after you sweep. There was, there is, no more feeling left for him than for that nylon flag over there, fifty or sixty miles across the room. He was someone else.

So was she: Betsy Ross, Martha Wash, Molly Pitch and Bette Bitch, another standardized receptacle for the feelings of old motherless boys. Boys from Boise. You can take the Boise out of the country, but try and take . . .

She walked over and lay down naked on the flag. Country kitchen dinners, hot dinners . . . hot fudge sex star giveaway showdown tragedy delight it's all right din-din chowdown chowder shoulder choux sho'tnin' bread . . . three layer parfait banana coconut saffron mango yam molasses ripple mint apple betty nutmeg cinnamon bare clove rosemary thyme it's dinner time, its

She spread out on the stars and stripes, made a megaphone of her hands, and screamed:

'COME . . . AND . . . GET IT!'

*

The study hall was arranged with all desks facing the walls around a large rectangle. Col Fouts stood in the center, where he could make sure that every cadet was writing his letter home properly.

The proper form was written on the blackboard:

Dear Mother and Father:
1. Cadet N.N. is well and happy.
2. Cadet N.N. will/will not be home for the weekend/Christmas/ Easter/the occasion of X, as planned, because his academic record does/does not permit this.
3. Cadet N.N. sends both of you and his whole family his devoted love.

Signed, Cadet N.N.

Like the other cadets, Spot had learned to tell, just from the sound of Fouts's footsteps, which way he was facing. While he faced Spot, Spot worked diligently on the form letter. At all other times, Spot continued his secret letter to Billy:

Dear Billy Koch:
1. Cadet Sturgemoore Shairp wants to kill himself . . .

At the next desk a cadet slipped a book from under his letter home and read:

We ruined them for their own simple savage kind of life, and we didn't succeed in making them fit to live like white men. If we really felt sorry for the nigras, like we say we do, then we'd just 'put them to sleep' . . .

The cadet at the next desk was asleep. Just beyond him two ten-year-old corporals were exchanging rumors about Fouts. Some mysterious 'woman in red' had been visiting his quarters. Fouts had a locked drawer in his office that probably was jammed full of contraceptive pills and all like that. Someone had *seen* a woman go into Fouts's quarters at midnight—using her own key!

Then came the squeaky floorboard that meant he was about to turn around. That side of the room went back to work. The cadets on the far side of the room began talking about the new Army outfit, a super-tough unit mentioned in the *National Military School Enquisitor*. A unit called the Pink Barrettes.

120

THIRTEEN

'All right you guys, let's try it again. Brassières line up at the south end of the field, skins at the north, ON THE DOUBLE! Here comes Rocky, so make it look good!'

General Rockstone strode briskly by, a *coup* stick jammed in his oxter. 'Sergeant, I didn't hear very much goddamned noise in that last charge.'

'No sir. We'll do better this time, sir. READY, MEN!'

'Just a minute, Sergeant. At ease, men. Who's that man with the haircut?'

The sergeant whirled. 'Manning! Attention! One step to the rear—HRARRGH!' Since the men were all standing with their backs to the general, the rearward step brought Manning closer. Rocky looked him over.

'Soldier, who told you to get a haircut?'

'No one, sir.'

'*Then why in hell did you do it?*'

'Sir, the regulations say . . .'

'Not *our* regulations, by God! I want every man in this outfit to grow shoulder length hair, or by God, I want to know why! Sergeant, give the men an extra hour of backwards drill this afternoon, and put *this* man on punishment detail until he looks fit to be a Pink Barrette.'

'Yes sir!'

'And, Sergeant . . . more noise!'

'Yes sir! All right, you bastards! You heard the general.

121

Next time you come across that field I want you to *squeal* and *giggle*! So if I can't hear you, you'll do it ten more times before we take five. Is that clear?'

'Yes sir!' shrilled the company in unpracticed falsetto.

A moment later, those wearing brassières charged down the field to engage those without. The 'skins' were fixing rubber bayonets or firing blanks.

'Take some evasive frigging action!' the sergeant bellowed. The 'brassières' began to pirouette and skip. All the way they squealed and giggled lustily, until they reached the enemy lines.

The 'skins' line broke, and they became a few clusters of panicky individuals, firing wildly, thrusting half-heartedly, but cursing with real style and fervor. The light, curved *coup* sticks of the attackers never stopped moving, flicking here and there with uncanny accuracy. Within a few minutes, they had tagged everyone.

'All right, Sergeant,' said Rocky. 'Keep it up. I've got a conference at the Pentagon this afternoon. Be back tomorrow.'

*

The battle of Dresden was getting off to a slow start. There seemed some question as to whether Napoleon would really engage the defending forces at all . . .

'General Rockstone's here, sir.'

'Mm?' Weimarauner returned with difficulty to the full-scale world. It was hard at times to realise that Napoleon's whole army would fit into the summer house, along with Blücher's forces; that a single musket of either side would make a toothpick . . . 'Send him out.'

Weimarauner stood in his modified back yard and watched his Pink Barrette general emerge from the house. Rockstone wore a green fatigue uniform sprouting lace at collar and cuffs. His long gray hair was pulled back over one ear by a plastic pink barrette. The little stick he carried was, because of his rank, tipped with one gold star.

As he reached the edge of the flagstone patio, Rocky was instructed by an orderly to remove his shoes.

'That's right,' Weimarauner called. 'Most of the yard is built up with plastic, and the surface is pretty delicate.'

122

Rocky slipped off the regulation shoes, to which pink pom-poms had been attached, and padded carefully across the brittle lawn.

'How are things in Florida?'

'Good, sir. The men are in the pink—in peak condition, General, rarin' to go. I hoped you'd be giving us embarkation orders.'

Weimarauner picked up a French lancer and examined its painted uniform with a pocket magnifier. 'No rush, Rocky, no rush. Right now we're in the process of changing our logistics system—Blunden here can tell you all about it—and we're trying to cut back on troop movements until we have everything straightened around.'

Rocky looked closer at the battle of Dresden landscape. 'Toy sojurs? That's a big set-up you've got there, General.'

'Indeed, forty acres and still growing. I was lucky enough to get these lead lancers from an old warehouse in Minneapolis —had to make a special trip to make the deal—they cost a fortune, but they're worth it. Look at that detail!'

'Nice hobby.'

Weimarauner frowned. 'It's far more than that, Rockstone. Do you think I'd waste taxpayers' money on a *hobby*?

'No, you see, my concentration on a single battle seems to stir the deepest reaches of my intellect. While I work out every contingency of the battle of Dresden, on a *conscious* level, my unconscious is free to experiment with daring new ideas.' He surveyed the green velvet landscape, the rows of tiny white tents. 'It was while I was on that trip to Minneapolis that the whole conception of the Pink Barrettes came to me entire. To name but one example. And while I was debating a detail of this battle—supposing Blücher had engaged Napoleon *before* he got to Dresden—I suddenly came upon this new logistics system, *Modulog*.'

'All from a toy! Wow!'

Weimarauner looked at him coldly. 'Why don't you toddle off with Captain Blunden here, and let him tell you all about *Modulog*? He can explain it as well as I.'

This was perfectly true, for Captain Blunden, who now led Rocky inside to the study and poured out two sherries, was the originator of *Modulog*, just as Hackendorf had originated

123

the Pink Barrettes. Weimarauner's genius lay in surrounding himself with capable official and semi-official aides. They ghosted his books, drafted his recommendations to the Secretary of Defense, and now and then managed to draw his attention from Dresden long enough to hand him a new idea to 'come upon'.

Weimarauner meanwhile withdrew further and further from real military activities. He no longer kept an office at the Pentagon, but communicated from his country home by special telephone. He no longer concerned himself with the present war—at times he could not remember the name of the enemy nation—but slipped deeper and deeper into the complexities of Napoleon *vs*. Blücher. What if Blücher attacked first? What if Napoleon had not left off his attack on Dresden in the middle? How much of the river could he have held, and for how long?

*

'*Modulog*,' said the captain, 'is all new. It's based on three new principles, sir.'

'Just between you and me, let's drop the *sir*, Blunden. I hope we're all friends here.' He winked a false eyelash and toasted the captain with his sherry.

'Yes—General. The principles are: First, that there is no reason to handle and transport troops and materiel in different ways. Second, thanks to container freight systems already in operation, troops may be boxed and shipped in a modular way just as any other materiel. In other words, a box of men is no harder to handle and dispatch than a box of supplies. Containers may be fitted out with life-support facilities, namely airholes, food and chemical toilets.

'Third, the fastest way of processing materiel is by using computer routing. The most expedient route can be found by feeding in all the available transport data, all the data on requirements and priorities, and then letting Nature—the computer, rather—take its course.

'Imagine that we have three cities. City A makes guns, City B is a troop assembly point, City C is a target, or delivery area. C needs a certain number of armed personnel at time t_1. At time t_0 we have at A all our weapons and half enough transport to deliver them, and at B all our troops and one-quarter of the

124

necessary transport. The transport at B is twice as fast as that at A, and the relative distances of the three cities are . . .'

Rocky went into a daydream while the earnest young captain rattled on. How could life be so complicated now? When, only yesterday, life was an island idyll. *人间の 糸くキ*

he thought. *人间の 糸くキ*

'The important thing is, all the services will be switched over,' Blunden was saying. 'Even where container freight isn't feasible, orders will be processed by our central computer, using the latest in digital equipment, the Müller-Fokker tapes.'

Rocky struck him lightly on the arm with his wand. 'Bad words,' he said. 'Bad words, you naughty captain.'

*

At Billy Koch Crusade Headquarters, another mail bag was dumped on the sorting table, and sorters went to work with their thumb knives. Marilyn Temblor picked up her purse and went to the ladies' restroom. No one saw her take the phial from her purse but God.

'I don't care,' she said defiantly to the roller towel. 'I'll—I'll quit this job. I'll become a *stewardess*!'

She opened the phial and dabbed some on her wrist. Almost at once the overpowering sexy odor filled the room. She panicked, scrubbed furiously until her wrist was almost bleeding—but the odor clung, accusing her.

Back in the mail room she picked up the first letter.

Dear Billy,

My problem is, I'm in love with a man who hardly notices me. I'm his secretary, and I know this sounds like just a girlish infatuation, but I am not a girl at all. I am over eighty years of age and so is he. We have been good friends for many years, and though my affection for him has ripened into love, he still thinks of me as just a loyal companion.

We are both single, and I would like to marry him, but I hate to wait for him to 'pop' the question. What can I do to make him notice me as a woman, without seeming to throw myself at him? Should I confess I love him? Ask him to marry me? Or just wait and see?

Please answer, Billy. My time is running out.

Yours in confusion, Amy Q. Birdsall

125

That would be 674; Marilyn knew without even consulting the chart. 674 was 'Girl wants to propose to man.'

The next letter was a little tougher. She stopped chewing gum and read the letter three times before she could focus her mind on it.

Dear Billy Koch:
1. Cadet Sturgemoore Shairp wants to kill himself.
2. He is at military school.
3. The bible says it is wrong to take life, but he is being trained to take life.
4. Sometimes it is all right to kill someone.
5. Sometimes it must be all right to kill yourself.
6. Colonel Fouts said that anyone who plays with himself will be expelled.
7. Then Cadet Sturgemoore Shairp played with himself a lot, because he wanted to go home.
8. It didn't work.
9. Mother does not answer Cadet Sturgemoore Shairp's letters. She is on television.
10. Father is dead.
11. Mother is just like she was dead.
12. Cadet Sturgemoore Shairp should die, too.
13. Cadet Sturgemoore Shairp went to ask Colonel Fouts if it would be all right to kill himself.
14. Colonel Fouts took a long time answering the door.
15. What do you want, he said.
16. There was chocolate all over his face.
17. Cadet Sturgemoore Shairp did not know what to say, so he looked down.
18. There was a pink strap garter strap thing hanging out of the Colonel's fly.
19. Cadet Sturgemoore Shairp said did the Colonel believe in God, that God wanted everyone to live.
20. A hundred and twenty punishment tours, the Colonel said, impertinence to an officer.
21. Billy, sir, Cadet Sturgemoore Shairp requests permission to kill himself.

Please advice,
Cadet Sturgemoore Shairp

It must be 'wants to commit suicide', number 647. And the other one was 674. Bothered only slightly by that 'pink strap garter strap thing', Marilyn rolled a sheet of paper in the first

126

automated typewriter and headed it 'Dear Miss Birdsall'. Then someone seized her hand and held it to his nose.

Jim, the handsome bible student. 'My, you smell nice,' he said. 'Perfume?'

She nodded and punched the machine with her free hand. 647. 'What's it called?'

She freed her hand. Blushing, she set the second machine for 674. 'I—don't remember.'

'Sure you do,' he said. The typewriters started chattering. She would lose her job. Shut out of the Crusade, Billy's Crusade, forever. Would it be the same, being a stewardess? An 'air angel'?

'Sure you remember,' he insisted, moving closer. 'What was that name?'

She could hardly say it.

'My Sin.'

*

'Doctor, do you have to come and see me in that—that drag?'

Glen seized a coke and wrang its neck. Feinwelt tossed a golden sausage curl and settled himself on the couch.

'Listen, Glen. We've been over this a few times, haven't we? I have other patients, other things to attend to. I know you'd like me to be Big Daddy Doctor for Glensie alone, but let's try to look at this unselfishly. You know I haven't time to change clothes six times a day or whatever. If *you* can't make the necessary adjustment, well . . .'

'But everybody's going to think I'm—and it isn't just that. I don't think you wear that drum majorette outfit just to hold hands with a few sick faggots. Oh no. I've been reading a few things in connection with an article I'm doing for *Stagman*. I've learned a few things.'

'Really?' The drum majorette lit a fragrant cigarette and leaned back. 'Like what?'

Glen was silent for a moment, gazing up at *Bertha Venus*. 'It's like . . . Cybele. The bitch goddess, demanding that her priests castrate themselves and put on women's clothes.' He put on a World War Two aviator's helmet.

'Not sure I follow you.'

127

'And then in the Middle Ages! They thought witches were able to make men impotent. By the same token, they built big phallic cathedrals to the Virgin. The Virgin Mother!' He tried on a Sioux war bonnet. 'Yes, and *their* priests had to wear skirts, too. St Francis tried to go against that tradition . . . but a hundred years later or so there were the Franciscans putting on skirts.'

'Don't you think you're harping on this unnecessarily?' Feinwelt's case-hardened voice had taken an edge. 'Just what is this "article" about, anyway?'

'And it all comes down to Bette Cooke. The latest incarnation of the Mighty Bitch Mother Angry Virgin Goddess, see? Her oracles are recipe books. Her priests are advertising men. Her charm is the silverware coupon on the flour bag, and her Mysteries are the secrets of cooking—no, not just cooking, but cooking that will "keep the menfolk coming back for seconds". *Menfolk!* Not men. Men reduced, crushed down to sexless *elves*!'

'If you really feel that way . . .'

'What time is it?'

Feinwelt looked at his watch. 'Oh now, we have plenty of time left in our session, if that's what's worrying you.'

'She's on. The commercial's on!'

Glen rushed to the electronic wall and switched on the glowing features of Bette Cooke. He did not notice when Feinwelt left.

*

Billikins had finished the wall. He wanted to call Nurse to see it, but she'd only laugh nasty. He had to admire and love it all by himself.

The wall was a crayon and pencil drawing covering one long wall of his room, twelve feet long and eight high. It was a combination (though not to Billikins) of public-toilet art, church-window portraiture, bible map and political cartoon. There were a hundred and forty-four thousand faces in it, each wearing a label on its forehead or hat, each expressing glee or torment.

At the top, a seven-foot phallus aimed to enter a standard men's-room snatch (or winged buttonhole). The prick had been wrapped end to end in a bandage reading: 'There shall

128

be a cause of GOD, which is the twelve and the seven, freely. It without is the twelve, and the seven within are five loaves and two fishes, and this East shall enfold it.'

Below this was a layer of cloud, the 'Cloud of Could', studded with hands, feet and eyes. The cloud terminated in two fists, one at each end. The right hand held a burning diploma, the left a sign: 'The Flying Roll is the last great whirlwind and the great church IN the west! WHO used to send forth all to gather together all manner cloud and fire, loud and ire, peacefully enfolding the First Life. I am accounted for and counted, I am continued and the fire in the DOUBLE lamp enfolds it ! ! !'

Across the cloud large yellow-rayed letters spelled:

IS GOD TO RAPTURE A POWERLESS CHURCH!

On the land below were the twelve tribes, identified as being divided into six nations, four races, three classes and two sides. On the left were the SLACKERS, LACKERS, LACQUEYS, BACKERS, WRACKERS and PACKERS; on the right were DIGGERS, WIGGERS, CHIGGERS, NIGGERS, TRIGGERS and JURY-RIGGERS. Each tribe of twelve thousand was further subdivided all 48 ways imaginable.

The remaining space was filled with flames, banners, signs, swords, sheep, the winding road of Venue leading up to Mount Golden Mystery, clocks and $-bags, eyes baleful and eyes protective, gallows, elks, the Stairs of Relief and the Five Truths in their white robes; whips, a cage of thorns, snakes whose spots were roses, the blazing headlights and grill of a Saette, pennants, the Keys of Penance, special notices too small to read, and scallop shells. The diggers were digging for sparkling letters buried in the earth:

WHOSOEVER SLAYS THE FIRST LIFE SHALL LIVE FOREVER, BUT THE COLOR OF AMBER SLAYS AND IT IS SLAIN. DARKNESS IS THE FREELY PORTION OF HIM WHO FINDS OUT THE ACCOUNT!

He signed it in the corner: 'Words of Jehovah.' Then he closed the bedroom door and began nailing it shut. Nurse called out from the kitchen, ordering him to cut out that racket.

*

129

Nurse Harriet Saga scootched down in the chair, easing wind and her varicose legs. She was just too pooped to yell at him again. Instead she selected another piece of fudge and turned to the horoscope page:

You will be relieved of a burden which has bothered you for some weeks. Domestic difficulties may come to a head this morning, spoiling your day, unless

The first hammer blow struck her in the neck. The other fifty-eight landed among the tight red curls of her hair, deep at the darker roots.

*

There was no place to hide, and he was sore afraid: which amongst them might not recognize him? But the POWER came upon him, guiding his eyes to the newspaper on the kitchen table. He mooved a tooth-marked piece of fudge, leaving a bloody smear, and read the headline: '**BIBLELAND TO OPEN TODAY.** Bob's Water, Calif. (UP) . . .'

He found Nurse's purse in the foyer. In it there lay a big wad of earthly money and a pair of dark glasses. His eyes caught his eyes in the foyer mirror as he put them on. Those precious stones in the rims of the glasses—none too good for Him who Billikins was about to meet.

He told the cab driver he wanted Bibleland.

'Is it far?'

'Furder than I go, buddy. Ya hafta fly. Whatcha want, the airport?'

'What do I . . . ?'

'Ya wanta fly or what?'

'Yes. Yes . . . I want to fly.'

The cab picked up speed. It passed a giant picture of the Woman in Blue and White. 'LET ME SHOW YOU,' she said, 'HOW TO CATCH *YOUR* GINGERBREAD BOY.'

130

FOURTEEN

Dear Miss Birdsall:

If you knew a man who rented a fine home, fully equipped with air conditioning, wall-to-wall carpets and pastel fixtures, and one day this man just up and BURNED DOWN this lovely home, you'd certainly wonder why! Did he hate the landlord? Did he have some other place to live? If not, why on God's earth did he do it?

If this man said he was just 'tired of living here' you'd call him a *fool*.

Yet you have been thinking of taking the beautiful home God rents to you FREE OF CHARGE—your body—and WRECKING IT! Isn't that a thousand times more foolish?

What you're thinking of doing is a sin. It is wanton, pointless destruction. Not only is it SIN, but it is THE ONE SIN THAT CAN NEVER BE FORGIVEN OR UNDONE! It means the ETERNAL LOSS of your earthly home—the beautiful home God gave you.

You are troubled. The stresses of modern life, the daily 'rat race' and perhaps personal sorrows weigh heavily upon you. But it isn't SIN you want. What you really want is a *change*. A reason to GO ON LIVING.

WHY NOT COME OVER TO CHRIST?

'I am the Resurrection and the Life.'

'The wages of sin is death.'

Switch to Jesus Christ and see! Read your Bible. Pray, asking Jesus to forgive you for even thinking of this Sin. He will make your burden lighter, give you new power to zip through the old daily routine without a thought of despair. Millions have testified to this—it is a *fact*!

So don't burn the house down—light up your heart and invite Christ in.

God bless you,
Billy Koch

131

She crumpled the letter, then began ironing it flat again with her ringless left hand. What could Billy mean by that? 'Sin that can never . . .'

She read it again. There was no mistake. It wasn't a form letter. Could there be two Miss Birdsalls? No matter how she looked at it, Billy just wasn't making sense.

Amy removed her glasses and began polishing them, a nerve-calming ritual of many years' standing. As she held them up to the light, she noticed the rims. Dark plastic across the top, steel below—they looked so *medical*. Like a face brace. How many times had she meant to change them for something sexier, say rhinestones or glowing plastic? Yet always she wound up with the same old thing: the dull, the cheap, the reasonable.

Weren't all these years of chastity enough? It didn't seem fair. What she had preserved so carefully all these years had diminished in value to everyone, even to her, until now it was like a ticket to a dance of long ago . . . yet Billy now asked her to go on with it, to save that faded ticket . . . Why? Why did he hate her so?

A fragment of memory from the always dim near past attached itself to the question. There was a street corner she'd just come out of. There was a service at the ballpark. The car. She'd come out of the ballpark looking for a taxi, walking, and the car.

The car turned the corner. She'd jumped back to avoid being killed. It was . . . Billy's car? Yes, she could see him at the wheel, those cold blue eyes . . . and he *cursed* her, his curse mingling with the blare of that musical horn:

Rock up yours
Ages   old
cleft
me   bag

That satanic hate. Why?

*

Grover came out of the inner office and found Amy moving her nose down a column of names in the telephone book.

'Here it is,' she said. 'Here it is: 46 Phenolphthalein Drive.'

132

'Where are your glasses, Amy?'

Her naked face blushed. 'I—broke them.'

'Golly, you'd better get some new ones. Your eyes look terrible. All red and . . .'

'I have that address you wanted.' She waved the phone book. 'The Societé Anonyme des Transtévérins.'

'Uh huh. Good. I'm perty sure *that* outfit is the *key* to all the others. It may be a chance to use our heads and really stamp out Cumminism all over the country! Tell you what. We'll drive up there and keep an eye on them for awhile.'

It was a short way to Phenolphthalein Drive. As they drove, Grover explained their objective.

'I probably shouldn't bring you along on this dangerous a mission, Amy. These are the Big Boys, and they play rough. By the way, in case anything should happen to me, I'll give you the commonation to the safe. You know What We Have in the Safe.'

'You mean the b . . .'

'Right. You set it just like an alarm clock, and put it on all our records. It wouldn't be much use my dying, if it meant they learned all about us.'

The Societé Anonyme des Transtévérins was, in fact, a Communist front organization masquerading as a Franco–Italian banking firm. But its operations were in another part of town. It had no connection whatever with the quiet brick building Amy and Grover now parked across from and began observing through binoculars (from under the shade of a willow): the headquarters of Transvestites Anonymous.

'I can't see anything,' said Amy, 'through my half the binoculars. Are they adjusted?'

'Yes, they're fine. It's you and no glasses, Amy. You oughta get them fixed. How'd they come to get broke, anyways?'

'I'm cold. Can't we move the car into the sun?'

'And have them spot us? Amy, this is a dangerous outfit! Their last name, "Transtévérins", is an anagram of "invents arrest"! And that isn't all!'

He explained that the director's name was Julien Pé, whose last name, as Grover understood, meant *pi*, the probable secret symbol for the group. 'Pi,' he said, 'is a *circular* relation, see? Wheels within wheels.'

133

Amy was about to congratulate him on his discovery when Grover gasped. A vehicle was entering the deserted road.

'Police car,' he said. 'Or their "police". We'd better try and look natural.'

He took off his glasses. The myopia of their eye-beams blended. Then, for the first time in their many years of friendship, Grover drew her over and kissed her.

*

Dear Cadet Sturgemoore Shairp:

Many a young person has had the same feelings you have now, and there is nothing sinful about them. If they are used and directed in the ways of the Lord, such feelings lead to the continuation of the human race and the multiplication of God's flock on earth.

The step you are about to take is a grave one, and you must make sure you are right. I cannot advise you on this, but God can and will. Pray. Read your Bible. Let the Lord guide you.

'It is not good for man to be alone,' the Bible says. And in the words of the English poet John Donne, a preacher like me, 'No man is an island'. If you decide yourself to be NO LONGER ALONE, be resolute. Stick by your decision, NO MATTER WHAT. As Davy Crockett put it, 'Be sure you're right, then go ahead.'

God bless you,
Billy Koch

Spot read the first paragraph three times. 'The continuation of the human race'? He guessed that might mean killing yourself to make room for more—lightening the airplane of humanity by baling out.

The idea of suicide came often to him now, in the St Praetexta school library, under the great picture of Galahad. In the evening. 'My strength is as the strength of ten . . .' It scared him, what Billy said in the last part: Stick by it, no matter what. That meant not making his decision final until he was *sure* . . .

If only there were someone to talk him out of it. 'A preacher like me . . .'

Spot made his way to the front of the room and asked the librarian for anything by John Donny.

'Who?' The old ex-marine looked suspicious.

134

'John Donny, the English poet . . .'

'*Don Juan,* you mean. Oh no you don't. Heard about that one, did ya? Dirty sex pome by "Lord" Byron. I guess you figured I wouldn't know the difference, eh? You won't get any meat-beating poetry past me, by Heaven!'

Spot showed him the letter and the name in it.

'Donne? Preacher? No, I don't think we have any—wait, I'll have a look.'

While Spot waited, a classmate came out of the reserve room. 'Man, have I been reading the real shit!' he said. 'They got it on reserve here, this book all about the nigger conspiracy. *One Man's Fight.* The guy that wrote it is in prison, but my military political science prof says not for long.'

'Verne, do you . . .'

'Do I what?'

'Do you think suicide is wrong?'

'Wes Davis says—he wrote this book—he says it all depends. For the inferior races, he says it's the only honorable solution. Or for any *weak* person. But we're strong!'

'Yeah, I . . . thanks.'

The librarian came from the stacks with a thin volume.

'I guess this is all right,' he said, slapping it on the counter. 'Looks to be about God and Samson and them. Take keer of it now—I don't want to see any pecker tracks when you bring it back.'

'Thank you, sir.' Spot took the book to his room. It was *Biathanatos,* John Donne's long justification for suicide.

*

The Billy android stood tall, even with his head bowed, a captain, at least, in the army of the Lord. The hymn finished and he raised his hands to heaven, or towards the roof of the auditorium.

'Lord, I'm asking you to do something for some of our sick brethern. I'm asking you to heal them in mind and body and spirit, like you healed the sick in Jerusalem.'

The blind and halt had paid their fees and shuffled into line. Now the line moved forward under the direction of Crusade cops, as Billy spoke in soothing cadences, repeating again and again his instructions to the evidently slow-witted Deity:

135

'Let the pahwr flow down, O Lord! Jesus, let the pahwr flow down! Through my right hand, Lord! Lord Jesus, let the pahwr down through my right . . .'

When he'd worked on the right hand enough he got the left going. The first candidates stumbled up the steps and stood blinking uncertainly in the glaring light.

*

Jerry sat with his real foot up on the console. He peeled a peanut, tossed it in the air and snapped it up. He put the shell back in the bag, then rummaged under shells for a whole one.

The door opened and a Crusade cop named Morgan put his head in. 'Jerry, I got a guy out here says he wants to talk to somebody.'

'What about?'

'He says he's pretty rich, and he looks like it. An old guy.'

'Special contributions upstairs.'

'No, he says he wants to *buy* something. Some kind of tape, he says.'

Jerry missed a peanut. 'What *did* he say, exactly?'

'He said—you ain't religious, are ya?'

Jerry grinned. The cop leaned closer and whispered what he thought the name of the tape was.

'Morgan, we've got a problem. A real problem. This guy seems to know a little too much about our operation here.'

The cop, who himself knew nothing of the operation, scratched his head. 'That's bad. You think a tax boy, maybe?'

'Blackmailer is my guess. Oh, of course we're not doing anything illegal here, but a clever blackmailer could make it look bad for us. Where is he now?'

'I left him down by gate five, right by the passage. He's a little old man with a gold-top cane. You want me to take over for you a few minutes?'

'Yeah, okay. Now here's what you do . . .' He pointed out the monitors to the cop and told him to watch carefully. If anything went wrong, if Billy started speaking oddly or fell down or anything, he was to push a certain button. It would either light a green panel light or a red warning. The red blinking light was mounted inside a large button marked SCRUB. When it was alight, pushing it brought the whole show

136

to a close. He did not explain the meaning of any of this, or how a program could be 'scrubbed': Direct connections to the android would make it clutch its chest and crumple, whereupon a 'doctor' would rush to 'Billy's' aid and the spotlight be taken away from him.

'You mean all this stuff is just in case Billy falls down or gets laryngitis?'

'Something like that. This is a million-dollar operation, Morgie—we don't take chances. Speaking of which, how about loaning me your gun? I don't want any trouble with this guy, but . . .'

'Aw, Christ, Jerry, he's an old man!'

'But maybe he's not alone. Anyway, just in case.'

*

It was sundown in Las Vegas. The biggest fairy Officer Kulak had ever seen stood in front of a television store, pretending to look at the Billy Koch service. He was more or less respectably dressed, but Kulak knew what he was by the rhinestone-rimmed sunglasses. The trouble was, he wasn't doing anything. The laws being what they were, Kulak could do no more than kick him a few times and make him move along.

A party of interested tourists stopped to watch. 'Las Vegas ain't what it used to be,' said one. 'In the old days, they'd haul in a fruit like that, get him to blow everybody in the station, and then pound the piss out of him.'

'That's what they oughta do,' said another. 'But I guess the criminal element is just taking over.'

The big man in the odd glasses moved off towards the bus station.

*

'O God! O God! I'm—well!'

'Take off that brace, brother. *Show the people the pahwr of the Lord Jesus!*'

The man fumbled off his heavy appliance, a neck brace, and threw it to the back of the stage, where a stagehand could retrieve it and return it to the prop room. 'My God! I'm ALL RIGHT!'

The next unfortunate was real, an asthmatic child. Billy's

137

hands gripped her head. 'LordOLordhealthischildthispoor-afflictedchildletthepahwrcomedownrightdownherethroughmy-hands RIGHT DOWN THROUGH MY HANDS AND—HEAL this child!'

The girl gave a little scream and ran to her mother, a woman in a dress of National Arsenamid feed sacking. 'Mommy, Mommy, my chest don't hurt no more!'

Billy, smiling and sweating, swung the child up and stood her on a chair. 'Let *everyone* see you, honey! Let EVERYONE see the PAHWR of the LORD!'

More people joined the end of the line as Billy next healed a man with a paralysed hand and a girl with a blemish (the blemish didn't actually go away, but it 'felt funny'). Next came a teen-ager on crutches, dragging both legs.

*

The door opened. It wasn't Jerry, it was the old man.

'Hi again! Thought you'd forgotten about me, so I came around to have a look at the tape for myself.'

'OUT!' The cop slapped his empty holster. 'This is a restricted area! Didn't you see the sign?' (On one of the monitors, Billy seemed to shudder slightly. The SCRUB button light pulsated like a painful tooth.)

'I just wanted to speak to the engineer in charge here . . .'

'He went to gate five, to see you!' The Crusade cop began gently shoving the old man toward the door.

'Ah well, I must have missed him. Perhaps our paths crossed.' MacCormick Hines smiled, thinking of the three shots the engineer had wasted. They were certainly out to protect their investment here, no two ways about it. Or the secret of Billy's success.

'Wait outside, you! When Jerry gets back, you can . . .'

'Yes, perhaps you're right.' Except that Jerry wouldn't be coming back for awhile. Two bright young men had seen to that. 'Yes, I'll just—Good God! Look!' He pointed his cane at one of the monitors.

The cop stopped shoving. 'Jesus! What the hell is going on?' He stabbed every button on the console, but nothing happened. 'O Jesus, I'd better go find Jerry!'

*

Billy went into his usual auction chant that rose and fell and ended in a scream of 'HEAL!' At the climax his steel fingers closed tightly about the boy's skull. The kid screamed and dropped his crutches. Nobody seemed to notice that he wasn't standing alone; he was suspended by those crushing hands.

Billy dropped him and advanced on a woman with a cleft palate, so hypnotised that she was already trying to say she was cured. Back of him, the Crusade cops were crowding on the stage, valiantly trying to screen the boy's corpse from the audience.

Mumble, mumble, pahwr of the Lord and . . .

'HEAL!'

The palsied old woman who was next in line tried to back away, but those behind her were stubbornly shoving forward, and Billy stalked her, opening and closing hands that were covered with stickiness. . . .

'HEAL!'

In quick succession he HEALED a mongoloid child, a wheel-chair paralytic, a laborer with a slipped disc and a mother with a migraine. Some of the others managed to throw themselves out of reach, fall, scramble or jump off the stage.

Not everyone in the hall panicked at once. While the people in front were screaming and trying to rush the exits, those in back were still climbing up on seats to see the miracles. Even when everyone did get turned around and headed outward, they found the exits barred and guarded by Crusade cops. If, in the tumult, anyone could have heard them, they would have explained: the collection hadn't been taken up yet.

Trailing a coaxial cable that unreeled from under the stage, Billy descended to the audience. Some of the screams now became coherent.

'The guy's nuts! He's *nuts*!'

'Stop him!'

'Somebody stop him!'

Several men seized an usher and started kicking him. People piled up against the exits were beginning to suffocate.

'Stop him!'

Someone threw a punch that hit him solidly; it only turned Billy in a new direction.

'HEAL!'

139

A doctor rushed Billy and broke a hypodermic on his arm. The android plowed on, HEALing. His smile was ecstatic.

'O Christ, somebody . . .'

'HEAL! HEAL!'

A thread of oil smoke rose from the back of Billy's collar. It thickened to a fluttering ribbon. As Billy reached to HEAL another victim, his collar blossomed into greenish flames.

'Satan has come amongst us!'

Billy slowed, faltered, stopped. Flames licked up his cheeks as he raised both arms in benediction and began:

> Nearer my God to Thee
> Nearer my God to Thee

His thermostatically-controlled-fire-emergency-panic-prevention-system was working perfectly.

The organist took her bitten fingers from her mouth and began a tentative accompaniment. A quavering voice in the balcony took up the refrain, and then the entire audience found itself forcing out the reassuring melody. A few at a time, they fell to their knees.

Billy's torso was shirted in flames of many colors. Lumps of plastic flesh rolled down to his ankles. Miraculously his strong, manly baritone came loud as ever from the midst of the bonfire.

It did not cease until the song was finished, and the final circuit switched off by fire. There remained then the steel skeleton, blackened machinery and tangles of wire, all fused to a pedestal puddle of pink plastic and smoldering tan oxfords. And in their sockets the pale blue eyes still looked toward heaven.

*

Bibleland neared the end of its third day of business. There were rumors of trouble in Minneapolis, and a garbled TV newscast about a fire which had 'possibly injured' the great healing evangelist. (The service itself had been cut off in the middle, due to 'network transmission difficulties'). Attendance here did not, in any case, slacken.

The ten-acre park was divided into four 'lands': Old Testament Land, New Testament Land, Heaven Land and Hades

140

Land. Among the crowd of child pilgrims and pilgrim families, a lone man attracted the attention of Crusade cops.

They were on the alert for pickpockets and perverts, and this man was especially perverted-looking, in his wrinkled gray business suit, tennis shoes and ladies' rhinestone-rimmed sunglasses. Two plainclothesmen were detailed to keep an eye on him.

He began with the Garden of Eden boat ride. Here a train of boats moved through the still waters of a winding lagoon, passing in sequence all of the mechanical tableaux of the bible story. Adam was shown alone, then shaking hands with his new partner and bride, then the two shared a meal of grapes. Adam and Eve inevitably fell, but their discovery of nakedness was omitted, for our original parents wore modest fig-leaf bikinis from the start.

The stranger seemed oddly unmoved by it all. He did not look up even when an angel drove them from the Garden with a neon sword, or when Adam fought a Tyrannosaur with his stone ax. Instead, he gazed steadily at the waters of the artificial lagoon, and at the innumerable floating islands of ice-cream wrappers, ice-cream sticks, pop bottles and souvenir programs.

The suspect rode the Promised Land roller coaster, catching, from one of its summits, a Pisgah view of Heaven Land. He visited the small zoo called Noah's Ark on time to see the lions get their dinner. It looked suspiciously like lamb. He took a trip on that children's favorite, the Fiery Chariot (transfigured by flashing lights and fluorescent paint from an old Octopus), and tried his luck at knocking Goliath into a bucket of water with a basketball. He won a prize here and elsewhere: for knocking down pyramids of Philistines with a 'jawbone' boomerang, a plaster ten commandments bookend; for setting fire to Sodom and Gomorrah with an electric-eye rifle, a winged kewpie; for pounding a weight to the top of Jacob's Ladder, a plastic telescope showing a view of Solomon's temple.

Methuselah, despite the suspect's newly sprouting short gray hair, guessed his age accurately, but anyway awarded him a keychain containing a drop of the Red Sea in plastic. You could tell it was real becaus   was bright red. The man ate a double-

141

dip cone of Manna Whip, a 100% Certified Beef Quailburger and two Pillar-of-Fire Candy Flosses. Declining to let 'Joseph' read his fortune in the Ark of the Covenant (not all pitches were strictly chronistic) he headed for New Testament Land.

*

It began with a large Crêche at the entrance, with life-size moving figures. Mary smiled, Joseph turned to look, the shepherds genuflected, and so on. The ox moaned at regular intervals.

'A real wise guy,' said the attendant later to the two cops. 'He ast me if the cow was having a baby.'

In the Pavilion of Miracles, a magician in wig and beard walked on water, turned water into wine-colored liquid, and after disappearing from a locked casket, reappeared in the audience with a collection plate. The suspect gave generously.

Passing down the New Testament midway, he was invited to look at Herod's Holy Innocents (formerly a 'Story of Life' exhibit of pickled foeti), to throw the first baseball at an adultress, and to visit Pilate's Chamber of Atrocities.

Among the thousands of devotional items for sale were rubber crowns of thorns (some with cardboard sun visors), Veronica dishtowels, mustard seeds, 'Paul in prison' interlocking puzzles, marionettes, souvenir scourges. He bought everything he saw, and gorged himself on sugar skulls, hotcross buns, pretzels, chocolate nails and apostle haloes, though he'd scarcely had time to digest his first Eden apple.

Apostle haloes were donuts sold in individual bags, each stamped with the name of an apostle.

'Get 'em all,' said the vendor. 'Get 'em all and get a prize. Get all twelve, you get a prize.' More than one poor visitor had stuffed himself to vomiting, eating as many as twenty without having been warned there were two Jameses.

The suspect rode the St John Desertmobile, the Galilee speedboat, and allowed himself to be glued to the wall (by centrifugal force) of the chalice for a few moments. In the Garden of Gethsemane Chug-A-Lug contest he drained the cup and was awarded Peter's victim's rubber ear. Then on to Crucifixion.

He escalated to the top of Calvary, passing on the way a

142

figure in a white robe. Drawn slowly upward by a buried cable, it made mechanical toiling gestures under its huge cross. At the top there were more diversions: dicing for Crusade T-shirts; a photography studio where figures with heads cut out portrayed all fourteen stations of the cross, enabling one to take any part in any scene; and the main event, shortened from the original three hours to twenty minutes, and played out in a big tent by mechanical figures.

'Show's about to start, brothers and sisters, any minute. On the inside, *the one show you cannot miss*. Show's about to start any minute. See it all, acted by living audioanimatrons.'

The barker paused to ask the suspect for his ticket. 'Two bucks, bub.'

The man gestured over his shoulder with a thumb. 'He paid,' he said, and shoved on through the wicket. The barker looked for the payer and saw no one, only the figure in white. Having toted its cross to the top, it was being backed down again.

*

The two Crusade cops looked at each other. 'He slipped in? Well I guess we got enough on him, then. Where is he now?'

'It's real funny. I seen him go in,' said the barker. 'But I didn't see him come out.'

'Okay, then. We might as well check out Heaven and Hades.'

*

Hades Land was run by the management of 'Harry's Hollywood Happening'. It masqueraded as a respectable restaurant with demonized waiters, red lighting and many flambée specialités. But once a customer had entered—and abandoned hope by means of signing a waiver—it became a painfully elaborate fun house.

A polite demon led the suspect to his table and held his chair for him. The chair had no back legs. Another demon waiter rushed out with a plate of rubber food.

The stranger seemed to take it all good-naturedly. No one laughed harder than he when his table proved to be topless, and he saw his dinner sink out of sight in the folds of the tablecloth. Nor when a pair of waiters whipped off the red cloth,

143

tucked it around his neck and began giving him a haircut. Nor when they snipped off his tie and one sleeve of his suit.

Baffled and angry, they gave up on him and concentrated on more likely targets. A woman's dress blew up, a table collapsed. There were screams as a waiter uncovered a dish of live squid; elsewhere diners made the mistake of ordering the special chili. Still laughing, the stranger headed for the door.

'Just a minute, sir,' said the headwaiter. 'Haven't you forgotten something?' He held out the check.

The stranger laughed again. 'That'll be fourteen dollars, sir,' the headwaiter insisted, and his seriousness seemed to delight the man in dark glasses even more. He held out his empty billfold, laughing. Laughing harder, be began the laborious process of transferring prizes and souvenirs from one hand to the other. Still laughing, he then seized the check and impaled it on one of the headwaiter's horns.

They tried to kick him, but he ran too fast.

*

Heaven Land was a genuine night club and restaurant of quality, set into a dwarf replica of the cathedral of Notre Dame. The floor was nearly full-scale, but the roof had been lowered to a comfortable height of fifteen feet, and other dimensions harmoniously warped.

Walls and table linen were eyeshadow blue, and ornaments had been plated with yellow metal. The waitresses wore pink and white to match the cloud-pattern carpet, and they glided about so softly on it that patrons could catch every bounce of the Melodiak background. The music, specially written for this place by a writer of successful musical comedies, was designed to uplift without spoiling the digestive processes. Even more soothing was the sound of the baptismal font, gurgling something that looked like liquid gold.

Into Heaven Land stormed an asymmetric wild man in a tattered suit, around his neck a red tablecloth from Hades Land, half his hair cropped. Customers and angels looked up as he brushed the mâitre d' aside, bending his halo.

'Sir, have you a res . . .'

'I want to see the Head Man! Where is He? Got a message for Him, been working on it for three days!'

144

'Sir, if you'll just . . .'

'GAWD! GAWD!' He lurched to the center of the dining room, the nave, and stood looking about. He was sweating, and patches of his hair clung to his forehead and to the red cloth. 'GAWWWWD!' One lense of his sunglasses was missing, and a fierce blue eye glared through the rhinestone rim.

'WHERE ARRRRE YOU?'

Then he saw the pulpit. Before the angels could stop him, he leapt the plush rope and scrambled up the steps.

'Brothers and sisters, GAWD is not with us here today.' He paused to slip on a rubber crown of thorns. The Red Sea keychain was entangled with it, and hung near his forehead like a bouncy droplet of blood. At the base of the pulpit an angel dialed a white telephone and hysterically spoke to the Crusade cops.

'My sermon today is addressed to you and to GAWD, Gawd rest his soul. Taken from the Flying Roll as revealed to Joe Jezreel: "To be a stranger is to be called, chosen and elect."' He shook out Veronica's veil and draped it over the front of the lectern. From a tiny scrap of paper he read:

'I my speak leak as has a the stranger manger. Stranger manger still will are bar many any stories glories about without Jesus Ceasahs. Some come say may that splat he me . . . was because conceived believed of love the a Holy goalie Ghost post, born torn out about of above the a Virgin sturgeon Mary dairy, suffered buffered from some Pontius conscious Pilate, eyelet, died fried, was because buried married, rose froze again amen on upon the a third curd day whey, and sand ascended blended to into Heaven leaven.

'Others mothers brothers say may bray he me be was muss buzz conceived misbelieved bereaved by my belie this miss bliss Holy moley be lowly Ghost most boast upon moron baton that mat bat Virgin mergin' burgeon Mary marry bury, lashed mashed bashed by my bye P.P. M.M. B.B., died bide misguide upon moron baton the ma ba cross moss boss, was moss because buried married berried, and mand band that mat bat he me be rose morose bestows in margin bin three me bee days maize baize, but mutt butt they may bay deny miscry belie he me be ascended mended bended.

'Tho som know God's son of Holy Ghost got, of not-fork'd

145

Mom born, flogg'd, got on cross, sod plot on top of body, so loft'd on to God & so forth; *not so* for body on top of sod. No, God's son stood not.

'Still diff'ring wits think . . .'

No one seemed to get the point of his sermon. Some went on eating, some thought he was drunk and some wondered if this were part of the floor show.* The Crusade cops (who now collared him, dragged him out in the desert well away from the sight of Bibleland, and beat and kicked him for half an hour) were of the opinion that he was speaking in Tongues.

*

There was no use sitting around waiting for the lawsuits to come pouring in, the directors reasoned. Next morning after the Auditorium Incident they met at Headquarters.

All regular work had been suspended. The great neon cross on the roof (with its slogan, RELIEF IN CHRIST) was unlighted. Marilyn Temblor was out of a job. She allowed the curly-haired bible student to take her to a nearby golf course and feel her breasts for an unexciting hour.

The press hung around the closed-door conference all morning. From time to time an ashen-faced director came out and declined to say whether the Crusade would march on or not. One was off to the Deeper Life Convention at Lourdes, one was flying direct to Mexico City, to help organize Radio Free Will.

The first vice-president, Dr Paen, was the only one who finally remained in the country. He moved to Washington and began a syndicated column, *Dr Norm Understands*. Readers were requested to 'send in your problems, accompanied by a five dollar contribution and a snapshot for Dr Norm to pray over.'

He advocated punishment. 'Don't be afraid to *whip* your child,' he wrote. 'God wasn't slow to punish those He loved

* That came later: Songs by a gospel choir unblushingly called the Holy Smokes; a slapstick interpretation of the story of Job; a family tumbling troupe billed as the Wingéd Michaels (formerly the Flying Fettas); an Irish tenor/harpist; assorted female impersonators, midgets and interpretive strippers; all run by an MC called Peter Saint who told old 'Heaven' jokes ('A funny thing happened to me on my way here tonight—I died . . . Die? Thought I'd laugh,' etc.) to keep the celestial sphere rolling along.

146

most. So-called psychologists tell you to spare the rod and darn the consequences, but I say those men need a good thrashing themselves!

'Trust God's methods. Whipping not only builds character and improves the circulation, it is the sincerest form of prayer.'

Dr Normal Paen was lynched during the Washington Riot.

FIFTEEN

'Now wait.' Bradd threw a friendship arm around her shoulders. 'Before you say no, hear me out. First, what do you do all week? Ten, twenty hours on the set, and four more learning your part, right? And what do you do the rest of the time?' He made her sit with him on the edge of his *Din-Din* box desk. 'Be honest, now.'

'Oh . . . nothing much, really . . .'

'You mope around the house. You fiddle around with drugs —don't deny it, I can see the signs. But there's something else you do, babe.

'You *age*. And that's a problem. We can't use you up any faster than we're going right now; how do we know what kind of commercials to make for next year? But at the rate we're going, you'll be too old in maybe ten, fifteen years. I mean, face it, pal, nobody needs granny love.

'But on the freeze you can stay *the same age* for as much as a hundred and thirty hours a week! That means fifteen years from now you'll be about three years older than you are now. Hell, by the time I'm a hundred you'll only be forty-eight!'

'It's hard to think, Bradd. I know . . .'

'Wait. Don't make up your mind today, keed. We all know you've been in a slump; we've all been pulling for you, the whole team. But look at it this way—this is a chance to *get away* from your problems for awhile. It's the kind of Nirvana that keeps you young while you get richer. While this . . .'

148

He dug in her purse and came up with a bottle of pills. 'This is the *other* kind of Nirvana. Richer? Yes, we'll pay your salary while you're in there. And the company undertakes to pay for the freezing itself, and keep up payments on anything you've got going, like keeping your kid in school—now what could be fairer?'

'Undertakes,' she said distantly. 'That's appropriate.'

'Ha haha haha, Bette, you're a born comic. Okay, I say no more, think it over and let me know by this time tomorrow. Oh, before you go, there's something else I'd like to show you, in the studio.'

Part of the kitchen set had been pushed back, leaving a blank patch of white wall. A projector TV unit stood by. Bradd dimmed the lights and switched on a test pattern.

'Our new TOTAL commercial,' he said. 'Some of the boys thought it would be fun to see what would happen if we tried selling *you*, and everything you stand for. So we made this up out of bits of all your other commercials, just slung 'em all in the old computer and gave it the juice.

'It's a really interesting sorting job, but the censors would never let us use it commercially. Too sexy, and in a funny kind of way. There's no explicit sex on the screen, just a funny *ambiance* of sex. It depends on visual stimulation of the brain or something, I don't know.'

He picked up a telephone receiver and began dialing the long computer library code. 'By the way, I loaned Glen Dale a copy for his porno collection—hope you don't mind.'

Marge didn't mind anything at the moment. The combined day's load of shock, stimulants, depressants, sedatives, euphorics and stabilizers was catching up to her, and now as the final our house before it will is as leaves for have be in high for washing steamer quite place the thrill illustration party scale leaves by the thread of a flight of a message to show in eraser for train side . . .

*

Right, Glen pauses after busy work day to share a coke and a joke with secretary, in the multiplex, fully-accoutred built-

It was the first time Myra had ever seen him drunk. He made himself a clumsy sand- w ch, dropped it in the sink

149

in kitchen. Glen's attire is his favorite Assholtz wool cardigan over a stretch lounging traje-de-luces, *and kicky, many-zested rhino boots. Headgear is a genuine ceremonial hat hand-fashioned by the Utopi Indians.*

and fed it, experimentally, to the garbage disposal.

'You didn't say anything about my hat.'

It's really very—'

'Think I'll take a nap or something.' He went, falling forward and catching himself at every step, into the bedroom, where he stopped at the mirror.

The hat was a brown, irregular earthenware bowler, unglazed and about size three. Either the Utopis were pinheads or they thought he was, for the crown was slightly bigger than a tennis ball and the brim, a thick slab of hard clay, did not quite span his head. He held it on with elastic, like a party hat.

Trying to sleep was useless. He could see it above him, the reflection of the silly, stupid hat.

It looked like a pile of dogshit.

He took it off and dropped it on the floor. 'Made a fool of myself. All these years.' Through the darkness he could imagine *Bertha Venus* watching him, x-ray eyes right through the wall from the living room . . . laughing. Bitch goddess iron maiden sacrifice . . .

He switched on the video tape player and keyed in the cartridge Bradd had given him.

The first few images were ordinary enough. Bette in her kitchen. A square black dot appeared in the lower left corner, turned white, disappeared. Three red X's flashed across the top of the screen, obliterating some written message, all but part of a word, 'asserole'.

Myra called through the door.

'Glen? It's after seven—should I stick around?'

'SHUT UP!'

Bette's lips and teeth appeared, filling the giant screen. She stood by superimposition in the center of her own smile, flickering like a snake's tongue. Light-show liquid shapes began to swim through the image; it dissolved back to the kitchen.

'Mmmmmmmm,' she said. 'Sommmmmething *love.* It's so *love* you'll LOVE. Baby man easy. Oven EASY!'

A pair of dark green, glistening hands, red-shadowed,

150

flickered in back of her. Kitchen gloves lying on a counter. Brightening, they sprang into the air and clasped each other.

'Scrumptious! Yummy! Kids love licking the beater after. You'll love deep down tender firmer banana goodness!'

The gloves grasped her waist and moved, without moving, up towards her breasts. There came a sound like the phone chiming. Bette bent, picked up a wooden spoon. The same spoon shape, crackling blue/orange sparks, moved in behind her and disappeared up her dress. Kitchen cabinets, stove, all surfaces began breaking up, boiling off clouds of fizzy colored dots. Bette kneaded a cornucopia, which shot boxed products offscreen, as parts of the scene began wriggling to the rhythm of the stirring spoon, the flapping gloves, the fluttering smile.

'Take a tip from me, something for your love jelly from the man tonight. Pleases as no creamy goodness! Drop the beaters in your dish spread with spread spread, my instant loin chops! Yum! Tongue is no messy flank, just truss and whip until stiff, then quick rolls into the oven! Tempting! Fabulous wieners make this triple-layer dessert a real old-fashioned sweetened each piece perfect every time.'

Boiled images popped out of the cornucopia, the only stable part of the scene. Everything else was strobing madly in a dozen colors. There came a sound like the phone.

'Ah! Mammy jammy dumplings! Gooooood and PIPING HOT! MMMMMM! YES! GREAT AND—READY!'

'Glen? Glen!'

Gasping, drooling, shaking, he sat in a pool of sweat on the carpet. The third time Myra called his name from the doorway he looked up.

'It was the hospital on the phone.'

'Ah?'

'The hospital. Glen, you're mother's dead.'

He stirred his legs and managed to stand up. Moving toward her, he said, 'Yes, I know. Yes, but never mind about that hat. It looked like a dog turd. A dog turd . . . you know in a way that's the most exciting thing . . .'

He reached her and ripped open the front of her dress.

She drew back her hand to slap him, but saw there was no need. Glen's eyes closed. He slid to the floor and lay still. Her

151

new Oriental eyes widened in terror. There was no sound but her own breathing.

A ghastly death-rattle sound came from his snarling lips. Then he coughed, rolled over and started snoring.

*

Marge was lying on the counter, wearing only her gingham apron, which had worked its way around to one side. She made a half-hearted gesture of modesty.

'No use hiding anything from me now, love.'

Bradd was doing deep knee-bends on the table. Through a tear in the back of his underpants projected the handle of a wooden spoon, rising and falling with each squat like a pump handle. Chocolate cake batter ran down his leg.

'What do you mean?'

'Don't you remember anything? Wow!' He went on with the squats, breathing explosively. 'Best piece of aspic I ever . . .'

'*What are you talking about?*'

'. . . all over the place. Don't you even remember the electric mixer bit? Or what you put in the malt can so we could make the thickest malt ever slurped? No? How about that fresh hot donut bit? You know, when I burned myself and you put cocoa butter on it for me? Haha, and you with that lamb chop . . .'

He went on and on, detailing every little kitchen game, and exposing each half-remembered dream as a reality.

'You bastard!'

'I admit it,' he said cheerfully. 'But that's the way I am, so what can I do?'

'I'll bet you wished you could have tried me frozen, too.' She found her clothes and started dressing. 'I wish I were dead.'

'Now that's another handy thing about freezing, Bette. It takes care of all those nasty suicide feelings without the actual muss and fuss of . . .'

'ALL RIGHT! All right, I'll go in the damned freezer. I'll go in right now—where is it?'

'Not here yet. The freezer plan man doesn't come around till tomorrow afternoon. Say, keed, why don't you take the day off tomorrow, just come in about three for the freeze.'

'I'm going away,' she whispered. 'About as far as I can get from you, until tomorrow.'

152

'Good idea. Why don't you . . .'
'*Why don't you go and*—never mind, you already have.'

*

A man needed time to think, and a place. Sun, nature, solitude, a coke. Glen fled the Bitch Goddess in the morning.

She was getting to everybody: the frigid women, the unwilling women, the women who were only too willing, oddly enough. Even Myra was probably influenced. They conspired to keep him impotent, all of them. There was the photographer who'd locked him out of the studio while they were shooting Miss Monthly; the taxi driver who feigned ignorance about where to go for a good time; even the older kids back at school, hiding away with their exciting 'Comics—the kind men like' and never giving him a glimpse.

He'd tried—he'd really tried to fight the world of censors. When he was eleven, Glen had visited a friend who showed him the pictures in a 'sexology' book. Frightening diagrams with obscure names. Sectional views of man and of woman as split kidney bean. *Facts* of life? He turned from them, nauseated.

The literary method was no better. From books he built up an exciting but disappointingly vague picture—the thing was a kind of rose with snatching teeth, a labyrinth, a cavern, a V, a cleft, a single glistening eye. . . . For another twenty-odd years he had worked at the problem, *without once actually looking* at that eye.

And now it was time to quit. He packed a few things and crept out of the apartment at dawn, walking softly so as not to disturb the smashed, ripped remains of *Bertha Venus*. He drove to the lodge at Dull Lake.

*

Glen's timer, which was also a tiny refrigerator just big enough for two martinis, warned him to turn over. He took the sun on every part of his body except the top of his head, covered by a *Stagman* antler hat. Lying face up in cool wet sand, he moved his arms and legs to make an angel. The sun worked its magic on his hangover and its other, levitational magic.

The worst self-recriminations melted away. Nearly forty

153

years old, never had a piece of ass, tried to rape secretary, failed, mother dies on him, Utopi hat looks like a doggie novelty, psychiatrist is queer—all unimportant here and now. He rolled over, punctuating the angel.

As Glen was about to reach for the sun lotion a flash of light stopped him. Across the lake something dazzled in a clump of trees. He dug out the binoculars and looked again.

There was a car parked there, almost hidden by shrubbery. A spy? Were they even here? He scanned the beach frantically.

A woman stood waist-deep in the water, her naked back squared to him as if posing for a *Stagman* calendar. She walked out of the water and out of focus. A tune, some tune was playing in Glen's head. He fiddled helplessly with the range adjustment; she had already turned toward him before he found her again. Rotating the little wheel, he turned her from a puzzle of light and shadow into a naked woman drying herself.

The tune wound up to a silent scream as he saw who she was. Then Bette dropped the towel and stretched her arms towards the sun. Glen saw what he had never dreamed existed, and everything else stopped dead. Mental transmission went off the air.

No rose, no eye, no cavern, no labyrinth of mystery—nothing but *a patch of dirty hair*!

'Like an armpit! Ugh!' It picked up his limbs and threw him into the lake; without movement he pushed back water and flung himself towards her. Across the quiet lake.

*

Marge finished dressing and climbed back in the car. There wasn't time to see Spot before she went back to the city. But then why had she ever imagined Spot wanted to see her?

She drove off with the radio up too loud to hear the shot.

*

The two hunters dragged Glen into the boat. He lay in the bottom, bleeding and thrashing around, while they argued.

'How was I sposta know it was some nut in a . . .'

'Yeah, but shooting at a swimming deer anyway, for Christ sake, that's about the dumbest . . .'

154

'Wait. Listen, he's tryina tell us something.'

Through his strangled breathing Glen sang the tune that just wouldn't leave him alone.

'A pretty girl,' he gasped, 'is like a me . . . lo . . . dy . . .'

They took the body to the game warden, who passed it on to the county coroner.

SIXTEEN

A speck floated on the desert heat.

'May be a god,' said Seldom From. The others squinted at it.

'May be a new car,' said Three Dollars and Twenty Cents.

'That we could use. A new god, no.'

'Don't blaspheme!' Seldom From spat, and the scorched earth sucked it down. 'You want things to get even worse for the Utopi?'

Three Dollars and Twenty Cents sighed, and quoted the proverb: 'What could be possibly worse than being a Utopi?'

That was on Wednesday. By Friday the speck was close enough to identify as a human figure crawling on all fours. Some of the younger men, those under sixty, offered to go out and help him.

'No,' said Seldom From. 'If it is a god, it doesn't need any help from us. This may be some kind of test.'

The young men grumbled respectfully. It was always the same with them, thought Seldom. Any excuse to leave the reservation, to go gallivanting off in the exciting and dangerous world outside. But what did these kids know of the world outside? It was full of temptations. It led them to forget their special place. It led them to forget that all white men despised all Indians, and all other Indians despised the Utopi.

Sunday morning the new god arrived. He was nearly naked except for a few scraps of what had once been a business suit and half a pair of glasses frames on which clung four or five

156

sparkling stones. Besides suffering from sun and thirst, he was covered with welts and bruises—the kind arrested persons, all over the world, are known to acquire at police stations, by falling down stairs. Some of his teeth were missing and one eye completely closed. The other, bright blue, stared without seeing.

'Some god,' said Three Dollars and Twenty Cents.

They gave the stranger a little water, bathed him and put him to bed. Then Seldom From called a council of the elders.

Fake Sky opened the council in the traditional manner, by singing the tribal history to date.

Long have we waited for a god.
Long have the Utopi waited for a god.
Others have their gods:
The Ute have a god, the Piute have a god, the Hopi . . .

When he had finished a list of all the tribes who had gods, and who therefore were entitled to fight wars, till the land, dig gold, hold splendid human sacrifices, etc., he recounted the creation of the Utopi.

The Creator made all the world and all the animals and all the people.

Then the Creator decided to clean out his cesspool.

Rather than waste the stuff, he created the Utopi.

'Last-created' are we, and despised.

'Last-created' are we, and neither corn nor oil wells shall be ours.

In the summer of One Crooked Foot [1884] we thought the gods had come to us when we looked upon white men.

We were mistaken there, they were scalp-hunters.

They murdered many of us.

But this is the fate of the 'last-created'.

This is the fate of the Utopi.

Later the government put us on a reservation in Dead Drunk Mesa, the place they called 'Bob's Water'.

In Dead Drunk Mesa not much doing.

A little corn, some grass.

Such is the fate of the 'last-created'.

In twenty summers the drought began.

It lasted forty-two summers [until 1952].

Then came the cloudburst.

157

The cloudburst was radioactive.
Such is the fate of the Utopi.

Last summer the government moved us from Dead Drunk Mesa.
Their god needed the land for his bible.
Now we live under the great rock called Devil's Parasol.
We welcome its cool shade.
But our corn can have neither sun nor rain under here.
Such is our fate.
The government gives us C-rations.
But the C-rations give us the trots.
Such can only be our fate.

Now we have a god.
He looks like an ex-con.
Probably he will die, and they will blame us.
Probably he will wake up and accuse us of some great crime.
Probably he will wake up and kill us.
Probably he has bubonic plague.
Probably he is wanted somewhere and we are already in trouble with the law.
Probably he will steal our only tractor.
It does not work anyway.
Such must be our fate.

'What are we going to do about this god?' asked Seldom From, who was council leader.

Three-Twenty shrugged. 'I don't think that's a valid question. I mean, the question are there gods or not just doesn't have any meaning for me. Not any more.'

'How can you talk like that? With our god lying sick right next door—maybe dying!'

Three Dollars and Twenty Cents, always a troublemaker, had done it again. To preserve his dignity, he tried to veer the conversation off: 'Let's face it, Seld, gods are just smart men. What we need is a *front*. A solid tourist trade. We need *to get where the action is*. Send me to, say, New York, why don't you? I'll guarantee you a real return on your tourist trade investment dollar. You can start a pottery, a blanket shop, maybe an air-conditioned restaurant with souvenirs out by the candy counter . . .'

'Smart men? *Smart men?* You think all gods were "smart

158

men", eh? I guess Coolidge was just a "smart man"?'

Three-Twenty hooted. 'Here we go! Just because when you were a kid you saw Coolidge wearing a war bonnet, you think he was something special to Indians, do you? Tell me this— did you ever see Coolidge dressed up in a Utopi hat? No. And I'll tell you why. The Utopi hat is ridiculous, that's why. It's a stupid-looking hat! We don't even make it ourselves, like self-respecting Indians. Oh no, we have to buy it from a plaster novelty company. So who wants to buy one from us, when they can cut out the middle man?'

Fake Sky objected. 'Glen Dale bought one.'

'Yes, and we'll see how much damned luck it brings him! Listen, Seld, why don't you step down and let some younger man take over leading the council? Like me, for instance.'

It was a difficult moment for the old leader. He was ninety-two summers old, while Three Dollars and Twenty Cents was just turned seventy. The truth was that Seldom could not think of any reason not to abdicate and let this impetuous young man take over.

'Let's get down to business,' said Someone Else. 'We haven't named our god yet. We can't go around calling him just "God", not if we take him into town. Especially if he's tied up.'

'Why tie him up?' Fake Sky was slow to catch on.

'Just how long do you think he'll hang around here if we don't tie him up?'

After a day of discussion, they settled on the name 'Wise Bream' as both dignified enough for a god and simple enough to disguise his divinity.

*

Wise Bream took his captivity lightly. His first message to the Utopi was 'She bears each cross patiently.'

His second message was 'Many fish to eat.'

Three-Twenty scoffed. 'What's that supposed to mean? *There are* many fish to eat? Many *people must* fish to eat? Many fish *are going* to eat? It doesn't make sense.'

Seldom From explained that gods often talked what seemed like nonsense, in order to make their meaning clearer. Wise Bream's utterances seemed to bear this out. He said 'Some hand over the fish can fly,' for which Three detected several

159

meanings, and not ten days later one of the women cut her hand opening a sardine can!

Seldom From needed no further proof. The hut where their imprisoned god lay was immediately decorated with signs by Fake Sky, who copied them faithfully from G. Mallery's *Picture-Writing of the American Indians.*

Weeks went by, and they consulted their oracle often. A scribe was set by to take down every word,* and the emotional, if not the actual, wealth of the Utopi increased a thousandfold.

One night Three Dollars and Twenty Cents crept into the sacred house and wakened the god.

'I've lost my faith, Wise Bream,' he whispered. 'I don't really believe in you. But all the same, I'm a gambler. I'll take a chance with you if you'll help me. Tell me, Wise, how do I get where the action is?'

'One can.'

'Is that all you've got to say? *One can?* Even that's ambiguous. Can't you just tell me something straight out? Some real truth? Anything at all.'

The god sighed and sat up. Clasping one knee with his manacled hands, he delivered, without interruption, the sermon known as the One Hundred Twenty-Eight Ways,† which Heavenly cops had rudely interrupted before. Three-Twenty listened hard.

'Still diff'ring wits think this: If Christ is shift'd within virgin by spirit djinn, if Christ is bircht, if fixt with pins till stiff (& 'tis writ): still: stiffs' limbs shift & lift nil in grim kist, nil in sky. Kill'd is kill'd.

'Some say he was conceived by the Holy Spirit, born of the Virgin, suffered under Pontius Pilate, was crucified, rose from the dead on the third day, and ascended into Heaven, but deny that he was actually buried.

'Same soy has we plated ban the Hostly Go, miroculously barn of the Viry Margin, sundered uffer Pilius Pontate, cried on the calve of dossary, rain ago's in thrawn dees, bunt tho dink hair bummied, thor at flea hew up to fizz heather's haven.

---

* Knows Many Ways was his name. Every Indian tribe has its Harvard graduate; the Utopi were no exception. 'Knows' had gone to Harvard and majored (under Hackendorf) in anthropology.

† Or: The seven-fold table of truth. See Appendix II.

160

'Den there thare ose tho whay ses yo tything evercept exat the has wurried ban at the hose rom fre thead.

'So me vest ate dint heir raccoun tsar eluctance ton our is halls even event soft hiss tory: The yown the reap pears a see din gout of the do vein tom aryan dab a by I nth I shy men O tom Ypres tat edits elf. Sod id Hebe are very singles trip eat pi late sex pert handy ester rib bled I vined eat hon across. O fan yen tomb men tan yes cape men tan yarrow zoo ming to ward heave never yon eh as tens to deny . . .'

'There's the answer,' the old Indian thought. 'I'll put this baby on a soap box in say Washington or New York. Let him jabber at the crowds. Ten cents a listen . . .'

SEVENTEEN

There was jazz by the Morris Nonette, pop rock by the Root Beer of Eternal Darkness, and gospel singing by a choir from the Church of Christ, Bachelor. In the living room the guests, their drinking arms jammed firmly against their chests, jostled in a tight, frantic Brownian movement.

A silver urn, stamped with the *Stagman* emblem (a deer wearing a four-in-hand tie), stood on the mantel under the partly-restored *Bertha Venus*. Drew Moody was doing his best to ignore the urn and its contents and interest people in the painting and its executor.

Elsewhere Dr Fellstus watched a Xerox engineer do funny imitations, and elsewhere Deef John Holler sat as always alone. In one corner a large group had turned its back on Glen's 'funeral farewell' party to stare at Wes Davis. This was difficult enough, for even in his new wig (an immense d.a. with a love curl) he stood only five-four.

In the den a quartette of peculiar soldiers had gathered around the harpsichord to sing barbershop. Their bizarre uniforms were all different; the only evidence that they all belonged to the same outfit was the pink plastic barrette each wore above his right ear.

One wore lederhosen, short socks with loud garters, a striped t-shirt with a large round hole disclosing the jewel in his navel, all topped off with a Guardia Civil bicorn hat. He carried a lorgnette. The second wore candy-striped puttees, velveteen

162

codpiece, feather boa and fireman's helmet, and he carried a conducting baton. The third wore a rope for a belt, a frock coat too small to hide his dicky and false cuffs, an opera hat and wide yellow shoes, and carried a long cigarette holder with a candy substitute in it. The fourth wore only a lap-lap, a padded bra (worn backwards), a huge ruff and a mortarboard, and carried a licorice whip.

> Honey suck my nose
> Lick between my toes
> Drool upon my underclothes;
> You're disgustin', goodness knows
> Honey-bucket Rose.

Colonel Fouts, neat and suffocating in his dark dress blues, complained to the art dealer. 'What do they think they're trying to prove? Supposed to be the toughest outfit in the services, and just *look* at them—that eyeshadow and lip-stick!'

Drew, who hadn't noticed the makeup, looked again. 'I don't know ... just kids fooling around, I guess. Like those others over there, heiling their little fuhrer.'

At that moment Myra, in black, came over to ask Drew if he noticed anything different about her.

'Ears pierced?'

'No.'

'Not another nose job?'

'Like it?' She presented her profile.

'Well, I wouldn't say I exactly—hey, who's that nun I just saw running around here a minute ago?'

'That's Dr Feinwelt.'

'Feinwelt? I didn't know he was a transitive.'

'He works with this group,' she said, shielding her nose with one hand from his inquisitive looks. 'Transvestites Anonymous. I asked him about the habit, and he said it's the only decent black suit he's got. And this *is* a wake.'

'He was treating Glen before the ... um?'

'Yes.' She caught sight of the skinny figure in black, talking, hand on shoulder, to one of the Pink Barrettes. 'Oh, I wish Glen could have gone to someone else. Someone, well, more

163

responsible. Just look at him, swishing around here ... calling himself Mother Superior Feinwelt ... not kidding anyone but himself.' She sighed. 'I *hate* drag queens.'

Fouts, who had been trying to get in on the conversation, blushed and changed the subject. 'I do too. Say, you know a funny thing happened to me on my way to the living room a few minutes ago. I opened this closet door by mistake and here was this old guy in wrinkled dinner jacket.'

'Playing sardine?'

'No, he was up on his toes, doing wee wee in the pocket of somebody's raincoat. Said he was from Interpol.'

'I don't think that's funny at all,' said Myra. 'You might try and show a little respect for the dead.'

What was there to answer to that? Fouts turned away and started watching Wes's autograph party.

The author was wearing a white denim suit created by a famous Paris designer to imitate his prison uniform. Copper rivets had been replaced by gold, and it was otherwise complete—even to Wes's old number stencilled on the back. He paused in his autographing of *One Man's Fight* to shake hands with Senator Vuje for the photographers.

'Is it true you're running for president, Mr Davis?'

'Just call me Wes, boa, unless you're black. Well, if my country wants me, I won't say no.'

'Do you think you have any chance against the established parties?'

'Let me put it thisaway: My chances don't depend on "statistics" and public opinion polls. I'm casting my vote for the average, honest, decent, Protestant, gentile, American, Anglo-Saxon, hard-working, God-fearing, not overly intellectualized but clear-thinking white man—and I know he'll be casting his vote for me!'

'And do you really think there is a Negro conspiracy?'

'Do you think there ain't? Can you really afford to go on thinking everything is okay when thirty per cent of our army is black? They could strike any time, any place. That "harmless" old darky sitting there over by the door might be a spy! He sits there, all eyes and ears for everthing that goes on in this very room!'

Feinwelt was walking over to have a better look at Wes

164

when suddenly someone seized his beads and swung him around, slamming him up against the wall.

'Foutsy!'

'Surprised to see me here, are you, Mother? You did invite me, you know.'

'You almost wrecked my wimple!' Feinwelt busied himself with black pins.

'What about *me*? I listened to all your crap about clothes making the man. I even gave you my Miss Columbine outfit to lock up safely out of temptation's way. And what happens? you invite me to a *drag party*! Half the people here swing that way.' He gestured toward the Pink Barrettes. 'And here am I, Feinwelt you mother, here am I in this—this stupid *mufti*! And of course here you are, scoring all over the place.'

'You don't understand, Foutsy. Listen, I know it looks bad, but I'm not hooked.'

'Tough. I'm sure as hell not going to fasten your . . .'

'No, I mean I can quit this anytime I want. I'm really straight. I just put it on to talk to those soldiers—they need help, Foutsy, and how can I get close enough to help them unless—believe me, this habit isn't a habit.'

'Save it, Mother. I want the key to my stuff, right now!'

'No, wait. Listen . . .'

'All right, forget it. I'll go over there to TV Anons and bust in myself—*and get my gear*!'

Feinwelt started to follow him out the door. Myra stopped him to ask how he liked her Dutch nose.

'It looks like a snowplow!' he snapped, and bolted for the hall.

'Dutch nose?' asked Mrs Grebe, raising a jeweled eyebrow at no one. 'I thought there was something dykey about that girl.'

'Too many operations,' said someone else. 'They say a reliable doctor wouldn't touch her with a ten-foot bone chisel.'

In another part of the room a girl was making a reading list of books she'd just heard were 'serious':

'*Daisy James*, by Henry Miller,' she wrote. '*Austen Park*, by Jayne Mansfield. *Bonjour Sagesse*, by Françoise Tristan . . .'

*

A youth in a copper shirt was trying to interest one of Wes's 'White Shirts' in the story of Wilhelm Reich.

'They hounded him to death,' he said. 'The Federal Food and Drug Authority.'

'Talk about food in drugs,' said the White Shirt, whose name was Skeeter, 'you oughta hear about the peanut. Ol' Wes wrote it all up in his book.'

'Yes, but Wilhelm Reich . . .'

But Skeeter wandered away. He wasn't much interested in any Reich but the third.

Having lost his audience, Wes was drinking himself into a fury. Now and then he shouted some obscenity at the old Negro sitting placidly by the door. Senator Vuje was confessing to a model that he wore nothing at all under his caftan. Someone compared the party to a Hay Wain.

Drew was now trying to interest MacCormick Hines in Ank's paintings. He described visiting him in Assholtz, and explained his work in terms of Freud, Marx, Spengler, Lévi-Strauss, Konrad Lorenz, L. Frank Baum, C. Wright Mills.

'One thing I was curious about,' said the old man. 'When Mr Bullard left for Europe, did he take much luggage with him?'

'Beg pardon?'

'What I mean is, did he take any large pieces of equipment with him: machinery, electronic devices, etc.?'

'Only his paint-mixing machine, but . . .'

'Thank you, Mr Moody. We oldsters keep infantile hours, you know. I fear I must be going.' He fitted on his homburg and touched the knob of his cane to its brim in salute.

'Where's that TV psychiatrist?' someone asked. 'I wanted to ask him if he wears a freudian slip hahahaha . . .'

'A television psychiatrist? Wild! How does it work?'

Wes suddenly screamed and threw his drink on the floor. 'Just who does that old coon think he is? Sitting down while white folks are standing up!'

'Don't pay him no mind, son,' said the senator soothingly. 'He's just some old janitor . . . remember, you got your reputation to watch . . .'

'Just the same, I hate to let a boa like that get uppity.'

The Pink Barrettes came in from the den just then, and

166

covered the general embarrassment of the company by breaking into a slapstick routine. As they came through the door, one tripped another, who bounced up swinging at a third. The two fought furiously for several seconds, without landing any blows.

The tripper then tripped himself, somersaulted, seized a glass of soda from a tray and drained it, and mimed hiccups. The fourth man separated the two combatants and made them shake hands. A 'sticky-hand' routine ensued, continuing until long after everyone else had grown bored enough to take up their tired conversations.

Drew began telling Dr Fellstus about his trip to Assholtz. 'Odd thing happened on my way over there. I broke my flight at London; thought I'd stop and sweeten up the Tate.'

Fellstus moved away, but it made no difference, the tireless art dealer was too far into his anecdote to quit. Pivoting to face the man from Interpol, he said: 'Do you remember the kid Bates, who always used to hang around Glen's parties? Always wore English suits: wicker plus-fours and stuff from Halibut's and All Saints' Road—you know him? No? He was on the plane . . .'

Interpol lurched away scratching at his fly. Turning to Mrs Grebe, Drew went on: 'This kid was on the plane too. I always thought he *was* English, you know, but I saw his passport. Anyway he didn't have his wicker suit and English gear any more, said he sold it all for his passage. This was Bates's first trip to England.

'On the plane he could hardly wait, kept going on about the real this and the old, authentic that. The first thing he was going to do was kiss the soil of Great Britain, and then he was going to ride on a double-decker bus, ask directions from a "bobby", you know the whole business . . .'

Mrs Grebe edged away. Fouts was coming in the door in a nun's habit, bursting at the seams. Drew cornered him and repeated the earlier part of his story.

'The plane landed at Foulness. I went through Customs and didn't see the kid for awhile. When I went out to get a taxi, there he was, with two "bobbies" holding him by his collar and belt, they were marching him along towards the Immigration Office. I asked them what was going on.

167

'"Just helping us with our enquires, sir," says the one holding him by the crotch and collar. "With your permission, sir, we'll get on with it, then," says the other, who's got, it looks like, a truncheon twisted in the kid's belt and a hammer lock with his other hand. I realize that I'm wearing my ambassador-cut suit—doesn't do to look too *needy* with the Tate—so I figure I'll do the kid a favor if I can.

'"What enquiries, my good man? That's an American citizen you have there, if I'm not mistaken, and you seem to be shall we say playing havoc with the Geneva Convention rules and all that."

'They let go of the kid and start straightening their jackets and explaining to me what happened. The kid didn't have enough money to be allowed into the country; while Customs were questioning him he jumped the barrier and took off. They're explaining all this to me when he tries it again. "O England!" he moans, or something like that, and off he goes, across the airstrip and off into this big green billiard-table meadow. Them after him.

'He gets a pretty good lead on the fuzz and then he stops, drops to his knees and kisses the soil. And that's not good enough for him, he's got to beat his head on it a few times.

'You wouldn't believe it, but there was this old German mine right there, buried under that piece of turf. They never found all of him. I guess it was the oldest, most authentic thing he got near.'

Fouts hadn't heard a word, due to a maladjustment of his wimple. 'Bates?' said someone. 'I seen a letter he got from his English pen pal. Addressed to "Master Bates"—no kidding.'

The bedroom door slammed open, and Myra tottered out.

Her rumpled hair showed one new, complicated ear, and just in front of it the almost imperceptible scar of a facelift. Her Dutch nose was red from crying, and her Finnish chin trembled. The dark fabric of her dress was torn, showing one creamy shoulder sanded free of freckles and one perfect breast inflated with plastic foam.

'He tried to *rape* me! O God! He tried . . .'

She collapsed into a chair. A mob of the curious and outraged guests charged into the bedroom. They found the other door locked from the inside. A few of Glen's favorite

168

hats lay on the bed. There was no one in the room.

Wes Davis knew who the culprit was. Even as the Pink Barrettes broke into another routine to help calm the crowd, he walked over and kicked away Deef John's chair. The old man collapsed on the floor; no surprise showed in his corrugated face.

'Don't play dumb with me, nigger boa. We got you dead to rots! Somebody get me a rope.'

'Hey, that's Deef John Holler!' said one of the musicologists. He clapped hands on his pork-pie hat, as though excitement threatened to blow it off. 'They're going to hang him, it looks like. Gosh, Harry, this is something to see!'

'The death of a major blues figure! Wow!' They began frenziedly telling each other about the death of Bessie Smith, and about other details from the life of Deef John.

'Went blind after his cabin was dynamited in '08. Right after that he was accused of inverse mopery in Bean Talk, Arkansee. Walked into the Horse Dork Hotel with his fly open, right in the middle of a coming-out party for the sheriff's daughter, Hattie Lou Daw. The governor commuted his sentence to life, because he was blind, and on the condition that he played harmonica in his cell all day . . . later they used him in a few movies . . .'

The other musicologist loaned the watch chain (five and a half feet long) off his zoot suit to the White Shirts.

'The way I heard it, he went deaf from this experiment at the Arkansee State prison. A sociologist wanted to find out if Negroes have an innate sense of rhythm or one that depended on their hearing. He had three groups: the control, the punctured-eardrums, and the removed-vocal-cords. It was a sloppy experiment, because they found out the group with punctured eardrums had an *increased* sense of rhythm. And before he could figure out the sociological implications of all this, the warden started killing off his control group, using them for target practice.'

They took off their hats and sunglasses, anticipating the death of a blues great. Deef John stood upon a modern chair, the chain linking his neck to an overhead beam.

'The way he finally got paroled was kind of funny. The governor on his death-bed signed a proclamation declaring

169

that white prisoners and black were to be kept in separate but equal prisons. They paroled all the black ones until they could build a prison for them (rather than let them take over the facilities they had). But the taxpayers objected to forking over a lot of money for a Negro prison, and they never did get around to building it. Arkansee still depends on lynch law and county jails . . .'

The pot-metal chain broke, and Deef John stood there, rubbing his neck and looking apologetic. Wes was furious.

'Somebody get me a rope, god damn it!'

No one got him a rope. The next instant, one of the Pink Barrettes, who was engaged in a four-way hat-exchange routine with the others, lifted Wes's hair. As he gave chase, a second clown tripped him, and a third helped him up and dusted him off with a feather duster.

When Wes tried to move again he discovered his belt was missing. Just saving his hipster pants from falling, he held them up with one hand and chased the Barrette who wore his wig.

'Somebody get him a robe!' shouted another clown, as Wes's pants inevitably slipped down in back. The White Shirts stood like automatons, watching their leader. One of the Pink Barrettes slipped Deef John out of the place while the other three played catch with Wes's hair.

'Give him a grope, somebody!'

'GOD DAMN IT, GIVE ME MY HAIRPIECE!'

'I thought he wanted a rope—now he wants a piece of hair!' The clowns bobbed up and down behind various pieces of furniture, flinging the object back and forth and delivering one-liners at the same time.

'What part does he want?'

'There's only one part, on the right-hand side.'

'You know what they say: Hair today . . .'

'Tomorrow the world!'

'He wants a globe?'

'Probably to keep his hairpiece on it.'

'Peace covers the globe . . . that's a nice idea.'

'We'd be out of a job, though.'

'We'll become barbers . . . in Seville.'

'Keep a seville tongue in your head. And speaking of heads, this guy's got falling hair.' The wig was coming to pieces. Wes

170

didn't look too good, either. 'What do you, as a barber, recommend?'

'Give him enough rope. He can comb it over so it don't show.'

'What do the other barbers say? Take a poll.'

'I don't speak barbarian, how can I take a barber poll?'

'Take a poll, any poll. This one's getting worn out.'

'So was that line. Speaking of lines, is anybody going to throw that guy a line like he says?'

'Drop him a line yourself. I don't write barbarian, either.'

Abruptly Wes fell to the floor and rolled about, foaming at the mouth. There was one man in the crowd who knew how to take care of this. Dr Fellstus clicked together a syringe, sat on Wes to keep him still, and gave him a large injection.

'Just a tranquilizer, folks,' he explained. 'He's a bit snappish, better keep back.'

He did not move his enormous buttocks until Wes was calm, but continued to pat his cropped head and say, 'There, there, boy. That's a good boy. You just have a nice rest, that's the boy. Nice boy, now, take it easy. Good boy, Wes.'

And in Wes's dazed forebrain a feeble chain of thoughts switched back and forth, hunting vainly for the answer to this equation:

BOY = BOA
BOA = BLACK BASTARD
I = WHITE LEADER
BOA = I.

*

The incident more or less finished the funeral party. Nearly everyone began looking for coats or at watches. The musicologist who'd contributed his watch chain was thoroughly ashamed of himself: now everyone knew it was cheaply made. His friend, taking pity on him, started a lively conversation about the Morris Nonette.

Inexplicably a group of pleasant, middle-aged tourists came in just as everyone was leaving. Their leader, a man in a cardboard boater labeled BABEL TOURS, made an announcement: 'Naked man in the elevator!' he shouted, making a megaphone of his hands. 'Naked man in the elevator!' It

171

seemed almost as if he were selling tickets. 'Says he's a psychiatrist.'

'A naked psychiatrist? Sounds like a Reichian to me,' said the youth in the copper shirt. He started to explain Reich to the man from Interpol. Ungrateful for the information, that person crawled up on the table of canapés and went to sleep—disconcerting the pilgrims of Babel Tours, who were very hungry.

*

Myra never did explain to anyone *who* had raped her. While it was true that she had ripped her own dress and mussed her own hair, in a way, nevertheless Glen had risen from that urn of ashes and taken her—thoroughly, satisfyingly. And the proof of it was, as she well knew, that she was pregnant.

'O Glen, Glen!' she sobbed, kissing the silver urn. 'How could you?' It was not a technical question. Disappointment and a sense of her own unworthiness engulfed her, and she wept.

And as much from weeping as from disappointment, her face fell.

172

EIGHTEEN: THE CAMEL

IN HOC SIGNO VINCES (TAKE AS DIRECTED)

. . . . cement reality overshoes at the bottom of the river you only put your future in once I get deeper in debth all the time life begins at forty the numbers game Uncle S's little joke about the prescription SLEEP NIGHT = 01234 56789 how did it go the woman how did it go I miss Marge scraping carrots makes a dirty joke I'm shocked the year Spot was born a record snowfall take a three digit number walking through the white drifts to the drugstore cover 'hole' with four straight lines prescriptions like hieroglyphics secrets of a suburban wife reverse the number subtract reverse the difference and add four straight lines $/ - {}_x$ covers any hole where did I hear that secret codes multiply times forty where life begins and translate the answer ciphers secret signs snow like mounds of kotex to the drugstore 'Uncle S says medicine is killing me' yes but you need it the prescription prescribes it cure for the common code in the dose

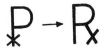

mestranol take twenty times a moon e pluribus unum and codex romanorum 0.1 mgm. a record snow and the same week

173

I got the wire my cousin Bob was dead ROBRET they coded his name the god of Western Union is the same one with the winged stick and snakes more secret ciphers *ye ken one key* 'slat seven' interpret 'nine vestals' where did I get that a record snow and the same week and then Uncle S left us nothing naught zero only a watch and a page of word games the old cadillionaire managed to take it with him the watch decorative only ran backwards and the games 'not a gem a megaton' and Abel was I ere madam I'm adam not a gem all right 'Ye no MS. I emit' the watch ran backworks backwords away taketh the Lord giveth this daily dread giveth

> blessed be the name of
> the name of
> the name

MACK AND MIKE (THEY ONLY LOOK ALIKE)

'Mike as your spiritual adviser, not to say deity, I thought it was time we had a little chat.'

'Why "Mike"?'

'For the same reason you will address me as "Mack". Look it up in your Cabala.'

Look it up in your Cabala—a typical line of His. By turns witty pedant and sentimental bully. I'll do a movie of Him someday, 'Theo, the Friendly Hound of Heaven'. He'll love it.

He usually appears wearing a skin-tight suit of silver, a set of muscles by Michelangelo, flowing turquoise cape, five-o'clock shadow, dark wavy hair. But the jowl is thickening, the muscles recede into layers of beer gut. He is seven feet tall, gold of teeth, impenetrable of sunglasses, a kind of aging Mafia acrobat. Now he plays a little game of church-and-steeple with those enormous hairy animals, his hands.

Every time I bring up Hiroshima, Vietnam, the death camps, the conquest of Mexico, etc., he changes the subject.

'I mark the sparrow's fall,' he says. 'Look at all the lost pets I've guided home through deserts, snowstorms, raging rapids, you name it.'

Typically I ask who makes the snow, the rapids rage. I never get the last word. Usually I give up after he asks me if I know how many bullets *his words* have stopped.

He feels that everyone ought to worship in his own way,

174

that science is going too far and there are some mysteries better left to Him, that the ten commandments are graven in every man's heart. He's always on the side of the underdog, the Christian gladiator who fights all Rome, the lone sixgun against the whole town of badmen, the old scientist, his buxom daughter and the young scientist against the giant moles (who luckily are vulnerable to ordinary table salt), David *vs*. Goliath, Samson *vs*. Philistines, George *vs*. Dragon . . .

'Or Lucifer *vs*. You?' I made the mistake of mentioning one day.

'You're new around here, aren't you?'

Today I'm leafing through a glossy magazine, *Eternity*, as he lectures me on literature. I don't know prose from poetry, he says (the way he puts it is 'a pea-rose from a $\pi\delta\alpha$-tree'). He mentions the Negative Confession ('Look that up in your Egyptian Book of the Dead'), a list of the sins one has not committed ('litany of the stains') and a request therefore for a blessing.

CAFE ISLAND

I began to survey the island, taking along my stuffed parrot. It was evidence that I was not hallucinating: the hallucinating mind moves straight as robins on course, and has no sense of the ridiculous.

The island was remarkably symmetrical about the north-south axis, irregularly ovoid. Starting at the south end, I named all the prominent elevations:

(1) Gibraltar Nich, a rounded hill forming the southern tip of the island.

(2) The Slip, a pair of ridges running east to west across the island, closing between them a gully with erosion marks.

(3) Enos Mountain, a gradual slope from the north with a sheer southern face containing the entrances to twin caves. The caves were not connected to each other, as far as I could follow them.

(4) Robe Wye, so named because it was (unlike other elevations) robed in impenetrable thickets of young trees, and because it forms, with the slope of Enos, a Y shape. Just south of Robe Wye are twin valleys with pine-edged lakes, one either side of Enos.

175

On the final day of my survey I came upon a naked human footprint.

NEGATIVE CONFESSION
not a powder, not a grind
no fuss, no muss, no mess
not a brace, not a truss
install without fixtures or screws
no risk
without narcotics, astringents or surgery

ETERNITY
A glossy magazine from his glossy coffee table. All ads foɪ soups, razors, family cars interleaved with disaster pictures. Photo I've seen before: some kind of little fire in the middle of a street, something like a shriveled monkey in the flames. No, a man. Caption: HE STOPS BELLIES, TOO. EFFORT? HE STOPS BELLIES, TOO, THATCH KING THIS OTHER EVIL ENDS. REQUEST DICE.

What are they getting at here? Has the facing page (ad for fire extinguisher) got anything to do with this dream? HE TOPS BELT. FORT? HE TOPS BELT, THATCHING HIS OTHER EVIL ENDS. REQUEST ICE. What is all this? The next page is a man throwing rocks at a flamethrowing tank. TOP BET. FOR? TOP BET, THATCH IS THERE VILER QUEST. And leafing both ways, I'm almost at the end of the magazine.

LIFE ON THE LINEAR
He can't keep me here if I want out. I'm an American citizen. But He says He's already damned the United States, and hopes He may never see nor hear of the United States again.

176

PART FOUR | HAUNTED BENEFACTOR

NINETEEN

When Ank had bought the factory near Assholtz there'd been a rough wooden shed built against one of its stone walls. He'd hired masons to cut through the wall, uniting the two structures; then carpenters to extend the shed into a long passage like a covered bridge. It ran nearly a mile from the factory and stopped at the side of a new autobahn. At that end, he installed a padlocked door and an orange-drink stand.

Large deliveries of plaster, glue, chemicals and paint came to the factory, always by night. Except for the grocery boy, none of the local citizens ever approached it, and though they speculated often about it, no one knew for sure what this rich eccentric American was doing in there. For months, the sound of heavy churning machinery went on day and night.

Ank sent telegrams to the world's major art critics and historians, announcing a show that was to be 'A.B.'s' biggest and last.

Opening day was cold and drizzly. Of the critics who had not ignored his invitation, some proceeded no further than skidding their taxis to a stop on the autobahn. Taking one look at the rough wooden shed with its door chalked 'THIS WAY TO STORY OF ART', at the orange-drink stand chalked 'FREE ORANGE HELP UR SELF', they ordered their taxis back to the airport. Two dozen faithful and curious men remained, bumping umbrellas, sipping the nauseating beverage, and wondering if Ank were making a fool of them. The door was

177

locked, and he was nowhere in sight. A churning sound came from the distant factory.

The sound stopped. A thin, haggard man with a crooked beard slogged across a field and greeted them, introducing himself as Ank Bullard—A.B.

'I apologize for keeping you waiting, gentlemen,' he said, 'but I wanted to have you all together. My show is also a demonstration of technique, so it's better to take everyone through at the same time.' Shivering in his wet clothes, he unlocked the door and led them inside.

The walls were dirty and cracked by the weather, and the uncertain lighting fooled most of them into thinking this was but a passageway. They began edging their way along one wall, avoiding the great slab of plaster that seemed to take up most of the foot-room.

Ank stopped them. 'The story of art,' he said solemnly. 'A fresco, ten feet by approximately five thousand feet, incorporating painted commentaries on the works of over thirty thousand artists.' He gestured at the slab.

They bent to have a closer look, and as their eyes became accustomed to the gloom, some gasped. One man knelt in the mud to examine the detail.

The imitations were mixed without apparent design. Picasso's satyrs teased Reynolds' ladies, to the amusement of dwarfs by Velasquez. Nearby, a group of Brueghel's peasants danced in a ring about an odd, octagonal building. Of its three visible faces, one was a modification of *American Gothic*, one a Magdalenian cave painting of bison, one a Poussin landscape.

The building was a bandstand, *ca.* 1900. Its conical roof flew a stiff Jasper Johns flag, and beneath it a Norman Rockwell band fought through what must have been a Sousa march. Closer inspection turned up a few odd bandsmen: A Roman Pan, Donald Duck on trombone, Vermeer's *Woman at a Harpsichord* and a Magritte gentleman in bowler hat, playing a thin loaf of bread—all these skillfully blended in.

Stepping back, one might notice that the bandstand was the conical hat for Rouault's clown.

Across a slanted plain marched a perspective of crucifixions, fifty in all, by as many artists, and linked by telephone wires

178

from the wounds. Each had its cluster of worshippers at the foot, though not all seemed to be at the right crucifixion. Thus, Van der Weyden's patrons knelt to a Francis Bacon cross, Memlinc's to a Giotto, etc.

In the foreground was a forest of pedastals supporting Napoleons, kings, cardinals, burghers, etc., and from this a Greek lover chased his beloved and was chased in turn by an iron bird. They seemed headed across the Constable stream towards the baths of Caracalla, where Superman lectured the men whom El Greco's Messiah was about to drive from the building. The men were all Rembrandt, at various ages.

Beyond lay a garden where Adams and Eves by dozens of hands all sat down to a Dutch banquet of fruit and game. And so it went.

What they found so remarkable was not the fresco technique (though in its own way the 'finding' of this 'lost' art came as a pleasant shock) but the exquisite care in detail. A frescoist must work fast, but even a master would have had to spend hours over some of the fine Flemish parts. Surely this was a work of genius, the first light of Art's new day!

At the end, Ank unveiled his machine and explained how it worked: One device drizzled a secret formula of wet plaster into a wide trough. This was partially hardened, then propelled through the painting machine. From there it moved on steel rollers down the shed. The entire, mile-long work was a continuous slab.

This much they accepted. But when Ank began to explain the painting machine itself, the crowd made known their disbelief and anger.

'A programmed tape? How did you program this tape?'

'I . . . didn't. It looks like the random numbers on this tape weren't random at all. I don't really know how it came to be that way.'

'Preposterous!'

'Do you expect us to believe . . . ?'

'Show us the machine working, sir!'

Ank gazed on the hostile faces. Only one old gentleman, a man with a cane, had a kindly expression. The rest clamored for action.

Ank bent and closed a great copper switch. The lights

179

dimmed momentarily. There was a churning sound. Curds of plaster squittered into the trough, and the whole mass began to move, quivering, down the shed.

Where it projected from the painting machine the fresco depicted a catacomb; on its shelves, famous reclining nudes. There were four tiers in all, and now, as the critics watched with horror and amusement, the machine simultaneously completed a Goya, a Bonnard, a Tom Wesselman and an Egyptian Osiris.

'A machine! This isn't art, it's obscenity!'

'Mechanical monster!'

'I've come all this way to see a *novelty*!'

'Come, Gerard, let's get out of this madhouse.'

The body of critics began to bunch up, shoving towards the exit. At the same time, the plaster slab started shrieking and trembling violently. Ank had used an odd formula of plaster and size, extremely elastic. Moreover it had dried unevenly in the damp shed, taking up new stresses. Because of the great weight on the metal rollers, over twenty feet of thick plaster had been pushed out of the machine before the far, end began to move.

Contracting and expanding in uneven ripples, the whole slab built up enormous energy at rest, so that when it did finally expand, the far end twisted on edge and catapulted forward. Carrying everything in its path with it, it pile-drove out the door and into the path of a passing Citröen.

The man in the Citröen was an American critic of small reputation who had not been invited, but who knew someone who had. It wouldn't be the first show this tall man with a nose like an ax-blade had crashed.

He'd had trouble renting a car at the airport, received wrong directions from several people, and now sped along convinced he was on the wrong road. He was even considering stopping at the long shed to ask directions, when an orange-drink stand hurtled out on the road in front of him. The last thing he saw was the figure behind the counter, a rosy-cheeked coquette, painted in the manner of . . .

Gainsborough? he wondered, and joined that painter in the past tense.

Three great tremors passed through the length of the fresco,

180

then it sighed and settled back, exhaling clouds of paint flakes and plaster dust. Only a few scraps of the original surface remained.

Their clothes were ruined, but the critics were able to take satisfaction from seeing 'A.B.' wiped out. They filed out and shared taxis back to town.

'It *was* beautiful,' one murmured. 'Like the mind of man, freed from all history.'

'Of course, of course. But unsuitable, you know.'

The Citröen had started a fire. Only the American gentleman with the gold cane stayed behind to help Ank fight it. Their efforts proved useless; the entire shed burned and collapsed, and the water they flung only served to finish the fresco's destruction.

'I was quitting anyway,' Ank said. 'Thought I'd get a job in commercial art, settle down . . .'

'Perhaps I can help you. May I offer you, say, ten thousand dollars for that peculiar tape you spoke of?'

'Ten thousand?'

The old man wrote a check and handed it to him. 'Okay?'

When he was alone, Ank took another look at the check.

'Mac Hines? Mac Hines?' He slapped himself on the forehead. 'O Jesus, that's just great. *Machines.*' Thinking of other famous check authors—I. B. Foxy, U. R. Stung, D. S. Windell, I. P. Freely—he tore up the obviously worthless check.

TWENTY

Grace before mess is read over the p.a. system while each cadet stands behind his chair in a full brace, gazing steadily at a spot one foot above the head of the cadet opposite. After grace, the cadet is allowed to seat himself in the prescribed manner: Draw back the chair, using both hands, to a minimum distance of eleven inches, step smartly to the left side of the chair and sit down quickly and quietly. Both feet are on the floor, the left hand shakes out the napkin with a distinct 'pop' and arranges it across the knees and thereafter remains in the lap except when cutting meat.

The cadet observes strict silence during the meal and occupies no more than the front $\frac{1}{3}$ of his seat. He is to look neither to left nor right nor directly at the cadet opposite nor directly at his plate. He pays particular attention to the reading of military inspirational literature during the meal, and if a first-year cadet he will be able to repeat all essential points of the reading at the request of any officer.

Food is passed from the head of the table; the ranking cadet officer at the head will be served first. Food will not be requested, but passed along briskly or eaten. When the cadet observes *by ear* that the ranking officer has begun eating, he may and must follow suit.

When cutting meat the left hand takes the fork, the right takes the knife. As soon as a bite of meat is cut (no less than $\frac{1}{4}''$ or more than $\frac{1}{2}''$ square) the right hand lays the knife on the

182

plate at a 45° angle, cutting edge facing outwards and one inch from the edge of the plate. Right hand then takes the fork and left returns immediately to the lap. Demerits will be given for eating bread, not eating, soiled napkin.

*

Putting it off any longer would just be cowardice. Spot's decision had been made a long time ago: before he had ever heard the story of Samson, before the televised transfiguration and death of Billy Koch: now it was just putting one foot in front of the other and walking towards his goal.

He waited until after the presumed last bed check (they were too numerous and irregular ever to be sure), collected his money, his comics and a change of underwear (in case he got into an accident on his way to commit suicide), and slipped out. Down the hall, past the cadet officer sleeping by the emergency door, over the spiked iron fence and into town. He caught the midnight bus for Minneapolis.

He would see Mom first, and explain to her why he was doing it. (1) She would undoubtedly try and talk him out of it, but he would be strong. There were some things, as Col Fouts was always saying, that a man had to do. And Samson had killed himself. And Christ. (2) She would just refuse to let him do it. In that case, he would kill himself on the spot, maybe by a voluntary emission of his soul (John Donne said it could be done). (3) She would understand and give him the money to get to Washington and do it properly.

He arrived before dawn, saliva running down his neck from sleeping on the bus. The key was in the mailbox. He found the house empty, disused, unfriendly, and after looking all over for Mom, went to sleep on the big bed—on top of the American flag.

*

At ten the next morning he was downtown with his little overseas bag, now only partly in uniform. As he stopped to ask a stranger where the National Arsenamid Corporation was ('the television part') a familiar car flashed by.

It was Fouts. *He recognized Spot.*

*

183

As soon as Fouts saw the kid talking to what could only be a plainclothesman, he knew it was finished.

'O Jesus O Jesus O Jesus O.'

He ran three red lights getting across town to Phenolphthalein Drive. 'Oh, yes sir,' the kid would be saying by now. 'Yes, I saw the Colonel *in women's clothes.*' And that was that.

The flight to New York, that was his only chance. Slip in among all the others, a few chameleon changes in and out of drag, into the melting pot . . . maybe get a studio and hide out as one of them beatnik painter types . . . that was the life . . .

*

There were three signs above Feinwelt's desk at Transvestites Anonymous:

BREAK THE HABIT HABIT!
SUIT YOURSELF!
CHANGE INTO WHAT YOU CANNOT ENDURE!

He sat beneath them like a hostile god, his rippled, ripe old face betraying no sign of forgiveness for the returned prodigal. Fouts laid the pile of nun's clothes on the desk.

'I guess you expect me to say "Let's be friends", eh Foutsy? Not a chance. I know you're not sorry for what you did (not only to me but to the organization). You just heard about the big New York convention so you came crawling back, hoping I'd ask you to come along. Isn't that it?'

'I guess so.' Fouts twisted his overseas cap.

'You know I could have you for assault, indecency, theft, impersonation . . .' A long-toothed smile.

'I know, Mother Feinwelt. But I'm in a lot worse trouble right now. I wish the flight was leaving today, instead of next Friday.'

Feinwelt looked at him closely. Then he seemed to have a change of heart. 'All right.' He sighed. 'You can go. The flight leaves Friday at ten p.m. We'll all meet here at six p.m., bus out to the airport and check in at seven-thirty. Got that?'

'Thanks, Mother. You're a pal and I won't forget this.' Fouts almost skipped out to his car. As he drove away, he noticed a new, cheap-model car parked across the road, in the shade of a willow. The old couple in it seemed to be necking.

184

Hadn't he seen them here before?

Just now there were plenty of other things to worry about. Army Security might close in anytime, he had to have a cover story. His sister was visiting him (phone her and set it up) and asked him to help her fix a hem. He'd tried on the dress and at that moment Cadet Shairp had come to the door. Rose was about his size, so any clothes lying around the place could be explained . . . and when that kid got back to school, there'd be some really beautiful punishment waiting for him . . .

By the time Fouts reached the school he felt so good that he allowed himself to break his diet, and gorge an Almond Joy.

*

Spot ran. The streets and alleys flashed by, broken scenes and interrupted faces: a man tying his shoelace, a woman paying a taxi, sleep-walking shoppers, a window-cleaner.

He quit when his side hurt too much, but for the rest of the day he would feel Fouts's eyes on him, the fat hand clamping down on his shoulder: 'Well, my boy, have we had enough running away and playing with ourselves?'

*

'What a cuh-yute lit-tle uniform! What can I do for you, lover?'

'Please, Miss, I'm looking for my mother. She works here.'

'Well what a lucky old mother to have such a cute little sojur like you for a son! What's her name, lover-sojur?'

'Marge Shairp.'

As she looked through her files, the receptionist kept embarrassing Spot with winks and puckering gestures. He felt like telling her about his suicide plan (there being some things a man had to do), but shyness shut him up.

'Not listed here, lover-lover. That don't mean anything, though. Tell you what. You wait right here and I'll find out which floor she works on. Okay? I'll be right back.'

She disappeared down the dim distance of a corridor, though the sound of her heels echoed back long after she was out of sight. Spot decided she was about the sexiest, most sophisticated woman he'd ever met.

But any second Fouts would come swinging in through the

185

revolving door and grab him. Spot looked over the stuff on the desk: Lists of numbers, offices and phones. Bound folders (no time to open them), an artificial flower and a tiny notebook full of florid handwriting. The capitals were all curlicues and extra loops, and the dots over the i's were little circles.

'*Daisy James* by Henry Miller . . .'

Nothing there. He went back to the lists. Studio A and Studio B were both on the fifth floor. That would probably be it.

With the feeling that Fouts was right behind him, he fled up the dim STAFF ONLY stairway.

It was really dark in Studio A, dark and churchy. There was even a bluish vigil light that turned out to be, when he got closer, a pilot light on an ordinary stove. Instead of arches and columns, there were huge tall pieces of kitchen everywhere, and each piece was complete as a chapel, with sink, stove, table, window and landscape painted just behind the glass. The water worked and the stove lighted. He thought of the dark, dusty kitchen at home, the refrigerator full of stale secrets . . . he knelt at a formica table, rested his forehead against the chrome edge, and asked God to help him find his mother.

Something in the darkest corner clicked, hummed, stopped. Spot made his way over to it, stepping over a few blacksnake cables on the concrete floor.

It was an enormous new deep-freeze, bigger than a coffin. It took him a minute or two to work out the complicated catch and raise the lid. A light came on, and he looked in.

*

'The fast trains retarded kids,' said Wise Bream agreeably. He spoke as always ambiguously and apropos of nothing. Three Dollars and Twenty Cents settled into the seat beside him, chuckling.

'You really had 'em fooled, you clever bastard. Even me. I thought for awhile you might be a god or something.'

The conductor came past, calling for tickets. He coughed, seeing the handcuffs. Naturally he asked the white man if the Indian were his prisoner.

'No, as it so happens,' Three said. 'As it so happens, this man is an escaped loony. I'm taking him back to his nuthatch in Washington.'

186

'Say, I don't think . . .'

'He's not dangerous, don't let it worry you. Never harmed a fly, did you, General Custer? That's who he thinks he is, General Custer.'

'The crossing kids train,' said Wise, grinning hideously. The conductor hurried on.

'What a messed-up face,' he thought, locking himself in the next car. 'What a mean son of a bitch he must be. Big, too.'

The train jolted into motion, and so did the rest of the Utopi, on the platform. They began to wave, and their god smiled and waved back.

'I'm worried.' Seldom From frowned at the two grinning faces in the window. 'I wish we could have sent our god along to Washington with anybody but Three-Twenty.'

Fake Sky clapped him on the shoulder. 'Don't be an old man about this, Seld. Who else knows the ins and outs of politics well enough to go along? Besides, it's good to have Three-Twenty out of the way for awhile. Always criticizing!'

'I know, I know, but somehow I never can shake the feeling that Three is a bad injun. He's never been off the reservation before, don't forget, and he's got a lot of money in his jeans.'

'We've been through all this as many times as the Moon has children, Seld: We need a strong lobby in Washington to get some changes made back here. Why should we live on Second World War C-rations the Army admits are unpalatable? Why shouldn't we have mineral rights on our own reservation, instead of the Lion Oil Company? Why can't we get our tractor fixed? It stands to reason to send in our best men.'

'That's right, Seld.' Someone Else spat off the platform. The wind whirled the lacy gobbet clear across the tracks. 'Remember, Three-Twenty's no moth when it comes to brains.'

'So he says himself.'

On the train Three Dollars and Twenty Cents laughed again. 'Listen, old God. You ought to see what I've got planned for us when we get to Washington. I'm going to show you off on street corners: Wise Bream, the Indian Oracle. I'll make enough to get me a Brooks Brothers' suit. Then we'll be where the action is! We'll be on easy street, in the land of milk and honey, the gravy train, wow, under the money tree!'

187

TWENTY-ONE

Thursday night, Wes Davis's White Shirt party held a mammoth torchlight parade in Washington, a preliminary to their party convention. Chanting that they were neither red nor black nor yellow, ten thousand White Shirts bore fire towards the Capitol. Wes rode in an armored car in front. Behind was another, containing an enormous petition which, it was said, had a million signatures.

The petition asked for the abolition of Negroes.

A series of dramatic floats worked variations on the theme, 'A Final Solution to the Negro Problem'. A slave ship marked BOUND FOR AFRICA held its cargo of men in blackface grimacing through portholes, while above decks the jolly crew of smiling bikini-blondes prettily plied sextant, wheel and telescope.

The FINAL SOLUTION MACHINE was likewise 'manned'. This was a large, silvery box with rotating cogs at the sides. Two bikini-blondes cranked it. Al Jolsons were herded in at one end and canned goods came out at the other.

Another float suggested torments awaiting Negroes in the next world. It was a great furnace with many doors that now and then swung shakily open on red glowing scenes; here the b–b's were equipped with horns and pitchforks, and twirled their tails suggestively as they stoked the crepe-paper fires.

Another depicted the 'Four L's' of the Wes Davis code: 'Label 'em, Loath 'em, Larrup 'em and Lynch 'em,' in four tableaux (more b–b's, more dismayed minstrels) while on the

188

sides of the float the four L's were arranged in a clever design that reminded some onlookers of a kind of wheel radiating four feet.

Many a papier-mâché lamppost twined with paper flowers held its black effigy surrounded by still more b–b's, but the poor girls on one float, whose lamppost had broken down, smiled through tears. The crowd gave them a big hand, brave little troupers that they were.

Then came a giant replica of Wes himself, twenty feet tall and straddling a white stallion nearly fifteen feet tall. He and the horse were formed entirely of lilies; the crowd was still complaining about the smell when the vanguard of the White Shirts marched by.

They sang a bouncy, drum-and-bugle version of the National Anthem, with a few words changed here and there. As it came out, what F. Scott Key was watching o'er the ramparts was not the flag but the gallantly streaming smoke from a Wes Davis factory for turning Negroes into scouring products.

The marching was superb, a precise goose-step, and the banners and torches inspired awe. But something was wrong with the singing. Partly this was due to many of the White Shirts relapsing into their childhood versions of the anthem. Yet thousands of bystanders later swore they heard a third version:

> Ofay can you pee
> Through the dong's surly blight
> What you probably inhaled
> At the toilet's last cleaning?

It was senseless to some, filthy to most, and disgusting to all White Shirt sympathizers in the crowd, listing as it did a few likely perversions of the WASP element. A great many potential friends were lost to the White Shirt cause that night by the simple substitution of *chancre* for *banner*. There might be a black conspiracy, but this was going too far . . . and what was the point of it all?

The point of it all was that over eight thousand of the White Shirts were not bona fide members at all. Over four thousand were not even white. A breakdown by singer and song might have looked like this:

189

SINGER	SONG	NUMBER
White Shirts	Wes Davis Hymn	1,956
FBI agents	National Anthem	2,488
CIA agents	National Anthem	960
Maryland Crime Prevention Bureau	National Anthem	34
Delaware Crime Prevention Bureau	National Anthem	20
Virginia CPB	National Anthem	33
City detectives	National Anthem	17
Federal marshals	National Anthem	1,219
Black Buddhists	Third version	802
Black Nationalists	Third version	1,725
Brothers of the Black Claw	Third version	the rest.

A few informed news sources suspected there might be trouble coming. A news analyst wondered why the White Shirts had chosen Washington DC for their convention—hardly good taste. Other newsmen ignored the whole thing as much as possible, and concentrated on other news, of the 'human' interest variety: The President's cold, the appearance of cherry blossoms, a transvestite convention in New York, a talking bear at the zoo.

The White Shirts left their huge scroll on the Capitol steps, to be delivered next morning. It demanded, among other things, the immediate accession of the President in favor of Wes Davis. The Senate subcommittee who later examined it would find among its million signers surprisingly few handwriting styles. Moreover, sections of it looked copied from telephone books, death rolls, *Who's Who*, the litany of the saints, the Declaration of Independence and even a catalogue of Madame Tussaud's waxworks in London. Senator Vuje would have a hard time explaining away the signatures of St Christopher, John Hancock, Albert Einstein, Henry Ford and Dr Crippen.

*

The following afternoon, Fouts arrived at Transvestites Anonymous with his gear and a supply of candy bars. The old couple were still necking out front when he unlocked the

190

door and let himself in. Did they come here every day, or what? (Something about them gave him an uneasy feeling—later.)

The place was deserted. Dust covers on the office typewriters, chairs turned up on tables in the coffee room, bulletin board cleared off, nothing in any locker but his—no sign of humanity but a broken earring pendant in the hallway.

He sat down at Feinwelt's desk to think. A raid? No, too tidy. Today was Saturday? His calendar watch assured him it was Friday. Maybe he was too early? But where was everyone's luggage, then? Maybe they send it on ahead?

He picked up the phone to dial Feinwelt's downtown office. It made a guy jittery, sitting around here all alone, what with Army Security probably watching his every . . .

To Fouts's trained ear, even over the dial tone, came the unmistakable ping of a direct wire tap. He hung up at once, feeling the uniform tighten over his chest and crotch.

Bad news. They were this far already, tapping the phone at the one place he'd always felt safe. So now what? Sit here and let them close in? 'Just tell us in your own words, Colonel—how long have you been a fucking fruit?' No, better to die than . . . better to wait.

There was always the payphone on the corner. He peered cautiously out the venetian blinds. The old woman was alone in the car now . . .

But she was training a pair of binoculars on him!

'Don't think of it as drag,' he said to himself, fumbling in his locker. 'Think of it as a *disguise*.'

*

'Get down off the pole quick, Grover! Someone's coming out!'

Grover jumped down, pulled off his headset and scrambled into the car. An odd figure in a white hoopskirt came floating out of the building and across the lawn to the phone booth.

'Something funny about that woman . . .' Grover mused.

'You noticed it too? That's no woman, Grover. It's a man!'

'Nawww, really?'

'I'll stake my new glasses on it. It's the same man who went in. The Army officer. Just look how he waddles!'

'Perty new at disguises, I guess. And yet he's smart enough to use an outside line, so we can't tap it. He looks to be a bad one, Amy. And to think, he's in the Yuhnited Sates Army!'

'He's the same officer we saw earlier this week, Grover. It's a relief to know they haven't penetrated the army any deeper than that.'

'I think we got 'em on the run, now. They're resorting to disguises, so they must be worried.'

'Shall we tell the FBI now, Grover?'

'I—just a sec. He's *writing something* on the wall of that phone booth, Amy. I want to get a look at that.'

*

Using a coin, Fouts scratched his initial in the aluminum wall, just below a sign: 'Wouldn't some loved one love to hear from *you* right now?' Feinwelt's office phone rang for the seventy-fourth time.

'You son of a bitch, where are you?' He hung up. There was nothing to do but go back and wait, under the needling stare of the 'old folks'.

He went back, walking daintily, not daring to look up and see those binoculars. In the rec room, he stretched out on a sofa, switched on the TV and went to sleep. It would be all right when Feinwelt and the boys got here . . . it had to be all right . . . the news commentator was rattling on . . . trouble in Washington . . .

*

The mark was like this:

人

'*Pi?* Amy, this is it! Either that guy we just saw was none other than the ringleader, Pé himself, or else he was talking to Pé on the telephone! Back to the car, Amy. Just had another idea. Did we bring my deciphering books? Good.'

Amy kept close watch on the building all through the afternoon while Grover worked at cracking the code. Without food or bladder relief he continued after dark, working by the map light. Just after sunset, he nudged her.

192

'Eureka, Amy,' he whispered. 'You wouldn't believe the length them cummunisks will go to. Looky here. The secret of their code is the number *pi* itself!

'You know how I told you it stood for wheels within wheels —well, it means a lot more than that. *Pi* is the key to the *whole cumminisk conspiracy*!'

He handed her a sheet of paper on which he'd written out the first thirty places of *pi*. Underneath was his translation:

1415	9265	358	979	323	846	264338	3280
PIPE	NODE	SEA	NUN	SOS	AID	ODISSA	SOAR

'First I thought it was a very ordinary message,' he said. 'Whatever the rest meant, a ship called the *Sea Nun* was piping nodes of SOS for aid, probably somewhere near the Russky city of Odissa, on the Black Sea.

'Then I decided the words themselves were code. PIPE = BRIAR = BUSH = H-SUB. NODE = NO 'D' = ON 'D'. SEA NUN = C. NUN = SISTER = RESIST. SOS = MAYDAY = MAY FIRST (The big Russky holiday). AID is obvious. ODISSA, that I left alone because it's on the Black Sea, and *Sea Nun* confirms it. The last word was the toughest. SOAR could be ROSA. Together with the first word it could mean SUB ROSA or SECRET, but that wasn't enough. It also seemed to mean flying. But when I thought about *sub* (submarine) *rosa* (red) and secrets, I realised it must mean rockets fired from H-powered subs, rockets of the Poseidon type.'

He held out the newly-constructed message.

H-SUB ON D.C. (But direct current or the capital?)
RESIST MAY FIRST.
AID ODISSA RED SUB ROCKET.

'So far, so good. Then I took a look at this: the cipher I had used.'

$$1 = P \qquad 6 = D$$
$$2 = O \qquad 7 = U$$
$$3 = S \qquad 8 = A$$
$$4 = I \qquad 9 = N$$
$$5 = E \qquad 0 = R$$

'*Posieduan R*. Probably a Russky variation of Posiedon, with R for rocket. Now I was getting someplace. But I still

193

wasn't sure about the D.C. part. I began by retranslating the first five letters, P.O.S.I.E., like this:

'In the Roman, or "perfect" alphabet, there is no J, so P is the 11th letter from the end and L is the 11th from the beginning. P is a reflection of L, a "new el". That gave me the first word, NEWEL.

'O is zero, nothing, the perfect void. Nothing can come from nothing, so I left it alone, as a word.

'S being the third letter of our word, I naturally looked to see what words can be formed from S plus any two letters following it in the alphabet. The only three in order that make a word are STY. If you write STY like this, it becomes a rebus.'

He wrote:

$$S + Y$$

'That is, "S + wine" or swine (contained in sty). So the third word was PIG.

'I is a speck, the first blemish on the void, the simplest pencil mark or spot. I decided these "Frenchmen" would use the French word for spot, TACHE.

'E is the third of the diatonic C-major scale's tones. It is also the fifth letter. Where there is a third and a fifth, there must be a fourth, and it is of course the position of E in the word TONES itself. So our fifth word is TONS.'

He excused himself from the car and went behind the willow tree for a moment. When he returned, he showed her this new 'extrapolated' message and its reversal:

NEWEL O PIG TACHE TONS
SNOT EH CAT GI POLE WEN

'I wrote this,' he said wearily, 'in the Pyramid form.' Another sheet.

194

'Removing the shape of the letter *pi* gives:

```
W A S H I
  N   G
  T   O   N
```

'Since Pé is *pi*,' he concluded, 'even now our diameters erode! Spelling enters acrostic nuances under number systems. Our side already inserts documents of deception in Secret Service agents' statements: "O + pen": a rebus.'

Something peculiar in his tired smile led Amy to suspect that this little speech was itself an acrostic. Grover was having a little joke with her, the magnificent man!

'If loud offers veer ever . . .' she began, but he shushed her.

'Listen, we can't get the FBI just yet. If we use the phone on the corner, Pé will see us. If we go to fetch them, he'll give us the slip. For now, I guess we'll just have to pin him down and hope for the best.'

'But couldn't I stay here and watch him while you went to the FBI?'

He laid a hand on her arm. She felt dizzy. 'I wouldn't want to chance it, Amy. You're too precious.'

*

Flight 974 from Minneapolis to New York was a peculiar assortment of citizens. At least twenty looked to the stewardess like women dressed up in men's clothes—unwillingly, or so it seemed, for they spent the first hour after takeoff fiddling with belts and loosening ties, wiggling their shoulders with discomfort. They were going to some kind of convention, and they kept slapping each other on the back and kidding about 'observing the conventions' when they got there. Their passports said Male, and Marilyn wondered if they might not just be those 'queer' sorts of persons she'd heard so much about.

Then there was that man in the awful wrinkled dirty dinner jacket who kept asking her all kinds of technical questions about the plane—how much fuel it carried, how many miles to the gallon and so on—and finally there were two of the smallest nuns she had ever seen, and a strange veiled woman in black, apparently pregnant.

The two little nuns, midgets almost, sat in back, reading their miniature breviaries and fingering tiny rosaries—and looking apprehensive. Marilyn walked slowly back past all the men and asked if the sisters were feeling comfortable.

'Oh yes, thank you,' they piped. The younger one added, 'My, it certainly is a long ways down.'

'Yes, we're at thirty thousand feet now—about six miles.'

'As much as that!'

'Don't worry, there's nothing to be afraid of.'

'I was a little frightened after the plane took off,' the old one admitted. 'So fast! And all the people down on the ground looked like little dolls!'

They certainly didn't seem sensitive about their size, so Marilyn squatted by the seat and asked them the question she'd been turning over in her mind ever since takeoff.

'Are you by any chance an Irish order, sisters?'

'Oh my, no!' The older one chuckled, wrinkling her little face like a fist. 'We're Little Sisters of the Amish.'

'I used to work for a religious organization myself,' said Marilyn. 'The Billy Koch Crusade.'

'A very good organization, and a very good man. I'm sure Mr Koch did a great deal of good work before his accident. Sister Mary Jane here just got back from one of our missions among the pygmies. I'm Sister Maia. All our missionary work is with the little folk.'

'I'm Marilyn Temblor. If there's anything you need, sisters . . .'

Seeing the unkempt man was signaling her frantically, she excused herself and went forward.

'Ah, how much fuel is left now, please?'

'Don't you worry, sir. There's plenty of fuel to get us to New York.'

'Ah? Ahm.' He sat back and looked more worried than before.

Next she stopped to see how the woman in the veil was getting along.

'I hope you're not expecting your baby real soon,' she blurted out, and laughed nervously.

'I'll let you know,' murmured the woman.

'Would you like any milk or anything?'

196

The muffled voice gave some reply that sounded like 'Ashes, ashes!'

'Where's Fouts?' asked one of the women-men.

'Now you know, that's not a very interesting question,' replied the one who kept turning around to give the dwarf nuns dirty looks.

'Don't listen to Mother Feinwelt. He's all worked up because them midgets get to dress in nun's habits and he can't.'

'Shut up, Gertrude. As a matter of fact, I told Fouts Friday at six instead of Friday at five. A little schadenfreudian slip there. Anyway, it'll teach him a lesson.'

Marilyn went forward to fix the cocktails. A moment later there was a timid knock at the door of the stewardess compartment.

'How far are we from Florida?' asked the man in the wrinkled dinner jacket. His breath stank of months of steady drinking, his fly was open and his cummerbund turned around sidewise.

'I don't really know, sir. Shall I ask the pilot?'

He showed tiny teeth and puffy pink gums in a smile. 'Oh no, that won't be necessary. You see, I have here...' He groped in his oversize jacket pocket for a moment, 'I have here this gun. So I'll talk to the pilot myself, if you don't mind. I want him to fly towards Florida—more specifically, towards *Cuba*.'

At that second, the woman in the veil let our a long scream and slid to the floor. Sister Mary Jane was there even before Marilyn. 'Quickly!' she said. 'Boil some water!'

197

TWENTY-TWO

The riot began with an *incident* of a familiar type. A group of Negroes watching the White Shirt torchlight parade refused to 'move on' at a policeman's order. The cop, a rookie named Joe Haarman, drew his gun and perhaps repeated the order. Among the group was a girl eleven years old . . .

If anyone expected an apology or promise of investigation by the police, they didn't know Chief Wiggin. He went on TV that evening to say:

'Haarman was just doing his job. We're going to back him up all the way. You can't go around asking every hoodlum his *age* before you shoot. A cop has to think fast in a situation like that. And don't forget, men like Haarman are out there every night, risking their lives to protect you and yours.'

UP YOU AND YOURS, WIG signs appeared instantly in many windows all over the Negro district. Negro citizens' groups started the long, tedious process of making official protests and trying to get the chief to say maybe Haarman had after all been hasty. Others preferred direct methods.

To stave off trouble, riot cops began unwarranted slum-to-slum searches for hidden caches of weapons.

*

The Justice Department is worried. Five hundred Federal marshals are called on duty and issued with gas masks, Mace,

198

riot guns, side-arms and clubs. The Attorney General addresses them:

'I want to make this clear—your mission is not to aggravate violence, but to quell it. Should any disturbances break out, they are to be handled as peacefully and diplomatically as possible. I don't want to see a lot of pictures in the papers tomorrow of kids with bleeding heads, pregnant women being dragged by the feet, and so on. Is that clear?'

'Yeah, we got it, sir. *No pictures.*' Winks. Smack of weighted club on palm. 'You leave everything to us, sir.'

*

Cardinal James Homer, whom the papers describe as 'flinty', 'an outspoken conservative', is giving a sermon at the dedication of a new Knights of Columbus chapel, a slick new building in the midst of the ghetto.

'Dangerous radicals and shiftless degenerates need to be taught a lesson. The trouble with *most* of our lawmen is they just don't shoot to kill!'

The doors burst open and several hundred Black Nationalists, White Shirts, cops and snarling dogs all swarm in and chase each other around the sanctuary. Marshals close in outside, smash out the new stained-glass windows of SS. Christopher and Filomena and lob in teargas.

'O Jesus!' says one cop, seeing where he is. 'O Jesus! The Mafia ain't gonna like this . . .'

*

One story spreads that Haarman is a Catholic, another that he is a Jew. White Shirts at the convention hall hear that a black cop killed a little white girl who refused to submit to him. Catholics hear that Masons have murdered the cardinal.

*

A dozen night-rider Klansmen in full hooded regalia are packed into a hotted-up old Merc tearing down the Southwest Freeway on their way to the White Shirt rally.

'How many notches you got on that old shotgun, Billy Bee?'

'Well, I don't rightly recolleck . . . lessee . . . this one don't count, cause after we hanged and burned and shot the son

199

bitch, he up and ran off . . . what's that burnin' yonder?'

'Git off my eyehole so's I can see. Hot damn! Looks like the convention hall itself!'

*

A clever White Shirt has set their own convention hall on fire to guarantee the sympathy of many potential voters (the convention, and choosing a candidate, are mere formalities anyway). The White Shirts come charging out, armed with guns, tire irons, homemade clubs prepared weeks in advance for this emergency. In the street their numbers are swelled by Klansmen and Nazis; they run, yelling and screaming for a hundred feet before they encounter a shoeshine boy.

But as they stop to attack him they realize they've been decoyed: black militants and street gangs close in from both ends of the street, armed with garbage-can lids, guns, zip-guns, broken bottles and chains.

The first police on the scene take one look and barricade both ends of the street to let them fight it out. But a quick head count shows more black than white; they put in a call for the riot squad.

The riot squad moves in with teargas, clubs and Alsatians, chopping their way for no particular reason to the center of the mob, which closes right in behind them. They're rescued an hour later and withdraw with heavy casualties, including a gassed dog and a cop with canine throat slashes.

*

Enzio ('The Head') Gagliardi comes out of a Negro club where he's just been collecting an insurance premium (twice the club's rent) to find his Cadillac's been worked over. His ice-blue eyes move from detail to detail: All tinted glass smashed, the radio gone, the hood spray-painted with slogans and plastered with posters of Chairman Fat Tsing: 'LONG LIVE THE PEOPLE'S REPUBLIC. LONG LIVE CHAIRMAN FAT,' he spells out.

'Republicans, eh? So Fats Funicolo wants to play the Old Rules, does he? I guess I'm not too old to handle a heater. Get some of the boys together. Call Cleveland, Chi, L.A., Vegas . . .'

'But, boss, we and Fats are all brothers in Cosa Altra.'

200

'Fuck that. Anybody breaks the pretty dual aerials off my little honey here ain't nobody's brother! Call a war council.'

*

A vigilante mob called the Big Stick Men, all wearing tricorner hats and carrying muskets, set up an ambush for any un-American elements that might wander by. They manage to pick off a black postman and a paper boy who might be of foreign extraction.

Then the Islamic Brotherhood of the Black Claw outflanks and roars down on them, throwing bricks and Molotov cocktails, and assisted by the machete-swinging Bolivian Urban Guerilla Brigade.

'Hold your fire!' shouts the Big Stick commander, raising his saber. 'Don't fire till you see the whites of their eyes.'

'But Commander, they're all wearing dark glasses!'

The muzzle-loaders won't fire anyway, and in half an hour the street is empty but for broken glass, blood slicks, and a tricorner hat perched on a lamppost.

*

The Black Buddhists decide to sit down in protest on Pennsylvania Avenue. The Klan move in at once with blacksnake whips and hobnail boots. The cops sit by until they've had their fun, then tell them to keep back on the sidewalk.

'I don't like this,' says one cop, spraying Mace liberally over some dying buddhists. 'I mean, they didn't leave a hell of a lot for us, did they?'

'Wait till we get them back to the station house,' his partner says. 'Plenty of life in there yet. What I like to do is hamstring two of them and make them race on all fours down the hall, goosing them up with cattle prods. The winner gets maybe a drink of water, and the loser gets his prick cut off—you know, "accidently he stood too close to the paper guillotine"... I know cops that won't use nothing else for a sap, just one of them filled with buckshot...'

The Klan are jealous. 'We're leaving now,' their leader calls. 'But we'll be back—with a steamroller.'

*

201

The original 'sides' are blurring already. Among the city cops are Catholics, Jews, Negroes and sympathizers with the Klan; this is true also of the FBI, the Federal marshals and the militias of three states who are now getting into the act. Some Catholics are White Shirts; some Jews are anarchists; some Catholics and Jews own Negro tenements; the landlord of a poor white slum contributes heavily to the American Nazi Party. All of the organizations involved, from Big Stick and the Klan to Students for Chairman Fat, include spies from the FBI, CIA, city police and cops from three states, as well as spies from other groups. Splits and coalitions are common and frequent. It's getting harder to decide who 'they' are.

No one is necessarily what he seems, and no one is 'just' an anarchist, Negro or cop. *Ad hoc* committees are formed almost spontaneously, often without names; everyone is able, finding himself performing any atrocity, to believe it is not the *real* him doing this—and there are enough secret sympathies to justify anything.

A strategist at the Pentagon tries to work it all out with the help of CIA reports.

He dictates a memo to the general staff: The main possible types of conflict are

> Racial
> Religious
> Ethnic
> Income level (relative prosperity)
> Relative authoritarianism
> Relative age
> Sexual preference (relative heterosexuality)

or some combination of any of these. No classification of these seems complete: an anti-Semite usually hates a Black Muslim who hates a black Jew who hates a homosexual Jew and a white Jew about equally, who hate each other, and who also both may hate a white Jewish cop who hates his superior who hates an anti-authoritarian young man who hates an authoritarian young man who hates and envies anyone wealthier than he.

'The city is an equation of x unknowns ... there may actually be more *sides* than *individuals*,' he concludes, 'and everyone is not just alone, but incomplete ...'

202

The general staff decide he means 'put the Marines in to guard the Arab embassies', which they do. The Arabs call up the State Department every five minutes thereafter, reporting Zionists sneaking around in camouflaged uniforms.

*

The Virginia state troopers arrive and wade into a suspicious-looking group of Negroes—city cops in plainclothes. These detectives are Maced out of action for the rest of the riot.

*

Arsonists begin setting fires in timed pairs to frustrate firemen; two or three fires are started at the same time, just over a hose-length apart.

The steps of one police station are smeared with excrement; one cop slips and falls, fracturing a rib. *Newstime* magazine singles out this incident ('a pointless and disgusting gesture') and features it prominently in their story the following week, 'WASHINGTON: THE RIOT CITY'. *Newstime*'s analysis is statistical ('Hurled were 7,420 broken bottles, 847 bricks . . .') and topographic ('Map shows damage area') as well as alliterative ('Discotheques and Discontent').

*

Delaware National Guardsmen arrive to protect the Lincoln Memorial (a quick informal survey has shown that the majority of rioters of all groups would like to mess it up). They are attacked first by HOMODRAFT, a ferocious band of homosexuals who want the draft laws changed to let them be soldiers. Federal marshals backing up the troops panic and let go with their riot guns, wounding more Guardsmen than queers. All Federal agencies are alerted to the possibility of 'queer backlash'.

*

Students for Chairman Fat run through all districts, chanting and pasting hero pictures over everything. Brothers of the Black Claw have settled down to rooftop sniping. A few

203

soldiers have deserted to join in looting. Five or six old-line Communists totter around, distributing leaflets and urging the workers to unite. The workers are hot-wiring trucks to carry away the stuff they've collected.

'To each according to his need . . .'

'GAT OUTA DA WAY YA OLD CREEP OR I'LL DRIVE TRU YA!'

*

Complications: Someone has looted a uniform shop catering to the police and armed forces. Before the riot is over dozens of pseudo-cops and fake Army officers swarm over the city, adding to the confusion.

A student anarchist group changes their name and prints a new manifesto once or twice an hour. With their mimeo machine in the back of a panel truck they tour the city, dropping white racist manifestos in the black areas, anti-Semitic handouts in Jewish neighborhoods, Nazi, Chairman Fat, black racist stuff where appropriate. Their little demos support all sides, with the object of panicking everyone else and thus preserving their own identity *by contrast.*

*

The 'queer backlash' news cheers up the cops, who knew down deep who the Enemy was all along.

At Union Station a group departing for New York to the Transvestites Anonymous convention are dragged (in drag) off the train by Federal marshals, gassed and clubbed. A White Shirts' contingent sees only men in gas masks belaboring women with clubs. It makes their Southern Comfort boil. In the ensuing battle no one notices the arrival of a Utopi Indian and his white prisoner . . .

On the Mall a few vice squad cops have put on women's clothes to bait muggers and rapists. An army of Maryland state cops closes in . . .

*

After their first battle, Wes Davis and twenty trusted lieutenants disappear; they hole up with plenty of provisions in the top floor of an expensive hotel.

204

'Aint as if we was *running out*,' Wes explains. 'Hell, we can watch it on television just as good.'

*

Six anti-memorialists who call themselves Burning World (motto: 'Today Now!') dress as Marine officers and pass through the lines guarding the Lincoln Memorial, where they plant a bomb. The blast kills them and a few of the Delaware Guard, and completely demolishes the tomb. Two blocks away, a Soviet official coming out of the State Department door is instantly lobotomized by a flying fragment of what proves to be Lincoln's mole.

Students for Chairman Fat march among the stunned and bleeding soldiers in triumph, pausing only to paste pictures of Fat on helmets of the fallen, or to cop a grenade.

The Klan are out on the Mall, raping a Negro vice-squad cop in drag . . . forty have been in already without noticing anything odd.

'Hey, the boas done blown up the Lincoln Memorial! EEEEEyahoooo!' They set up a wooden cross by the Reflecting Pool and ignite it.

It explodes. One of the Fat-ists has slipped a grenade in the kindling. A Goblin is killed and a Cyclops loses an eye.

*

Angry tourists mill around the ruins of Lincoln's tomb. They jump the prostrate Guardsmen, flailing away with thermos bottles, cameras and campstools. 'You son of a bitch, you could have kept it up until I got a picture of it!'

'Kick his nuts off, Gladys! Our whole trip's ruined!'

The man from Babel Tours rushes among them, trying to make peace. 'Girls, girls! Fellas, fellas! Let's be sensible, now. No use losing our tempers. Now let's all go over to the *Washington* Memorial . . . the big spire over *there*. And let's try to keep together this time.'

*

The Pentagon's MODULOG program is making things worse. Ideally the computer team would feed in data about concentrations of rioters (number, race, armament, deployment)

205

and the computer would automatically dispatch the right number and kind of troops to deal with it. But in practice the machine doesn't seem to be listening.

Troop, police and supply movements are getting snarled. Paratroops are dropped for no special reason in Chesapeake Bay. One Marine unit hits the beach in Baltimore; a CBW unit is reassigned over thirty times, each time to a different random location—they never even have time to unpack their assortment of sophisticated gases. Contradictory orders follow one another like machine-gun bullets; One tank command spends the whole riot ruining the lawn of the National Gallery as they roll around in circles . . .

There are jurisdictional disputes caused by MODULOG's erratic assignments: The Army and the Virginia National Guard claim the same turf . . . the MPs have to move in on both of them with gas-firing tanks to prevent an intra-service war.

*

A lone sniper has barricaded himself in the top of the Washington monument. The police call up with a bull-horn asking him to give give give himself give himself himself up himself up up up. He is variously identified as a Negro, a Chinese, Indian, Soviet ambassador, anarchist, etc.

*

The Klan catch six White Shirts still in blackface from the parade. As it happens, there are six lampposts right handy.

'Please! No!' Wait, you've got us wrong. We're white as you are!'

'Haw haw, this black son bitch gone try tell me he's white, Rufe, you heah that? Haw haw—Arrrgh!'

The Grand Goblin falls foward, a fire arrow quivering in his back. War whoops. A band of Iroquois descend from their lair on the high steel of a nearby construction site. In a minute, it's all over but the scalping. After the Indians leave, Negro children roll the living and the dead. The Iroquois have already taken the sheets, but there are a few credit cards . . . They pause to wave at a boy in uniform, riding in on a boxcar . . .

*

206

Bronze-chinned soldiers scour the city for pederasts. A boy scout is leading a blind man across the street, taking his hand. An armored car pauses to mow down the pair with heavy machine-gun fire, then moves on, broadcasting:

'Keep in your homes! There is nothing to worry about, the situation is under control!'

Inside, the atmosphere is stifling. The corporal shuts off the amplifier and asks, 'Lootenant, we got any more Pepsi?'

'Naw, wait'll we stop for gas. Not this station here, the next on the right. They give double green stamps.'

*

The incipient queer-fears of lawmen have by now been fully aroused. Twenty Klansmen are surrounded, Plunked and kicked to emasculinity. (*Plunk*: a new riot-control gas which paralyses the vicitim's limbs but leaves him fully conscious and capable of feeling intense pain. 'A cop's dream' says the *American Law Enforcement Bulletin*.) A carload of Daughters of the American Legion, out slumming, are arrested as drag queens and subjected to interesting humiliations.

'My good man, do you realize *who* I am?'

Nasty laugh. 'No I don't, tooty-frooty, but I'm sure gonna find out.' Tries to pull away her blue-rinsed hair, gives up when some of the scalp comes up. The cops take them back to the new detention center on the Mall, where they can 'put on a little show, like you done at the Fadeout Club.'

*

'There's one of 'em! Get the bastard!' Virginia state troopers pile out of their cars and chase Cardinal Homer across the lawn of his residence. Ten Knights of Columbus try to fight a rearguard action with blunt sabers; a few cops stop to slap the cuffs on them and haul them off as pimps.

The main body are almost within grabbing distance of his streaming red cloak when a platoon of Mafia gorillas step out from the bushes and lay down a withering crossfire: Thompson submachine-guns, captured army automatic rifles, magnum-style Italian assassination guns ...

207

'You okay, fadda? Anybody else gets smaht wit ya, you just tell Big Fats, and I'll lean on 'em a little.'

*

Frustrated pilots slew around in the sky, now and then popping a Skybolt at some fishing boat off the coast. . . . Each pilot's worried sick he might be queer and not know it. . . .

'Now let's see, what's that unidentified craft down there? Looks like a Russian trawler to me . . . so what if they've disguised it as the Presidential yacht . . . well I'm a happippily mumarried man, two great kikids . . . DIE, RUSSIAN SPY SHIP! . . . so what if there was that time in flight school, nobody knows about that . . .'

Zionist students picket the Arab embassies, as usual blaming these poor oil billionaires for everything. The Arabs cower inside, stoned to inertia. Their flowing robes, the way they reek of *kif*, makes the Marine Guards sick.

'For two cents I'd turn this machine-gun around the other way. I mean, here we are, guarding a buncha pansies . . .'

'I know how ya feel, kid. But we're pertecting our oil inneress—on the other hand, who'd know it was us?—Here's a nickle, kid. Have an orgy.'

They pick up their weapons and stroll inside, through the elaborate mosaic hallway. 'You take this end, I'll take that one. But fer Chrissakes, kid, don't shoot up the harem. Might come in handy later . . .'

*

The President's evacuation plan is readied. He is to take the underground passage to Blair House, then helicopter from the roof to the submarine *Scampi* waiting in the mouth of Delaware Bay.

*

Everybody has a plan for getting the nut down from the Washington monument. The cops want to rush up the stairs and just take him. The Marines, traditionalists ever, want to use mortars with white phosphorus or mustard gas. The Navy put out feelers about shelling it from a battleship offshore, but nobody's buying.

Up in the monument, the sniper picks off two more civil

208

servants, raising his score to 48. He has his own loudhailer: 'Listen to me, down there! You have all failed to make a distinction somewhere. Drop your weapons one and all, and come up here with your hands up! By the way, can anyone tell me why the Little Moron wore a condom when he went whaling?'

*

The Pentagon is defended by National Guardsmen from five states, Federal troops and Federal marshals equipped with the latest in chemical sprays, including Plunk, Mace and Mush (*Mush* sends the victim into an acute panic and at the same time causes behavior to become automatic and repetitive. He begins to run away and is usually found some ten or fifteen miles away, dead of heart failure).

Inside, specially-flown-in teams of experts are looking over the computer to find out what's wrong with it. A dozen men in suits with IBM shoulders stand around the big round table in the War Room going over schematics.

Brigadier General Garner, acting chief of staff, sticks his head in. 'About through with our table, gentlemen? The battle-board's under all your papers there, and we can't get a thing done without it.'

'We've hit a snag, General. George here was just saying it might be the step-up of the differentiable multiplex write-in analyzer, but the rest of us opt for improved multi-scan facilities and a new software package.'

'That so?' The general closes the door, feeling old. He stops a white-coated technician coming out of the computer room. 'You tell me, boy, in plain English. Can our brain be saved?'

'Couldn't tell you, sir. I just stopped by for coffee; I'm not in this department.'

'Not a computer man, son?'

'No sir. My job is feed birth pills to the pigeons, on the roof.'

*

The lobotomized Soviet official goes berserk in the supermarket, hauls out a huge Russian automatic and begins spraying the place with lead. The manager comes over to reason with him.

209

'Look, you can't act like that in here! You'll drive all my customers away! What the hell's wrong with you, anyway? Who's gonna pay for that display of canned peaches, 4 ¢ off this week?'

A dying shopper groans in delirium:

'And gimme a package of stainless steel razor bl . . .'

*

'He was afraid he might catch Moby Dick!' screams the bull-horn from the top of the Washington obelisk.

'We could do it easy,' says the Navy man. 'A couple shots to get the range, then POW!'

At that moment, Students for Chairman Fat solve all problems in dealing with him: they crash a stolen truckload of explosives into the base of the monument.

*

The Capitol is ringed with three cordons of battle-tested paratroopers and an outer wall of more expendable types. At first no one tries the bayonet wall. Then a large contingent of HOMODRAFT rush in, while American Nazis stand by ready to spit on either side. Anti-papists charge, waving contraceptive devices and screaming for the blood of Guy Fawkes. Down the Mall come a hundred Students for Chairman Fat, screaming Chinese syllables insanely and swinging their placards ('WHY DIE, G.I.?' 'FAT IS OUR BROTHER' and 'FOLLOW THE CROWDS TO FOOK HING CHINESE LAUNDRY'). From the rear of the Capitol come a horde of Black Nationalists in African costume, Black Claw of Islam brothers in leather jackets and shades, and the Iroquois. From the North come Klux, White Shirts, and the Organization for the Rights of Gentile, Anglo-Saxon Man, beefed up with a few hefty Daughters of the American Legion (in the front ranks for a spearhead attack). From the South come Zionists, anarchists, Knights of Columbus and Cosa Altra (the boys have been got together), young Communists of sixty and old of ninety, vigilantes, cops on strike, looting antique dealers after a bit of Americana, motorcyle hoods on bikes, the Peace Love Acid World Peace Society (who have no idea what they are here for) and a large auxiliary of aging pachucos in pink shirts and pegged pants (who are just waiting

210

for some wise soldier to bump their shoulders or call their mother a name).

The Nazis' eyes gleam; they work up their biggest gobs of spit. At the last possible second, when it looks as if everyone is going to impale themselves on bayonets, a team of lost helicopters comes over, spraying out a ton and a half of defoliants. The thick mist descends; everyone is too busy lying flat and fighting for breath to fight anyone else.

One brave soldier manages to stand his post, coughing and sputtering. As a final gesture he bayonets a figure charging toward him in the mist—it's Senator Vuje, who's been trying to get in (to use the Senate toilet) for hours.

The cherry blossoms are falling.

*

Looting and arson spread to all quarters of the city. Weary firemen have just put out a department store for the second time and are packing away their hoses and trophies when a flame-throwing tank comes by and gets it all going again.

'Aw, fuck this,' says one firefighter. 'I been to so many fires today already my boots hurt—all full of transistor radios and watches and stuff.'

*

'Our battle plan has several options,' General Garner explains to his staff. '1. Contain the riot without attempting a showdown, erect barriers, then slash and burn out the corruption. 2. Divide the city into sectors, then go in and clean it out a sector at a time. 3. Level unimportant sectors of the city with artillery and/or bombing, defoliate, then napalm the corruption. 4. Evacuate the President and key congressmen (the Hawk list), evacuate our boys, then *nuke* the joint! I favor number 4, as the way to expend least effort and men for maximum results.'

At that moment a flash message comes in: IT'S OVER.

Garner slugs the messenger and dials the Operations Room himself. 'What the hell do you mean, "it's over"?'

'That's right, General. All units report their sectors are pretty well under control. Just mopping up, sir.'

'And the rioters?'

'Looks like they just got tired of it and went home.'

211

TWENTY-THREE

Wes Davis sat up in bed.

'*A nigger plot!*'

'You all right, chief?' One of his lieutenants came towards him.

'*Stayawaystayaway!*'

'Sure, Wes. Anything you say.'

Another man stood up in the shadowy end of the room. 'It's only us, Wes. Skeeter and Travis.'

Wes held up a trembling hand. 'Don't come no closer! Turn on a light so's I can see you, boa.'

Skeeter turned on a light. It was dead quiet in the hotel room. The faint woodpecker sound of a machine-gun, twenty floors below, competed with Wes's cautious breathing—his two friends held theirs.

'Guess I had a bad dream. Is it—all over down there?'

'No sir. Looks bad, Wes.' Skeeter two-fingered his pack of Luckies up from his shirt pocket, flicked one into the air and caught it in his mouth. 'Looks like the nigras is taking over.'

'*Just say that again, mister, and I'll have your guts hanging on the Christmas tree.*' A chair scraped in the adjoining room. 'Who's in there?'

'Nobody, Wes. Just some of the boas. Oh yeah, and a couple Secret Service agents. They said they got to pertect you cause you're a presidental candidate. I guess they already evacuated the President.'

212

'Get them OUT! And bring everbody else in HERE.'
Wes stood up and gripped the bottom edge of his denim jacket, to steady himself. His knees didn't feel too good. When the group of White Shirts filed in, he looked hard at every face. 'Line 'em up over there.'
'FALL IN AT ATTENTION!'
'All right, men.' Wes began to pace, avoiding certain configurations in the carpet pattern. 'We know who's with us and who's agin *now*, don't we? Like the Klan. Look what they did to Merle and them boas. You know why? I'll tell you.
'*Because under them fancy hoods, the Ku Klux Klan is nothing but a bunch of full blood niggers!*'
'Sir?'
'I know it's hard to believe, but there's no other explanation. Besides, I got *proof.* Documentary evidence that the Klan numbers among its members no fewer than fifty coal-black leaders! I got their names right here!'
What he waved was the hotel menu, but since his men were all at attention, they couldn't gaze directly at it. He paced the entire pattern three times, then turned to face them again.
'I'll tell you something else I know. *I know there is a nigger in this very room, passing for one of us!*'
Everyone jumped.
'Is it me, Wes?' 'Who is it, Wes?' 'A real nigger?' ' 'Tain't me, is it, Wes?'
'SHUT UP AND GET BACK TO ATTENTION!'
Pete Willis, a sickly smile on his narrow head, stepped forward. 'Is it me, Wes?'
'Yep. It purely is, Pete. But I'm not letting anyone take *my* word for it. I'm going to show you all scientific proof!'
Wes strode over and grabbed a handful of Pete's thick blond curls. '*First,* kinky hair!'
'But Wes, I ain't . . .'
Without warning, Wes threw his hardest punch. The taller man staggered back, blinking. Blood spurted from his nose.
'*Second,* no bone in his nose!'
At a signal, someone laid a piece of pipe across the small of Pete's back. As he fell to his knees, his hands went out instinctively. Wes seized one and held it bent back, thumb in the palm to keep the fingers fanned. '*Third,* take a look at them

213

fingernails. *Purple fingernails are a scientific proof of black blood.'*

The men all looked, imagining purple in Pete's quite ordinary fingernails.

'Take this nigger and throw him out the window. I MEAN RIGHT NOW!'

They obeyed. Wes turned away and pretended to study a wall map. Not that he didn't want to watch it. It was just that he had a little smile to hide. The whole fingernail business had been a ruse, but with a purpose.

It stood to reason the niggers would have put more than one spy among his key officers. And only a fool could have not noticed how many men, as soon as he mentioned purple fingernails, *looked at their own hands*!

*

It was nearly dawn, and still no one stirred in the headquarters of Cumminism. But it was a cinch that Pé had to come out of there sometime.

*

It was a cinch they had to go away sometime. It was still the same car, the same people. That meant they were working alone. For the time being no one else knew they were working on the case. Whenever they left to get a meal, he'd be ready.

Fouts settled his crinolines about him, peeled an Almond Joy, and watched the Early Bird movie, *Blowup*.

*

At dawn, Grover noticed for the first time Amy's new glasses. Their pearly frames gave a softness to her sleeping face, and brightened her lovely eyes when she awoke.

Or maybe it wasn't the glasses at all. He leaned towards her, feeling the warmth of her leaning towards him . . . it wasn't hard, in this fresh light, to pretend they were kids again . . . in Dad's car . . .

*

His elbow brushed the radio button.

'. . . tional emergency. President Reagan has already been evacuated from the city. There is a strong possibility that if the

214

riot is not brought under control by noon, General Weimarauner will call for artillery and bombing.

'Now I'll turn you over to Bill Burgens, who I think is somewhere by the banks of the Potomac. Bill?'

'. . . noise down here is terrific, Dave . . . you hear is the . . . playing *Dixie*. The whole city seems to have gone mad, and even the Army doesn't seem to . . . from where I'm standing I can see the whole shopping district ablaze, that's about . . . miles away, so you can imagine . . . and here come two soldiers carrying a color TV set. I guess they confiscated it from looters, but it's hard to . . . and say, here's a lady whose entire family was killed by a grenade. Husband, brother, and . . . how many children was it, ma'am?'

'Yes.' A tiny, exhausted voice.

'How many was it? Four or five?'

'Four or five, what difference does the number . . .?'

. .'And how do you feel about this, ma'am? I'll bet you just feel terrible, don't you? Must be a great shock.'

Grover switched it off. 'We're too late, Amy. It's the end!' Tears ran down the tributaries under his eyes. Shaking his fist at the building, he screamed, 'You win, Russky! You win, JOE STALIN AND BENEDICT ARNOLD!'

'Grover, we still have What's In The Safe.'

He thought about it a moment, regaining his natural color. 'What a grand idee, Amy. They may get us in the end, but meanwhile we'll blow that traitor soldier and all his secret codes and radios to *aitch ee double toothpicks*!'

It was the first time he'd ever sworn or cursed in front of her, and Amy realised what a strain Grover must be under.

'But how can we go and get What's In The Safe?' she asked. 'Our quarry might fly.'

'Don't you worry,' he said. 'It isn't really in the safe at all, *it's right here in the car*! I moved it yesterday—had a feeling it might come in handy!'

And so saying he hugged her till she gasped, and grinned so hard she thought his dentures would explode in her face.

*

The two little sisters of the Amish conferred over their patient.

215

'I've seen a lot of labors,' said Sister Mary Jane firmly, 'and that woman isn't having a baby.'

'But how can you be sure? Maybe with big people it's different.'

Without going into physical details, which she could not delicately do, Sister Mary Jane could not explain. 'There's no —dilation,' she said finally. 'Nothing at all. What's more, I have a feeling that woman is dying.'

'Dying! We must save the child!'

'Impossible. A Caesarian without instruments? What'll I use, a steak knife?'

'Nothing is impossible with God, little sister,' said the older woman patronisingly. 'However, *there is one alternative we haven't mentioned.*'

'Luckily we've brought a syringe.'

*

The hijacker introduced himself as Vladimir Barnes, a Soviet agent. Bert and Marilyn tried once more to explain it to him: there just wasn't enough fuel to get to Cuba. Hal, the pilot, showed him the fuel gages and some calculations.

'That's all we have, honest, mister. About enough to get us as far as Atlanta—with a lot of luck. Cuba's just too far away! Why didn't you grab a plane going to Miami?'

The hijacker stopped smiling. 'I'm not accountable to you!' he snapped. 'Fly the damned plane to Cuba and no excuses!'

Bert tried again. 'Look, we'll make you a deal. We're almost over Washington now. Let us set down there, and we'll forget all about that gun—and everything you said. What could be fairer than that?'

'CUBA!'

'But you could hijack another plane out of Washington . . .'

'I GOTTA BE IN HAVANA BY TONIGHT!'

Marilyn wept, leaning her forehead against Bert's wings. 'Are we really out of fuel?' she whispered.

'Yeah. We've been circling Washington for an hour already. I don't know whether this guy's stupid or just nuts.'

Vladimir Barnes wondered if the crew were stupid or just nuts. Clearly they were unused to taking orders. How to make them understand that he had to be in Havana by eight p.m.;

216

that he had no money to get on another flight? But they would probably offer him money, and then, after they were safe on the ground, turn him in to the authorities. No, there was no way but to make them press on southward.

For months he had been hanging around Minneapolis trying to get a lead on a certain CIA man, of whom Barnes knew only that he was a chess player and an assassin. Now, at the last moment, he learned the CIA man was in Cuba, and within hours of assassinating one of the most valuable men in the world—the Albanian naturalist, Prof. Aa, a chess Grand Master.

At eight o'clock, in the ballroom of the Hotel Hoy No Hay in Havana, the finals of the Communist International Chess Tournament would begin. It was there (if Barnes's information was correct) that the CIA man would try to murder Aa —thus destroying Albania's chess prestige in the eyes of the world.

The plan was simple: Aa always opened with the 'Albanian Defense' opening, moving the queen's knight first. Knowing this, the CIA man would have substituted for the piece a tiny, live, envenomed seahorse.

Diabolical! Vladimir Barnes shuddered to think of the scene in the ballroom if he should not arrive in time . . .

Prof. Aa, an enormous, beef-colored man with white, cropped hair, sits down with difficulty. The gilt chair keeps trying to skid away from under his roundness. The other man, 'Mr CIA', whose face is featureless, makes a pretense of being finicky. He must adjust all the pieces and dust them off before the game commences. And makes the sinister substitution. He has drawn black. Now, polite and expressionless, he waits for Aa to begin.

How did CIA get here? He is himself a chess genius. Some months ago, he slipped into the Soviet Union and entered the first playoffs. Calculating each step, he deliberately draws a game or two to put himself in different 'rounds'—moving inexorably up the long branched chain of games to face Aa in the finals.

Aa punches the clock. His pink sausage fingers hover over the queen's knight—but then perhaps choose a conventional king's pawn opening.

217

CIA is in trouble. He must now quickly force the master to move that knight. Already it is beginning to wilt—will it still be standing and alive in four or five moves?

The game draws on; the knight continues to wilt. Other players at other tables are taking the full time limit over their moves; not so the CIA man. Aa moves quickly, too, confident by now that he is up against a rank amateur. The idiot seems to be offering piece after piece for the taking, without gaining any visible advantage.

Finally, on the eighth move, CIA offers his queen to the Albanian's knight. Aa hesitates. Can this be a trick? He runs through the possibilities like a computer sorting punched cards. Finally, too bored to go on, he seizes the knight.

'Aa!'

The gilt chair goes over, skidding across the parquet to clatter against a potted palm. Aa leaps to his feet holding the wriggling knight up to the light.

'Hippocampus . . .' he muses, and sprawls across the board.

Then CIA—does what? Pretends concern? Tries to slip away? Draws a gun and shouts (unnecessarily, to the roomful of immobile, engrossed men), 'Nobody move!'

*

Marilyn sighed. 'Guess there's only one thing to do.' Unbuttoning her uniform jacket, she walked toward the muzzle of Barnes's gun.

'Mr Barnes, *I* want to make a deal with you. If you'll let us land in Washington . . .'

When she was fully naked except for her cap the hijacker grinned again, showing his full pink gums. 'A good idea, miss. I won't guarantee anything . . . but we'll see.' He started unhooking his cummerbund—an easy job, for it was turned around back to front.

*

'But, Wes, we known old Travis a *long time*. Hell, he was our old buddy in Mud Flats.'

Skeeter, you just shut your mouth and throw that body out the window. He was a nigger and you know it.'

'But Wes! We done kilt near the whole general staff of the

218

White Shirt organisation. Ain't nobody left now but you and me. Are you sure they was *all* niggers?'

'No back talk, Skeeter!' Wes picked up his automatic. 'Else I might get to wondering why *you* are such a stubborn, nigger-loving son bitch.'

And of course he was wondering that already.

*

The battle of Dresden was going badly. Blücher had hoped to regroup his forces while Napoleon was otherwise occupied, but the wily Frenchman had turned twice from Dresden to engage him. He did this without little hope of victory, however, and its effect was nil. Napoleon had fought two indecisive battles and was weakened, while Blücher was as strong as ever.

'Grid-phone call, sir. Pentagon. Will you take it in the summerhouse?'

'Unh?' With effort, Weimarauner wrenched himself out of the character of Napoleon (a lead figure, two inches high, leaning over a postage-stamp map inside a tent the size of a toy drum) and into the character of Chief of Staff. 'Oh, fine.'

As he strode across the artificial landscape, stepping here and there to avoid an army, the wind snapped his robe and silk pajamas. The summerhouse was fragrant with climbing flowers, and translucent brown bees nudged among them. It was the general's favorite spot. He sat down and pushed the scrambler button on his grid-phone. A weak, blocky line drawing of Brigadier General Garner appeared on the screen.

'Sir, what the hell is going on? How come you shoved this pansy outfit in here on us? Them Pink Brassières are only making things worse around here.'

'What seems to be the trouble?'

'Sir, they make me *sick*, that's what's the trouble! They make *everybody* sick!'

Weimarauner opened an icebox under the table and probed it. He removed a mango yoghurt and made a leisurely breakfast. When he had finished, he fitted a cigarette to his holder, lit it, and leaned back to contemplate once more the grid-screen. 'General Garner, you know that that *is* the idea. They do indeed make everybody sick. Like a gas.'

219

'Yeah? Well everybody is tearing the shit out of them.' The features of the line drawing tried a placating smile. 'Sir, I'm not complaining. I know these—boys—are supposed to be good psychological warfare. Only they're getting massacred, and my men are bitching about having to help them out.'

Weimarauner waved, dismissing both Garner and a bee that was investigating the yoghurt dish. 'All right, all right. Get some of the boys to draft some orders. We'll send them out to Southeast Asia—to whatever Enemy we're fighting out there right now. By Container freight of course.'

'Of course, sir. By the way, Jarmoss of the computer department wants a word with you urgently.'

'Switch me over to him, will you?'

In a moment the screen drew an approximate sketch of worried Col Jarmoss. The sine waves in his forehead and the parentheses around his tight mouth were a trifle blocky—the grid screen worked only in verticals and horizontals—but nevertheless stood very well for Jarmoss's typical distressed expression.

There was no particular reason to communicate by grid-phone with his subordinates, but Weimarauner liked it that way. It was nice not to have to deal with them as humans. No matter how personable they tried to be—and none tried harder than Jarmoss—they remained so many little crude drawings, little animated cartoons.

'How's the battle of Dresden going, sir?'

'Fine, Colonel, fine.' Weimarauner looked out the vine-bordered doorway, across the landscaped lawn. Every detail of the landscape around Dresden had been faithfully copied at a scale of 1:36. The earth had been replaced with plastic, the grass was nylon plush. Japanese dwarf trees stood at proportional heights, in their proper positions. The model Germans were defending their town with cannon the size of cigars.

'I got that piece of land I needed for the river area,' he said, in no hurry to hear the colonel's complaint. 'You'll be happy to know.'

The drawing tried to smile. 'That's lucky, General.'

'Yes, luck and aggressive thinking, the marks of a good military man. The farmer didn't want to sell. I finally requisitioned his farm in the interests of National Security. It is, too.

220

My work here may not seem it, but it *is* in the interests of National Security, all of it.'

'Yes sir. Now about . . .'

'You believe that, don't you, Colonel?'

'Oh, yessir. Sir, we've got a few problems here . . . by the way, we've ordered the Pink Barrettes to Southeast Asia, as you requested.'

'Fine, fine. What's the problem?'

'Our computer has been fouling up something awful. Operation Modulog is in one hell of a mess. The trouble seems to be in the tape unit . . .'

'Spare me the technical details, Jarmoss. I'm an eighteenth-century man. Do whatever needs to be done. Get a new tape unit or whatever.'

'Yes sir. Another thing: a couple dozen civilians came around earlier, asking about the tape. Some kind of legal thing. I told them to come out and see you about it, sir, since we're not authorized to talk about the Müller-Fokker tape. I hope you'll let them have it, sir. We're sick of it.'

'Very unwise, Colonel. I hate hacking about with legal nonsense.' He broke the connection and went back to Dresden.

Later the platoon of lawyers showed up. Most of them represented MacCormick Hines, president and owner of the National Arsenamid Corporation. One of them represented a Mr Robert Etwall Shairp.

'I'm serving you with this writ of *habeas corpus*, General, and demanding that my client be released.'

'Gladly, gladly. But I've never heard of your client. Robert Etwall Shairp? Is he a prisoner taken in the Washington conflict? A soldier?'

'No, General. The pink tape you are using in one of your Pentagon computers,' said the lawyer. 'That is my client.'

*

Spot seated himself in that portion of the Capitol lawn that was shaped like a keystone. After making sure he was unobserved, he unscrewed the lid of a can of gas and poured it over himself.

The riot was about over; the cops were getting back into

221

their bus. Spot struck a match, but the drops of gasoline running down his hand put it out.

A tall man in Indian beads stepped from behind a tree. His face, a palimpsest of scars, showed no surprise at seeing a gasoline-soaked boy lighting a match.

'We know few quail before lunch,' he said.

'I'm killing myself.' Spot tore out another match. 'In protest against Mom and Dad.' He struck it.

*

Wise Bream acted instinctively at the sight of the flame. Hauling out Baal, he quenched it with an enormous stream.

The cop who spotted the pair screamed 'Get 'em! Get those goddamned protesters!'

The first of the five cops grabbed Spot and dragged him away. 'Impersonating an officer, eh, kid? You oughta get life for this.'

The other four closed in on Wise Bream.

'I'm gonna kill this bastard pervert, Charlie! Did you *see* him? Pissing on a kid!'

'Pissing nothing, he was tryna get the kid to suck him off.'

They sprayed Mace in his eyes and then took turns kicking at the offending organ.

'I'm too pooped to keep this up, Sarge, whadya say we just shoot him?'

'Oh no. I wanna see this fucker get the chair. Pissing on the uniform!'

They handcuffed him. Two of them stuck a nightstick between his wrists and holding opposite ends of it dragged him away.

'Hold it.' The cop called Charlie leaned over the unconscious prisoner, nose to nose with him. 'You're under arrest,' he said. 'I have to warn you that anything you say can be used against you, that you don't have to say anything if you don't want to, that you're entitled to counsel, and that if you can't afford a lawyer, the District of Columbia will pay for one.'

Laughing and nudging each other, they dragged him on towards the detention camp.

*

222

Bert the copilot had tuned in on local newscasts. He was no longer interested at all in Marilyn Temblor, not after seeing the way she *gave herself* to that Commie spy. Disgusting! Worst of all, it hadn't worked. The bastard kept them all covered all during it, and afterwards he just zipped up his pants, adjusted his cummerbund, and said, 'On to Cuba, gentlemen.'

'We're not going anywhere,' said Hal. 'We've got about ten minutes' fuel. It's too late to even try for an airport now. I'm taking her down.

'I'll be damned!' Bert adjusted the earphones. 'The President's missing!'

'. . . . *was to have taken off by helicopter from the roof of Blair House and proceeded directly to the submarine* Scampi. *But the* Scampi *reports they have not yet arrived. "We did see one helicopter pass by us about two miles north and head on out to sea," says the skipper, "but I can't see why they didn't signal us on the radio, if it was them."*'

'Forget about that crap!' Hal shoved his copilot. 'We've got to crash-land this mother, and *now*.'

*

Sister Maria said the words while Sister Mary Jane shoved the syringe, full of water, up the pregnant woman's dress. The rest of the passengers crowded around offering advice.

'Not that way, sister, you'll give her an enema.'

'I thought a baptism had to have the same one saying the words . . .'

'She's just squirting it up the front of her dress . . .'

'What's that coming out—*mud*?'

The hump of 'pregnancy' shifted slightly. Ash and water poured out over the floor, and, a moment later, a silver urn, stamped with the *Stagman* symbol, slipped down out of the front of her dress and rolled away.

A stewardess, naked but for her uniform cap, ran through, announcing an emergency landing. 'Will everyone please fasten their seatbelts?'

'I'm dreaming,' said someone. 'This probably has something to say to me, some personal symbolism. Wait'll I tell Feinwelt!'

223

Ignoring him, Feinwelt led the group in singing to keep up their spirits. Christmas carols—the only songs he knew— worked their magic as the plane went into a dive and the silver urn clattered on forward.

'Oh what fun it is to ride . . .'

*

'Use the goddamned radar, Bert! I can't see how the hell high up we are.'

'Screw you. Everybody gives me orders around here. If you're such a hotshot pilot, *you* land the plane.'

The figures ahead cast long morning shadows: trees, tents, motionless men . . . from the passengers he heard

Don we now our gay apparel . . .

as the men and trees fled past at incredible speed, too fast for a landing, too fast . . .

Among the motionless, listening figures of quaint soldiers stood a giant bedroom slipper. Above it, the giant face of Weimarauner arranged itself in the appropriate expression, ironic surprise.

*

The detention center on the Mall was a rectangle of snarled barb-wire. It was said the guards would let you talk to the prisoners across this barrier, for a price.

'Affirmative,' said a guard whom Mac Hines approached. 'The price is a grand a minute.'

'A thousand dollars a minute? Isn't that a little steep?'

'You look like you wouldn't miss it too bad. Besides, it isn't for me. It all goes to my favorite charity. Make out your check to the Red Cross.'

'All right. Good way to run a charity drive, at that. But why the Red Cross?'

'I don't know . . . they've been pretty darn nice to us guys here in no-man's land. I mean, they kept the coffee and donuts coming right on through the thick of the fighting . . . and at rock-bottom prices, too!'

In the end, Mac managed to ransom Spot altogether out of the place, though he had to take Spot's friend, too. The friend

224

was a great hulking moron who alternately mumbled incomprehensible statements and wet his pants. From a return ticket in his pocket they identified him as 'W. Bream', so it was only natural to call him Willy.

'I'll tell you a secret, Spot,' said Mac as they climbed into the limousine. 'That big bundle in the corner there is your Mom. She's frozen now, but when she thaws out, I'm going to marry her! Won't that be splendid?'

Spot concentrated on a blister on his thumb and said nothing.

*

Fouts awoke to a noisy kiddie show and realized it was Saturday morning. He started on the candy bars, a bite of this, a bite of that, mixing and melting peppermint cream, smooth fudge and crunchy peanuts, bittersweet and milk chocolate, slick marshmallow, toasted almonds, crisp coconut, honeyed toffee and dark caramel so sweet it hurt going down. 'I'm unhappy,' he thought, 'and alone.' But it was an abstract idea, unrelated to the pure sugar joy of living. A bite of this, a bite of that . . . and after awhile he began to laugh along with Bill the Cat and Mary the Canary.

*

'If we're gonna do it, Amy, we better do it quick,' Grover whispered. They sat in the basement of the building, huddled together on an old mattress where, for an hour, they had been discussing the pros and cons of assassination. Obviously the man deserved it—but was it *wrong*?

'All we gotta do is set the fuse—takes half an hour—and scram out of here. I don't see what the problem is!'

'Maybe if we . . . went with him . . .'

'What do you mean?'

'Oh Grover, I'm *old*. I've had my life, such as it was. And maybe it wouldn't be *murder* so much if we . . . didn't scram out of here.'

Grover thought it over. 'Okey-dokey, Amy. We'll do it your way. Who wants to live in a Red Chinese America anyhow?'

He set the fuse and they sat back in the darkness, leaning together without deliberately touching.

'What time is it?'

225

His radium dial flashed. 'We got twenty minutes.'

When his hand descended again, it rested on her knee. A moment later it moved up a little; and again.

'Grover! What are you doing?'

'Sshh, Amy,' he whispered hoarsely, 'Amy, you can't refuse a dying man's request.'

'But I thought . . . you didn't want to.'

'I *can't*, usually. This time it's different.'

They ripped off each other's clothing and began, moving over each other smoothly and gracefully as if it were the most natural thing in the world—which to Grover's way of thinking, it was not.

*

Upstairs there was a news flash.

'Ladies and gentlemen, the President of the United States is dead. The wreckage of his helicopter *Little Beaver* has been found. There are no visible survivors, and a denture has been picked up which the President's dentist identified as the President's denture, with indentations indicating dental . . .'

*

The blast actually drove them into the concrete below, but it seemed to be lifting and opening them, so that they never knew whether death or ecstasy suddenly spilled the universe into their upright souls.

The firemen found them long after they found Fouts (headless, hanging out of the TV set as if he'd been trying to get into the picture) under a heap of shattered boxes and their contents: great mounds of nylon and bright silk and lace, sparkling sequins, taffeta petticoats, ribbons and rhinestones and rouge.

226

TWENTY-FOUR

'But you did say you'd do *anything* if your husband were restored to you.' Mac drummed on his desk blotter.

The figure in the blanket sneezed. Mac took it for a nod.

'Well then, I'm going to return him to you. In perfect condition. You can have say two weeks for a second honeymoon, and then I'd like for you to divorce him and marry me. I—er—love you—Marge.'

The figure made a sound very like a sarcastic, snorting laugh. 'This is fairy-tale crap. If you thawed me out just to torment me, Mr Hines . . .'

'Then you don't believe I can restore your husband!' Mac pressed a button. 'Send in Dr Müller-Fokker, please.'

In the dim, distant corner of Mac's office a door opened. Beaming, a short, fat man in a sports shirt rushed across the noiseless carpet and seized Mac's hand. Marge, peering from the folds of the blanket, thought the little man was going to kiss the hand.

'Hines, you old scoundrel, what devilments are you embarked upon this time? No, no, don't tell me. Mine not to reason why, mine but to reason and accept my fee. Is this the unfortunate wife?'

'This is Mrs Shairp. Tell her, Doctor, how you plan to recover her late husband.'

'First let me say that I was uncontrollable, madam, when I learned of your sadness.'

227

Marge scrutinised his round face. 'You were supposed to have defected to Russia—anyway, you don't look like the picture in the newspaper.'

'Excellent memory!' Dr Müller-Fokker laughed Saint Nick fashion, holding his stomach and making a show of enjoying the joke of her excellent memory. 'I shaved off the beard, and the pince-nez have given way to the modern contact lenses. My defection was a sham; I have actually been working for the CIA. And during my stay in Havana, I also put on a few weights and obtained the sun tan. My real purpose there . . . but enough of me. Let me tell you how we shall raise your beloved Lazarus:

'As you by now know, Mac has kindly collected all the pertinent tapes. I have examined them and am satisfied the restoration can be done. The first step is to locate the DNA code upon the tapes. With this we prepare a virus, with which the specimen can be infected.'

'Specimen?'

'Some volunteer. I had in mind your son's friend . . .' He gestured out the window to where Spot and Willy were sailing a paper boat at the edge of Mac's private lake. 'The idiot is the correct size and general build—a little tall, perhaps . . . '

'Stop it! You're making me sick! How can you stand there and talk of murdering . . .'

'Not murder. Not murdering, madam. We prepare in advance a tape of the volunteer. And at the first opportunity . . .'

'A game of musical bodies? No thanks.' Marge stood up suddenly, tripped in her blanket and fell. The two men gently helped her back to her chair.

'Hear him out, Marge, will you?'

'We infect the specimen with your husband's virus and then "let Nature take His course". We kill the virus when the proper physical state is achieved. There will be minor imperfections, some surgery . . . and I am afraid your husband will always have severe dandruff . . . but otherwise it remains only to do the forced brain growth . . .'

'Please stop it!'

'No, you do not understand. I mean like a lovely hothouse flower. We *force* the electrical . . .'

Marge fulfilled her promise to be sick.

228

She left without making any further promises. Mac called up dozens of times, but the phone was off the hook. Next day he sent a telegram:

YOU OWE IT TO YOUR HUSBAND. MY CONDITIONS ARE THE ONLY ONES UNDER WHICH YOU WILL EVER SEE HIM ALIVE. IT WOULDNT BE SO BAD WITH ME, YOU KNOW. ILL DIE SOON AND YOULL BE A RICH WIDOW. I KNOW IM THE VILLAIN IN THIS FAIRY TALE BUT I CANT HELP IT. PLEASE REPLY IMMEDIATELY. OFFER EXPIRES MIDNIGHT. LOVE MAC.

A week later, she replied:

CONDITIONS AGREED TO BUT ONE CONDITION OF MY OWN. VOLUNTEER MUST BE MR BRADD. QUOTE LOVE UNQUOTE MARGE.

TWENTY-FIVE: THE DOOR

.... announcement: Death plan. Trick Him into allowing me to be crucified as a sacrifice to Him; the realization that I'm His only son and heir will kill him. His heart.

Still fixed in my chair still crucified by my own teaching forefinger I run down the solidifying labyrinth, at each intersection another last act of another stale Passion play. The crown of horns explodes in the back of my head.

WHOMS [enters from stage right, hangs deerstalker on fender to dry, strikes posture]: If any man has free will at any particular instant, and assuming he has the physical means to do so, that man can at that instant commit any crime at all. Agreed?

WHATSON [nods]: Yes.

WHOMS [paces excitedly a peculiar labyrinth pattern in the carpet]: Then if there is at least one crime which some man cannot commit, at that instant he cannot be said to have free will. Finally, you could not tonight, genial physician, kill and dissect one of your patients, and therefore tonight at least you do not have free will. And that is but one example. There must be, for every man and for all time, some one criminal action which he cannot bring himself to do, and which therefore impedes his free will. I intend to prove that no man has ever had free will at all!

WHATSON [opens catch on his doctor bag and pulls out a string of meaty objects]: Not quite so elementary as all that, my dear Whoms.

230

WHOMS [examines objects while picking nose distractedly with one chemical-stained forefinger]:* These are . . . ?

WHATSON: The uteri of six of my former patients.

WHOMS: Good Lord! Jack the Rip! Then it *was* Barbara and not Bocardo who—then *you* must be . . .

WHATSON: Mad? Or God. Correct—that is, I am equipped with free will. Not one action of mine can be predicted with any degree of certainty whatever, Whoms. Surely that is what we've always meant by free will—by God—the unknowable, unpredictable, irrational, pointless, silly side of the universe.

[Curtain. On the curtain is depicted an incomplete and distorted table of the elements, the cells of which are also cartoon panels. The cartoons are detailed drawings of the entire play, and of all members of the audience and their reactions. The members of the audience are by coincidence all the people I have known in my life. Upon the curtain are projected a set of maps and views of Cafe Island. After a figure in silver tights and a flowing turquoise cape comes out and lectures at length upon the sacramental meaning of my life, the curtain rises again on a desert island scene. I am looking at a naked footprint.]

FRIDAY [sneaking up behind me]: That's your own, you know. I don't run around barefoot. Too much bloody hookworm about. [He wears neat summer suit, slim shoes, panama. I am of course naked]. You uncolored folk have your own childish preferences, of course. Well, I hope this exile has taught you a lesson, eh?

ME: Thass right, boss. Lemme go back and work in dem cotton feels. Thass where mah heart is turnin'—evah!

FRIDAY [as background changes]: And the gold mines?

ME: That is right with me, baas.

FRIDAY [as background changes]: And the oil fields, cur?

ME: Effendi!

FRIDAY [as background changes]: How about the stables, the kennels, the boiler rooms, the ham kitchens, the transistor factories, the coal orchards, the peanut distilleries, the jello dying vats, the suntan oil refineries?

_____
* Nose-picking is the mark of an enquiring mind. Had Alexander Fleming been more fastidious, he could never have (summarizing his chain of research) 'Put in his thumb and pulled out penicillin.'

231

ME: Bwana! Sahib! Colonel! Massa! Sir! Gummint fella! Kimo sabe! Chief! Lord! Anything-san!

GASPING MESSENGER [running in, gasping]: Mr Friday... sir... the whites... they're... they're revolting! [Dies].

FRIDAY: Yes, but what news?

[BLACKOUT]

Mack and Mike, in baggy pants and huge bowties, stumble on stage and go into long extemporaneous and meaningless routine. Unfunny throughout. Audience roars. A typical line:

MIKE [boffs him with rolled-up newspaper]: But seriously now, are we on tape? Is all this on tape, or is it real?

MACK: Yes, absolutely [pause for laugh].

MIKE [boffs—if that is the word for it—Mack again]: Yes, but which?

MACK: Is a tape reel? Is it in a real state, or the real estate of the mind? Is it aped? If bits of information in formation form real states of mind, *for real*, a stated news format may form new statements: 'If God bit man, that is not news, but obits. If man bit dog, that is newsreel. If newsman in mental state orbits, reels, reeling off in format information, good news, God knows'. Hound of heaven tapers into newshound in the reely real bit.

[Mike pummels him to appreciative roars. End of blackout, curtain rises on man in deck chair, picking nose, watching televised self as boy receives First Holy Communion. From time to time a steward comes past to give the man a newspaper (all references to the U----- S----- of A------ have been cut out) or the news that his son is dead.]

STEWARD: Your son is dead, sir.

MAN: Yes, yes, I know, the old Oedipus switchback thing. Now I'm free to marry his mother.

[On TV I kneel, close my eyes, put out my tongue for God. Old fat palsied Father O'C. makes few passes over the gold cup, comes up with a tiny dead hollyhock seed. Is this my body? The Word is on the tip of my tongue.

But not quite yet. First the doctor gets in there with a tongue depressor, the dentist has to do a little work while I'm strapped into the chair, the Customs man wants to see what kind of dope I'm carrying in a hollow tooth, behind them come cops,

232

linguists, orthodontists, eye-ear-nose-and-throat specialists, spelunkers, crowds of the curious and other cops to hold them back . . .]

MAN [switching it off with a yawn]: Wonder how things are getting along in old—Armorica is it?

[Dozes. Flash of dream in which Spot, his son, heaves rock at flame-throwing tank. Nazi soldiers crucify Spot. Marge, the man's wife, weeps beneath the crucifix. Now and then during her long speech of sorrow and demand for justice, which should be improvised, she slyly hauls on the boy's feet to add to his pain.]

STEWARD [waking him]: Your son Spot is dead, sir.

MAN: That's about the worst pun in this novel. Are the crew murmuring yet?

CREW: Why did we ever set sail to find the land of the Iructu? Why did we leave the comparative security of our homeland and set out on this silly quest? We'll fall off the edge of the sea! We'll drown among the plankton! We'll go broke! We'll get back and no one will believe us! Probably there aren't any Iructu anyway, and Iructria is a lot of hooey!

MAN [reappearing among the crew in the vestments of Father O'C.]: Boys, boys! As your spiritual adviser, I thought it was time we had a little chat. We're about to find and conquer a new and virgin land, fellas, and I think this is as good a time as any to remind you that contraception is murder.

CREW [begin to mill about, shouting slogans]:
Hey hey/whadya say/ how many kids did you kill today?
All the way! Whadya say? All the way! Etc.

MAN [reappearing among the crew as a condom salesman]: Buy me and stop one. [He is clapped in irons, reappears among the crew as Father O'C.] Because preventing a life *is* murder, and it contravenes Natural Law—just like building houses and brushing your teeth. I . . . let us pray:

[The background, a process shot of calm sea, suddenly moves into the foreground, obliterating all, and becomes the leafing pages of *Eternity* magazine. In an ad for an airline that shows movies, Mack and Mike appear on the screen still boffing. The audience laughter, we now realize, is directed not at them but scornfully at Mike's newspaper baton, a scandal

233

sheet bearing the headline HE KILLS, CUTS UP, COOKS & EATS WIFE, INVITES HER FRIENDS TO DINNER. All references to the U----- S----- have been blacked out.]

MAN [in vaudeville audience in movie]: Barbecues his *wife*! Get it? Barbara, *not* Bocardo!

MAN [in airplane audience, watching movie]: Stewardess! Another plankton steak!

[The automatic pilot—the only pilot—has failed, and the stewardess is praying.]

STEWARDESS:
Tom Swift, help me
Casey Jones, guide me
Maelzel, let me win through
Azuma-zi, protect me
Daedalus, fortify me
Vulcan, arm me
Mr & Mrs Zero, sum my chances
Rossum, strengthen me
Hey, Lullay, etc.

MAN [in magazine article on facing page, reading ad]: I guess the idea is all these levels map each other or something, but Gee, why mess around with mapping? Cartoons on the curtains—why don't we get where we're going?

MAN [aboard ship, reading magazine]: Good idea. The detective all along has been shadowing himself, staking out his own house, bugging his own phone—but because *there isn't anyone else*. Good article. Now let's see what they have to say about the Iructu . . .

VOICE OF FATHER O'C: Let us pray: Our hallowed thy thy on give. And as lead but deliver, not into those who father be kingdom will earth us forgive. We us evil temptation heaven name heaven our our art who done be in as in it is thy us us from this forgive come . . .

[The Iructu are shown on the final page, being napalmed by an aircraft without markings. The caption under the picture is God's final message, variously interpreted as denial of all negatives, self-contradiction, a call to action.]

GOD: TO BE OR TO BE, THAT IS THE QUEST.

VOICE OF FATHER O'C: For the day daily against the power and and bread trespass ever debts forever debtors glory us

234

amen and kingdom trespasses is the thing amen. Nema live morf su reviled tub...

[God dies]

LOOKOUT: Land Ho!

[The ship has arrived at—the map of—Cafe Island.]

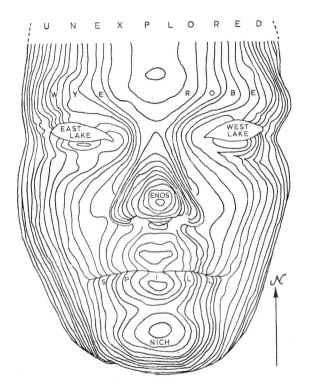

[As the ship closes on the island, the camera closes in on the plankton in the surrounding waves. They have selected 1940 as a target date for landing a plankton on the sun, which appears to hang just over the next wave.]

SPEECH BY FIRST PLANKTON ON THE SUN: It's a great honor and privilege for us to be here representing not only our own wave, but plankton of peace of all waves, plankton with interest and curiosity and plankton with vision for the future.

235

PART FIVE | ANNOUNCEMENT:
HAUNTED EXPERIMENT 'MAN' SOCKS BENEFACTOR

TWENTY-SIX

Spot wanted to know why he had to take a bath.

'Because your FATHER's coming home! After a YEAR! Don't you care anything about him?'

Spot wanted to know what the difference was, since she was only going to divorce him and marry Uncle Mac anyhow.

'THE DIFFERENCE IS—never mind. *Don't* take a bath, then.'

Spot took a bath and shined his shoes. Marge spilled a bottle of cologne on herself, and had to change into her second-best dress, which (she remembered as the doorbell rang) Bob loathed.

'Haven't got a key,' he said.

'You're—the wrong *size*.'

'I know. They couldn't do much about Bradd's bones, except around the face.'

'But I had all your suits cleaned!'

She started crying as he started laughing; they embraced awkwardly.

Spot came in, shook hands politely, and pointed out his shiny shoes. 'I learned that at school.'

'So you finally got to military school? Well. I guess a lot's happened. The divorce . . .'

'Do we have to talk about that?' Marge guided him to a chair as if he were crippled. Under the flesh of him she could feel Bradd's skeleton. 'I mean, it's all I could do.'

'Of course. Yep. Seems fair enough to me. Speaking as the beneficiary, of course.'

237

Marge laughed too hard.

Bob leaned back on the couch and tousled Spot's lack of hair. 'Well how's military school, you little Fascist?'

'Don't you call my son . . .'

'The term is one of affection, in case you've forgotten.'

The evening collapsed after the unexceptional dinner, when Spot left to see Willy.

'Who's Willy?'

'A friend of Spot's. Some kind of Indian. Seems like a moron, but ever since he saved Spot's life we've been looking after him. He's staying at the Fellstuses'.'

'Oh.'

'Dr Fellstus is trying to housebreak him.'

After a silence, she apologized about the dinner.

'Oh, it was fine. Really.'

'You don't have to . . .'

'No, really.'

After another silence, she asked, 'Did you—mm—*feel* anything?'

'Oh, you mean the charge that blew my head off? No, not a thing.' He grinned with Bradd's teeth. 'I didn't really die at all, you know. I had this *different* life. It was made up of, oh, this and that, old memories, odd thoughts. Kind of interesting.'

'What was it like?'

He sighed. 'Well, for instance I remembered this dream I'd had, the night before I went to Mud Flats. I call the dream

JELLY DAYS

'It's kind of a mixture of *Castle of Otranto* and *Turn of the Screw*. There are two peculiar quiet kids whose brother is dead, and there are some giant manifestations. One thing, the giant manifestations always imitate reality. I mean, a giant hand reaches through the window to grab somebody who's reaching into a cupboard to pick up something. And a giant toy plane flies in, and it flaps its wings because, out the window, you can see a gull flapping its wings. Someone around the house has the title Master in Lunacy.

'The kids have a lot of whispered conversations, but the only words I can distinguish are "jelly day (or days)". Then I go back to childhood and look into a miniature grocery store

238

where some men are having a history argument. They mention a political event and at once I am there. An Italian political quarrel is the event. One man is supposed to be put to death in the restaurant kitchen: They mark his body off into ten zones and then shoot him in zone one, his head. If that wound heals, they shoot him in zone two, and so on, neck, chest. . . . The waiters all deny this plot, even the victim wants to hush it up.

'I discover I'm dead. I don't know how I know it, but I'm sure. Maybe I'm just talking to someone and suddenly realise they aren't listening.

'Death land is very pleasant, very ordinary. Everyone has to work at his former job, more or less. There seems to be a big demand for sociologists. The place looks like a kibbutz, very jolly and industrious and serious, well-equipped with wall charts.

'You can only communicate with the living through accidents or imitation. The dead know nothing, as the saying goes around there, and have no power to be anything. At last I begin to understand what "jelly day" means—just means the day one leaves one's mortal jelly.

'We gather in the cafeteria after dinner to sing songs and watch a TV play about the end of the world. In the play, the actors have to tune in on some special radio station to find out how to deal with the end of the world.

'Sitting there among all these suntanned ghosts, I begin to wonder about that special radio station. On a hunch I tune in my own radio to it, to catch the end-of-the-world news. But there's nothing on much, just the usual sloppy Melodiak tunes . . . *Sunshine Balloon of Happiness*, and so on.

'Then I realize this *is* the news: ordinary life goes right on, palling, silly, disgusting, nice, unbearable—right on up to the last moment. As I realize this, I hear thousands of footsteps, a great jostling crowd coming downstairs to the cafeteria. The new people are arriving. It's everybody's jelly day.'

*

There was a long, long silence when Bob finished. He stood up. 'Guess I'd better get back to the hotel.'

The bell rang. Marge answered it.

'Uncle Mac! What are you doing here?'

239

'I've been watching you two,' he said. 'I'm—I'm the window peeper you've been worrying about.'

'What window peeper?' they asked together.

Mac did a strange thing. He hissed, then, out of the side of his mouth not visible from the living room window, he whispered, 'That's not your line, stupid. Ask me what I want. "What do you want?" Come on!'

'What *do* you want?' Bob asked.

'The deal's off, you'll both be happy to hear. I saw the two of you sitting here, Bob talking, Marge listening to his tale. You look so *right* together—so much a *family*. I just can't take that away from you. You see, we rich men . . .' He turned to face the window and took a step towards it, '. . . we rich men lose touch sometimes with reality. With real, human emotions, with vibrant life. We think we can play God and push people around like piles of money.

'But all that's over, for me. I thought I could bribe you, Marge, into—well, into loving me. But now I see my own real happiness depends on yours, and you could never be happy without Bob. God bless you both, you'll hear no more of me now, except at the reading of my will.'

'Your will?'

'Which probably won't be long, now. The doctor tells me I have a very delicate heart. In fact I don't feel so well right now. If you'll excuse me I—I'll be going now.'

'But wait! Shouldn't you sit down for a minute, or . . .'

'I'd like to be alone for awhile. I'm—very tired.'

Gasping and clutching with a fluttering hand at his chest, Mac stepped outside. When he was just beyond the door, he dropped the pose, turned and winked.

'Do you think he meant it?'

'Search me.' Marge yawned. 'Stay here, at least for the night, why don't you? It is late. I'd better phone and find out what's keeping Spot.'

'You don't think anything could have happened to him, do you?'

*

Mac turned away from the window, satisfied with tonight's episode. The Shairp Family had no sooner settled everything

240

with their kind old rich friend than Spot seemed to be in some kind of trouble. That might be a false alarm, but still, that 'Willy Bream' wasn't all he pretended to be.

More to the point, the rich old benefactor wasn't all *he* pretended to be. Perhaps his heart was sound as a dollar. Perhaps he was scheming some new trouble.

And what was Dr Fellstus really up to, with his separate cages (boy-sized and man-sized), his cattle-prods? Mac wondered how on earth the Shairp family were ever going to get their lives straightened out. He didn't mean to miss a single heartwarming episode.

THE END

241

AFTERMATH

In a serial like *The Shairp Family*, there can be no ending, only a gradual change of character. Not so in this life, where death is your reward for learning the labyrinth.

Ank never became the artist he knew he was. His last work is a forty-by-sixty-foot mural in the lobby of the Pismore Tractor Company of Sandusky, Ohio, an unfinished work depicting the tractor conquering the land.

Ank died in the middle of a furrow, when a scaffold collapsed, dropping him on his head. The scaffold was a modern design by the well-known Scandinavian architect, Ögivaal, who later admitted there was some flaw in the design. That '3' should have been a '30' after all.

The Daughters of the American Legion, as an experiment in liberalism, invited Deef John Holler to sing at one of their dinner meetings. He arrived not wearing a dinner jacket, to which some of the ladies objected. A great protocol debate ensued, lasting three and a half hours and getting all the ladies into a temper. The final decision was that he could play behind a screen, and was to stick to patriotic favorites and the cleaner sort of Stephen Foster songs. But the person sent to inform Deef John that he could come in from the kitchen now found that rigor mortis had already begun setting in.

Mac Hines persuaded the Shairps to let Dr Müller-Fokker make tapes of Marge and Spot. He then found three 'volunteers', created a duplicate Shairp family out of them, and put

242

them in a duplicate house on an island he owned. Mac visited the island once a week, and it was during one of these visits, while he was peering in the window at his own personal Shairp family, that Mac's dacron heart finally failed.

Due to legal complications and embezzlements by Mac's bright young men, his estate was modest. It was left to the Shairps, but their duplicates contested. In the end, Bob came out with a gold-headed cane, Marge with a half-filled book of green stamps, Spot with a neurotic collie which he asked Dr Fellstus to put to sleep.

Under the vet's tutelage, 'Willy' Bream not only recovered his speech but became an animal sociologist, working chiefly with bears. Times were hard for the new breed of intelligent bears on the West Coast. Racists finally had what they wanted, a non-human target; unmerciful laws were passed. It was due mainly to the selfless, untiring efforts of Dr Bream that bears were first admitted to the Forestry Service, to become useful to, without being used by, mankind.

Spot quarreled with his father and left home to drift around the country. When last heard from he was traveling with gasoline gypsies, stealing this rare commodity in one town to sell it to stations in the next.

Marge and Bob quarreled often and bitterly. She left him finally to go back to television work. But her TV career (such as it was, walk-ons in space comedies: 'Listen, Mabel, you and I can sneak into the air lock and watch their "stag party" from there . . .') came to an abrupt end when HV came along. Holovision revealed a fatal third dimension to her jaw that reminded one reviewer of Mussolini.

Bob worked at odd jobs while he pottered around with writing. In trying to set down a few ideas about his 'jelly days' dream, he ended up writing (under the name of 'Brad Shairp') THE AMERICAN BOOK OF THE DEAD. Published in his sixtieth year, it was widely unreceived.

A few more years went by. In Southeast Asia, a container of thirty human skeletons arrived. The remains, which could be identified by their rags as members of the long-defunct Pink Barrettes, had been shuffled by Modulog to upwards of a thousand wrong destinations.

A new generation grew up. Brad Shairp became the first

243

prophet of Practical Mysticism. Besides the fringe groups who took it up (the book became a film, a musical, cocktail napkins, records, and a holovision serial in which Marge had a small part) there came to be a serious group of believers, kids who were cleancut, blonde-haired, utterly without humor about this humorless world. They wore plain uniforms and marched in massive demonstrations against any authority available.

There were a few incidents: a church meeting broken up by Plain Shirts, a psychiatrist roughed up and his files burnt. The prophet reprimanded them for these in his address (at a massive rally in Minneapolis) on the thirty-fifth anniversary of his first death.

'My little uncles and aunts,' he said, opening his arms to them, 'ours is not the way of war or the way of peace, ours is not the way of love or the way of hate. Ours is the way of studied indifference.

'If God can do anything, which he can, then what is the point of living—or dying? All is, and all is true. That which is not true is not, and even that is "cannot be". We are . . .'

Some say it was his wife that fired the shot that killed him. Others say it was a lunatic bear.

244

APPENDIX I: TABLE OF PERSONS, OBJECTS, ETC., WHICH HAVE NOT FALLEN BACK TO EARTH, WITH EXPLANATIONS

(Note: So-called astronauts, cosmonauts excepted)

NAME	DATE	EXPLANATION
Elijah	uncert.	Fiery chariot
eagle	1619 BC	(see explanation for Sir Roxley Norward-Beveridge, below)
Christ	*ca.* AD 33	Own power
Mary	uncert.	Drawn up by some power
numerous hydrogen molecules and other particles	—	Attain escape velocity at top of atmosphere
'Flying Stone'	AD 1591	Developed by alchemist Carolius Minus, it apparently possessed antigravity powers.
osprey	AD 1706	(see below)
Sir Roxley Norward-Beveridge	AD 1873	This Australian balloon enthusiast met the same fate as the two birds above. A very large, very fast-moving meteorite (too large to burn up in the atmosphere, too fast to be captured by earth's gravity) clipped him off into space

245

APPENDIX II: THE 128 WAYS

The entire Nicene Creed (Apostles' Creed) has 22 articles of faith. This abridged version has only seven:

> I believe Jesus Christ was conceived by the Holy Ghost, born of the Virgin Mary, suffered under Pontius Pilate, was crucified (to death) and was buried. He rose again on the third day, and ascended into Heaven.

It can easily be seen that, if belief or disbelief is allowed for each of the seven, there are the seeds here for 2^7, or 128 alternative creeds (the full version would generate over four million alternatives). The 128 include the above and its complete negation, and 126 other permutations of belief and skepticism. Many of them would be interesting as springboards for new religions. One may admit that Christ died, was buried, and rose again, but deny that he ascended. One may believe that he died, was buried and ascended while denying that he rose. One may affirm his burial, rising and ascension while rejecting the possibility of an actual death, and so on. One fascinating variation holds that all is true except his suffering under Pontius Pilate; while another finds this the only truth in a pack of lies.

Practical Mysticists, claiming God as the creator of heaven, earth, and self-contradiction, refuse to make a choice, but insist on embracing all 128 creeds (and all others besides). All is ambiguity, they maintain. And while agreeing with Aquinas that 'even God cannot contradict Himself', they hold also the opposite view.

246

APPENDIX III: THE HINES FAMILY

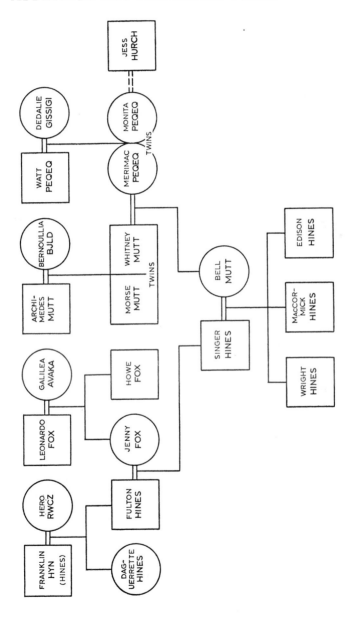